Who's the fairest
of them all—
the duke…
or his irascible,
irresistible twin?

Strong hands grabbed Char . . .

Whitridge threw her around and against the wall to face him. Her air left her body in a whoosh.

"Hand over the purse you stole," Whitridge ordered.

Char couldn't speak. She was trying to breathe. He took her by her shoulders and gave her a shake for emphasis. Her head rocked back and forth and her hat tumbled off her head. Her blond braid, the color of moonbeams, fell down to her shoulder, pins scattering everywhere.

"What the bloody—?" Whitridge started. The blazing anger in his eyes turned to confusion, then shock. They dropped to her chest as if wanting to confirm the surprise. His hands loosened their rough hold.

Charlene took full advantage.

She could not be caught. She doubled her fist and, fear giving her strength, punched him right in the gut with all she had.

Well, she'd aimed for the gut.

In truth, her blow had fallen lower, to a place most gentlewomen would not touch in public.

And his reaction had been all she could have asked for.

By Cathy Maxwell

THE SEDUCTION OF SCANDAL
HIS CHRISTMAS PLEASURE • THE MARRIAGE RING
THE EARL CLAIMS HIS WIFE
A SEDUCTION AT CHRISTMAS
IN THE HIGHLANDER'S BED • BEDDING THE HEIRESS
IN THE BED OF A DUKE
THE PRICE OF INDISCRETION
TEMPTATION OF A PROPER GOVERNESS
THE SEDUCTION OF AN ENGLISH LADY
ADVENTURES OF A SCOTTISH HEIRESS
THE LADY IS TEMPTED • THE WEDDING WAGER
THE MARRIAGE CONTRACT
A SCANDALOUS MARRIAGE
MARRIED IN HASTE
BECAUSE OF YOU • WHEN DREAMS COME TRUE
FALLING IN LOVE AGAIN • YOU AND NO OTHER
TREASURED VOWS • ALL THINGS BEAUTIFUL

Marrying the Duke
THE FAIREST OF THEM ALL
THE MATCH OF THE CENTURY

The Brides of Wishmore
THE GROOM SAYS YES
THE BRIDE SAYS MAYBE
THE BRIDE SAYS NO

The Chattan Curse
THE DEVIL'S HEART
THE SCOTTISH WITCH
LYON'S BRIDE

CATHY MAXWELL

The Fairest of Them All

MARRYING THE DUKE

AVONBOOKS

An Imprint of HarperCollinsPublishers

This is a work of fiction. Names, characters, places, and incidents are products of the author's imagination or are used fictitiously and are not to be construed as real. Any resemblance to actual events, locales, organizations, or persons, living or dead, is entirely coincidental.

AVON BOOKS
An Imprint of HarperCollins*Publishers*
195 Broadway
New York, New York 10007

Copyright © 2016 by Catherine Maxwell, Inc.
Excerpt from *A Date at the Altar* copyright © 2016 by Catherine Maxwell, Inc.
ISBN 978-0-06-238863-6
www.avonromance.com

First Avon Books mass market printing: June 2016

Avon Trademark Reg. U.S. Pat. Off. and in Other Countries, Marca Registrada, Hecho en U.S.A.
Avon, Avon Books, and the Avon logo are trademarks of HarperCollins Publishers.
HarperCollins® is a registered trademark of HarperCollins Publishers.

Printed in the U.S.A.

10 9 8 7 6 5 4 3 2 1

To a generous Seven:
Kathe Robin, Kate Voorsanger Ryan,
Sandi Cararo, Kelly Justice,
Sarah and Gwen Reyes,
and
PJ Ausdenmore

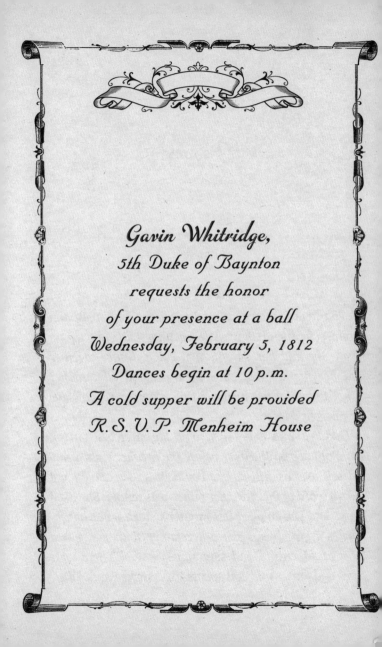

Gavin Whitridge,
5th Duke of Baynton
requests the honor
of your presence at a ball
Wednesday, February 5, 1812
Dances begin at 10 p.m.
A cold supper will be provided
R. S. V. P. Menheim House

Dragons

Charlene's father was rarely at home, so having him promise to spend the whole evening with her was a treat. She and her parents had eaten dinner together and her mother had even splurged and allowed her father to light a fire in the sitting room hearth to stave off the cold damp.

Cuddled into her father, who lay stretched out on some pillows on the floor before the fire, her eight-year-old self was as still as she could be so she would not miss a word of the story her father was telling. She liked books and she enjoyed her mother's stories, but her favorites were always those her father told. He shared tales of adventure and sometimes magic. There were elves and fairies and evil spirits like banshees and "little devils."

Tonight he spoke of a noble prince who slew the dragon terrorizing the kingdom of a beautiful princess. In the end, they married and everyone in the kingdom came to their wedding and danced.

"Like they came to your wedding feast?" Charlene asked.

"Oh, this was grander than what your mother and I had. We only had a village," he answered.

"Why didn't the princess slay the dragon, Papa?"

Her mother laughed, a bitter sound. "Yes, Dearne. Why must it always be a prince who wins the day?"

"Because, my love, that is the way of the world." He mimicked her mother's tone, and Charlene began to regret asking her question. "Men slay dragons."

"And if they don't, Dearne?" her mother pressed, leaning forward in the chair where she sat, her legs covered with blankets. "What if they can't or refuse to slay the dragon eating us up from the inside? Then what happens to the princess?"

Anger pulsated in the air, as dangerous as a dragon who could devour a whole village. Charlene clenched her father's jacket.

Her father covered her hand with his, its warmth reassuring. "Be at peace, Julie," he said to her mother. "You are upsetting our lovely Char." He pressed a kiss on her forehead and Charlene let herself relax in this haven of his comforting presence.

"I just want you to be my prince, Dearne."

"And I am, Julie. I try."

Her mother's mouth opened as if she would say something, and then she looked away without speaking, her brow furrowed in concern.

"I want to marry you, Papa," Charlene chimed in, anxious for there to be peace. Then her father would stay with them always and not disappear for days, sometimes weeks at a time. Charlene wanted no more of the arguments that sent her mother into tears.

Her father liked her comment. He gently pulled her braid and laughed. "You can't marry me, poppet."

"Then who shall I marry?" she asked, the question suddenly important.

He leaned close and whispered in her ear advice she would never forget. "Marry the man who slays a dragon for you, my little love. That is the man you can trust, and don't settle for anyone less."

"There are no dragons in London, Papa."

"There are, but one does not see them immediately," he answered. "They come upon us unawares . . ." His voice trailed off into silence, one that was heavy with sadness for both her parents, and Charlene knew it was her fault.

She should not have pestered her father with talk of dragons. Why, everyone knew dragons were evil and evil thrived on unhappiness. That is what her mother said.

Charlene started to ask for another story, one that

would take away the sorrow in the room, but it was too late.

Her father gently slid his arm out from under her head and came to his feet. "I must go out." He spoke to her mother. "Don't wait for me."

Her mother nodded, accepting, angry.

Charlene did not want to accept. She jumped to her feet, tears coming to her eyes. "No, Papa, don't go. Stay. I won't ask any more questions. You can be right here with Mother and me."

He tilted her head up to look at him. "Tears, Charlene? Tears don't solve anything." He dried her cheek with the pad of his thumb. He was a handsome man. From him she'd received her white blond hair and blue eyes. "And I do want you to ask questions. It is what I adore about you. Now be good and mind your mother. I have a dragon to slay." He patted her head and left the room as he had time and time again, except this night was different.

This night, the dragon destroyed the prince.

Chapter One

January 21, 1812

*L*ady Charlene Blanchard didn't know why the memory of her last evening with her father was tickling her mind. Perhaps it was because it had been on just this sort of dreary overcast day that they had pulled his body from the Thames.

Or perhaps it was because she now slew her own dragons.

Disguised as a lad in breeches, stockings, and buckled shoes, minus the buckles, she stood in the late afternoon's lengthening shadows along Threadneedle Street. She hid the curves of her nineteen-year-old body with a loose shirt and even bigger coat. Her braid was wrapped around her head and tucked beneath a wide-brimmed hat of the sort an ostler would wear.

She watched with interest what was happening in front of the Bank of England. Three men had stepped out of the bank's doors. She had seen them go in and had been close enough to hear their speech. They were Americans.

Lady Charlene smiled. Americans or any foreigners were always good marks. They weren't wise to the ways of the city.

Her eye went to the heavy, brown leather coin purse the youngest of their number tossed into the air and then caught as if he hadn't a care in the world. He grinned at his friends. "I plan on enjoying London."

"With wine and song?" the oldest suggested sardonically. He wore a bagwig and carried an ebony walking stick with a silver head. He was little taller than Char's own five feet four. His shoulders were back and his head high. He had a bored expression, accentuated by his beaked nose and flat mouth. He dressed with an eye to detail.

"No, with *women*," the young one crowed. He had guileless good looks, the sort of man who usually married young and bred a gaggle of children.

If Charlene had been in skirts, she had no doubt he'd be one of those hanging his tongue out for her. However, dressed as she was, she escaped his notice. She was one of thousands of street lads scurrying about London. The threesome hadn't even given her a look as she moved closer to watch the purse.

Her mark confirmed her suspicions. "I'm marrying in three months," he informed his mates. "I have wild oats to sow and a ready cock." He threw the coin purse in the air again but the tallest of his companions reached out and snatched it out of the air.

A quick movement. A confident one.

This man was no fool.

He was thirtyish, tall, broad-shouldered, with overlong dark hair and a square jaw. He was obviously the leader of the trio. There was a presence about him, a determination.

The man also had a distinctive voice. There was a depth to it, a sound that set him apart from the others.

Like Char, he wore a brimmed hat down over his eyes. She was hiding her abundance of white-gold hair and long, dark, feminine lashes. She wondered what he was hiding.

"We are not here to feed your pecker," the man said, offering the purse back to his companion. "Or for you to catch the French disease."

"Sod off, Whitridge," was the answer. The younger man tucked the purse into the deep pocket of his greatcoat. *On the left side. And he didn't button it.* "I can take care of myself. And the first thing I am going to do is put as much distance as possible between you and me. Seven weeks on a ship with your constant criticism is all I can stand. I need at least seven weeks apart from you."

"We are here in the serv—"

"*I know*, I know, we are here in the service of our country. You really are a prig, Whitridge. Isn't he, Lawrence?"

Lawrence had been stifling a yawn. "Men with responsibilities usually are. I'm heading to our rooms. I want a good supper and a bed that doesn't rock, which is the exact opposite of what you crave, Matthew. Until the morning, lads." He didn't wait for a response but went briskly off, swinging his walking stick.

Matthew said, "Lawrence has the right idea. I'm off on my own." Without a glance at Whitridge for approval, he charged into the flow of afternoon traffic.

Char made her way after him, the man with the purse. She was confident in her disguise. She'd been dressing as a lad for two months now and enjoyed the freedom. No one had noticed she was female yet, proving her aunt Sarah wasn't the only actress in the family.

She was also taking pride in her new talent.

Char, Lady Charlene Blanchard, was a pickpocket and a good one.

The idea of her doing a bit of larceny had come from Lady Baldwin. Her Ladyship was a frequent visitor to the house on Mulberry Street where Char lived with her aunt Sarah Pettijohn. Before marrying Lord Baldwin and stepping up into the ranks of Society, Lady Baldwin had been an actress like Sarah and had also apparently dabbled in a bit of crime.

"Sometimes a girl has to do what she must to survive," Lady Baldwin had confided to Char. "Sarah has too much pride, but you understand the way the world works."

And Char did. The daughter of the infamous Lord Dearne knew very well how precarious life could be. Six months ago, her uncle Davies had stopped sending the monthly funds he'd promised for Char's living. Even with Sarah working several positions at Haymarket theater, from roles on the stage to sewing costumes to even writing plays that the theater manager took credit for, money was tight and Char felt guilty. Her aunt could have made a very good living for herself if she hadn't taken Char in.

"We shall just slip a bit from those who can afford it," Lady Baldwin had suggested. "It will be a balancing of the scales, so to speak."

That idea had appealed to Char. There had been those who had preyed on her father's weaknesses to steal all that he owned. Now Char could repay them in kind.

"You have quick hands and a bright mind. Between the two of us, we'll have that rent paid," Lady Baldwin had predicted.

Of course, it had taken time for Char to learn the art of picking a pocket. Fortunately, Lady Baldwin was a good teacher and they had met with initial success. Claiming the money was from Uncle Davies, Char had given Sarah enough to keep the landlord from tossing them out.

She was a bit short this month. The fat money purse Matthew had tucked into his open coat would make up the difference in the rent and more.

Matthew was a cocky one. He turned toward the wharves and the hubbub always going on there. This was life in London at its rawest and Matthew fit in. He gawked at every female bosom that passed him by, shouldered his way through crowds gathered by pub doors, and generally behaved as if he owned the street.

Char kept close without drawing his attention to her. She skirted around those Matthew offended. She trusted her disguise, and few noticed her.

"Wait until the mark is properly distracted," Lady Baldwin always advised. *"Then you can lift his purse without his knowledge. His attention will be on something else. The secret to a good pickpocket is patience and the right moment."*

The right moment for Matthew arrived when a tavern wench stepped out from the dark doorway of her establishment. She was a slatternly thing—all bosom and chins—but had the dark, sloe-eyed look Char had observed men liked. The wench's gaze met Matthew's and then, with a shrug of her shoulder, her blouse fell down over one shoulder, revealing a good amount of bosom topped by a dark brown nipple.

The American stopped dead in his tracks. The bawd grinned and nodded for him to follow her.

At the same time, a woman carrying flapping headless chickens in both hands attempted to pass between Matthew and his coveted nipple.

A better distraction could never be found.

Char moved forward so that when Matthew practically fell over the woman with her chickens, she could pretend he had also shoved into her. His weight fell against her. Pushing back with one hand, she slid her other into his inside pocket.

Her fingers closed over his purse. She pulled it

out without him the wiser and elbowed her way past him. Now, she would hurry home—

"Stop, *thief.*"

On those words, everyone on the street tensed— even the bawd, the headless chickens, and most certainly, Matthew.

But not Char.

She recognized the deep voice. She did not need to turn to know that Whitridge had seen her take the purse. She took off running, fear giving her feet wings.

For his size, Whitridge was fast. He was practically right on her heels. She could hear him breathe.

She dodged in, out, and around the pedestrians on the crowded street. Whitridge barreled over people, earning him some rough responses. He kept shouting the order to "grab the boy." Fortunately no one wished to be involved. They stepped out of his way, but they moved out of Char's way as well.

Matthew had realized he had been robbed. He shouted his outrage but he was well behind Char and Whitridge.

Rounding a corner, she dashed down an alley and grabbing at a rain barrel as she passed. She threw it into Whitridge's path. There was the sound of wood on stone, a grunt of pain, and strong curses.

Char grinned at her success but did not indulge in a backward glance. Instead, she escaped onto a more crowded street, praying she had lost him.

She hadn't. She could *feel* his presence. The rain barrel had delayed him but had not stopped him.

This street was busy with coaches, carriages, drays, and even sedan chairs and dogcarts. She zigzagged her way around them. Her chest hurt from running so hard. The leather soles of her shoes slid on the cobblestones. She had managed to tuck the purse inside her jacket because she needed to use her hands for balance and to ensure her hat didn't fly off her head. Revealing her sex would be the ultimate disaster.

She was moving toward home, toward safety. Soon they would be in neighborhoods where she could be recognized. For a moment, she debated running in the opposite direction, but couldn't. She yearned for the haven of her bedroom, to throw on her skirts and safely return to being who she was supposed to be.

But first, she had to escape Whitridge. The man was a bloodhound.

Now it was Charlene who swore.

She ducked down another alley that was only

wide enough for her shoulders. Certainly the giant Whitridge could not follow her here—and she was right.

He tried to squeeze himself into the narrow space between buildings, and failed. She hurried on, hating the feeling of having the buildings close in around her. She had no idea what was at the other end of this alley but it didn't matter. In ten minutes, she would be home.

Home, home, home, *home*.

Coming out on the other side, she found herself on a strange street, but sensed she was within blocks of her house. This street was not as crowded as the others.

Her chest hurt and her heart pounded in her ears. She gasped for breath but forced herself to walk and act as if she didn't have a care in the world. Her disguise was intact; her hat firmly over her head. No one gave her strange looks and a burly man carrying a leather pouch filled with papers brushed by her with the rudeness men used on each other.

At last, she let herself smile.

She'd gotten away with it. The purse weighed down her coat. It was hers.

Coming out onto a connecting street, Char realized where she was. Yes, home was only a short distance from here. She couldn't wait to—

A tall, loathsome figure stepped out on the path in front of her as if he had anticipated she would be coming in this direction. *Whitridge.*

He'd lost his hat during their chase. She could see his eyes clearly now. They were angry blue shards. His fists were clenched.

Charlene whirled around and ran, this time in panic. She shoved an orange girl and her patron aside and then almost ran over a child carrying eggs. Whitridge no longer hurled accusations at her. He was intent upon capturing her.

And if she hadn't been so stunned by his sudden appearance, by his dogged determination, Char would have been more aware of where she was going. Instead, she made a fatal error. She turned down another alley, and realized too late this one had a closed passage. Worse, she could not turn back, not without running right into her pursuer's arms.

The stone foundation of a building facing another street loomed in front of her. Charlene ran to the wall, placing her hands on the cold rock as if she could find a secret exit, a doorway, a window, a crack—

Strong hands grabbed her arm. Whitridge threw her around and against the wall to face him. Her air left her body in a whoosh.

"Hand over the purse," Whitridge ordered.

Char couldn't speak. She was trying to breathe. He took her by her shoulders and gave her a shake for emphasis. Her head rocked back and forth and her hat tumbled off her head. Her blond braid, the color of moonbeams, fell down to her shoulder, pins scattering everywhere.

Chapter Two

"What the bloody—?" Whitridge started. The blazing anger in his eyes turned to confusion, then shock. They dropped to her chest as if wanting to confirm the surprise. His hands loosened their rough hold.

Charlene took full advantage.

She could not be caught. She doubled her fist and, fear giving her strength, punched him right in the gut with all she had.

Well, she'd aimed for the gut.

In truth, her blow had fallen lower, to a place most gentlewomen would not touch in public.

And his reaction was all she could have asked for.

He released his grip, doubling over. His breath came out in a grunt of pain.

Char was shocked. Who knew that men were

that vulnerable in their private areas? This was a trick she would not forget.

She snatched up her hat from the ground and took off running, pulling her jacket up around her neck to hide her hair. Whitridge did not, or could not, follow, and she found herself looking back, hoping he wasn't mortally wounded.

He leaned a shoulder against the wall. For the briefest moment their gazes met. He was furious.

"I'm sorry. Sorry."

Whitridge didn't appear in the mood for an apology, so she kept running. She burst out into the street and once again tried to walk, but discovered she now had new problems.

As she made her way to Mulberry Street, first one boy of age ten or so and then another fell into step beside her. A bit later, a third, older boy followed close behind.

These *were* street lads, angelic, albeit dirty-faced, ruffians who roved London in a pack known as the Seven because of their number. They were far better pickpockets than she.

She hoped to ignore them, to keep walking until she reached the back garden gate of her home and safety.

They would not let her.

After a few minutes, the boy on her right, a lad they called Pinky, crossed in her path. Char had to stop.

"What?" she said, letting her exasperation show. It was better than allowing them to see her fear.

"Leo wants you," Pinky said solemnly.

"Tell him I will talk to him later. We will make an appointment." She tried to sound cheery.

"Leo wants you now," the boy behind her said. He was Danny and had been her first contact at meeting Leo. He was as tall as she and far stronger. "The sooner you see him, the sooner you can be finished, my lady," Danny said.

Of course they knew who she was. The Seven knew everything that happened in the area around Mulberry Street.

With a great show of impatience, she nodded. "Let us go then." She was certain of what Leo wanted and knew she could not escape this interview.

She'd run afoul of the gang the first time she'd gone out to pick pockets. Apparently, the criminals of London had divided the city into territories. She was in the Seven's territory for petty crimes.

The Seven were children really. Leo was the oldest and he could not be more than sixteen, which didn't truly make him a boy, but the others were as young as eight. They all had one thing in common; life had made them hard.

The boys took her to another long, narrow alley that was much the same as the one she'd used to escape Whitridge. One had to walk sideways in order to pass through this one. The alley gave way to a large courtyard hemmed in by buildings. Wooden boxes, barrels, and crates were stacked together as if they formed small rooms against the far wall. As her party entered the courtyard, boys crawled out of their hiding places. Three pairs of eyes solemnly watched her approach the largest of the boxes. A cloth flap on one side was pushed out and Leo emerged.

He was rapier-thin and wore what had once been a gentleman's green velvet evening jacket. Around his neck he'd knotted a black scarf, and he sported a *chapeau bras* on his head so that he reminded her of nothing less than a very young, slyly menacing Napoleon. He liked to carry a riding crop, which she had witnessed him use on the younger boys. He had his crop in his hand now.

His voice was always soft but she had a sense that he could harm her. To date, he had been careful with her, almost respectful, and she prayed her luck held.

"Lady Charlene," he said, bowing with a courtier's mocking grace.

"What do you want, Leo?" she answered, taking this moment to push her hair up under her hat.

"Besides the money you owe me for working in the Seven's territory last month? It was a guinea, my lady. A fair price and you have not paid it yet. However, today you have cost me extra. You went over the boundary into someone else's territory this afternoon. They want tribute from me. They want four guineas."

"Four guineas? For nothing?" she protested.

"They claim you were successful."

"I wish I had been." She wondered if lying was a sin if one lied to criminals. She needed the money in that purse. "I thought I had a fat pigeon but those flapping chickens the girl was carrying were in my way. I missed the purse."

"Why did that man call you thief?"

"Because he thought I had nabbed it. I didn't. Once he realized his mistake he let me go. Pinky can tell you the truth of what I say if he saw me chased into the alley. I walked out as cool as you please."

Leo studied her a moment. She couldn't tell if he believed her. She did know one thing; if he did place his hands on that purse, he would take it all. She would not give it up without a fight.

Suddenly he turned and walked back to his lair. "Very well. I want a fiver from you, my lady, along with what you already owe."

She waited for him to demand she pay it by a certain date, but he didn't. Instead, at the "door" to his abode, he faced her and said, "You are going into debt quickly. That seems to be a family trait. Some of the gents were very familiar with your father."

Whenever he spoke of "gents," she knew he spoke of those on the next level up from him. He aspired to be one of their number.

"They were there when he was pulled from the Thames. Bad luck that." There was no sympathy in his voice. "Be wise, my lady. Be very wise." He let his words sink in and then said, "You are free to go."

He did not have to repeat himself. Char backed up, keeping her eye on all seven of them. She tried to appear calm but inside, she was shaking.

Did Leo suggest that her father had owed money to the criminal element in London? That his death might not have been a suicide but a murder? That she, too, could meet such a fate?

She did not want to think on it. She ducked into the alley and once on the road, almost ran home to Mulberry Street. Now she didn't know if she was fortunate to still have the money purse.

When she reached her back gate, she looked around to be certain no one was watching before letting herself through. She ran across the damp ground to the door leading into the kitchen.

Mulberry Street was a shabby but respectable neighborhood. The house had two floors other than the ground floor and a basement. There were three bedrooms, a front room, a dining room, and then the kitchen. The foyer was little more than a landing with steps leading upstairs. A second set of stairs behind a door ran up from the kitchen. The rooms on the ground floor all opened up to each other, and overall, it was a cozy place to call home.

Char didn't believe she'd ever been so happy to be here. She pulled the money purse from her pocket and practically stumbled over to the kitchen table, where she threw it down and, bracing her hands against the hard wood, allowed herself a moment of blessed relief. She'd done it. She'd kept her prize—

Footsteps could be heard coming down the hall.

"Char?" her aunt Sarah called.

What was she doing here? She had left for the theater hours ago and should not have returned until late evening. Char would never have left the house if she'd anticipated Sarah returning at this hour—and she knew better than to let her aunt catch her wearing breeches.

Sarah may be an independent thinker, but Char would wager she would draw the line at her niece parading through London as a lad, or a pickpocket.

Forgetting the money purse on the table, Char

ran to the kitchen door. She had just closed it behind her when she heard Sarah in the kitchen, calling her name.

As quickly and quietly as she could, Char climbed the stairs. Her bedroom was the first closed door to the right of them. She raced into her room and shut the door behind her.

She yanked off her jacket and drew up the shirt, kicking her shoes off at the same time, which was not effective at removing either. Blinded by material, she fell onto her bed. Jerking the shirt off, she tossed it toward the wall behind her bed, threw each shoe after it, and fumbled with the buttons of her breeches—

A knock sounded on the door. "Char? Are you in your room?"

There was no time to completely undress. She also could not avoid Sarah. Her aunt was known for her persistence.

Breeches loose around her hips so that she had to hold them up, Char cracked open the door. She peered outside at her aunt.

Sarah Pettijohn was four-and-thirty and had flawless skin and deep red, red hair that she twisted into a heavy, thick chignon at the nape of her neck. She was quite simply the most wonderful, wisest person Char knew.

After Char's mother, Julie, had died, Sarah had

swept into her life and saved her when no one in the world appeared to give a care for her twelve-year-old self. Sarah had proved her wrong.

It hadn't been easy for Sarah to take her on. Sarah was actually Julie's half sister, having been born on the wrong side of the blanket, so to speak. At one point, long before Char had memory, Julie had insisted Dearne let her take in her half sister. That was when Sarah herself was thirteen.

"One act of kindness always kindles another," Sarah liked to say. "When I heard that you had been turned over to that disgusting man Davies for no other reason than that he was considered your only kin, I knew I had to do what I could to help you. He has a terrible reputation around London, especially for young girls."

Char hadn't been certain what her aunt meant but she did know she did not feel comfortable around her uncle and decidedly did not like his wife. Her aunt May constantly complained about how much feeding Char cost no matter how little Char tried to eat to keep her happy.

Back then, Char had been afraid of everything. Losing both of her parents had been beyond painful and it had left her destitute. Sarah had encouraged her to be brave. "Your truth is what you believe of yourself," she'd told Char until the words were engraved in her soul.

Under Sarah's tutelage, Char had blossomed. Her aunt believed that a woman should seek knowledge. She was fiercely passionate about all aspects of life, especially the theater. Her one goal was to see her plays under *her* name someday performed on the London stage, or anywhere else for that matter. "I know it will happen," she would say to Char, "as long as I don't give up."

Char admired her aunt so much, she had once tried writing plays as well, but she had lost interest. Writing was hard work and she didn't have anything to say.

Instead, she had contented herself with taking care of their house, well, until she'd discovered the adventure of pickpocketing—and then something had opened up inside Char. She didn't know what she exactly wanted out of life except she knew she rather enjoyed living by her wits—save for when her aunt was standing at the door and could, possibly, learn what mischief she'd been about.

For all that had happened in her own adventurous life, Sarah could be very moral. She would not approve of pickpocketing.

"Yes?" Char said, and rubbed her eyes as if she had been woken from sleep. Of course she had to let go of the breeches and they fell to the floor at her feet, but Sarah didn't notice.

She was focused on Char. "Are you all right?"

"Of course. Why do you ask?"

"I've been calling you. In fact I knocked on your door not minutes ago."

"Oh, that might be why I woke up. I was napping."

"You never nap."

"I did today. By the way, why are you here? Shouldn't you be at the theater?"

Sarah grabbed the change of subject. "I should but Lady Baldwin came to me with such good news, I told Colman I had to go home. I was only the understudy tonight and Melissa has already arrived so I knew I would not be needed. Well, he would *find* something for me to do—you know how he is—but he let me off tonight."

Her aunt never missed a performance, even when all she had to do was stand backstage.

Curious now, Char asked, "What news did Lady Baldwin have?"

"Something that involves you." Sarah's green eyes lit with excitement. "She's downstairs. I will let her tell you herself. However, this is your chance, Char. *At last*, you have an opportunity to take your place in Society where you belong."

"What do you mean?"

"Come downstairs and find out. I can't wait to see your expression when you learn what it is." She started to turn away but then stopped. She held up her hand to show Char the money purse.

"By the way, I found this on the kitchen table. Is it from Davies?"

Char could have cried.

The money was now in her aunt's hands. There would be no opportunity to remove five guineas. Sarah kept a strict accounting of expenses.

"Um, yes. A servant delivered it earlier."

"I didn't see it on the table when I first came in this afternoon," Sarah said, puzzled.

"Perhaps you missed it?" Char suggested.

Her aunt shrugged. "You might be right. I'm so excited about Lady Baldwin's news, I'm giddy. I could have looked right over it. Thank heavens it is here and it feels as if he is making up for what he hasn't sent."

"Have you looked to see how much is in it?"

"I'll count it while you dress. Hurry and join us." Sarah went down the hall to the front stairs.

Char shut the door and leaned back against it, annoyed with herself. *Why hadn't she carried the purse upstairs with her?*

Perhaps there would be a moment when she could filch five guineas. She could hope, although, in truth, Leo hadn't pushed her to pay. It was almost as if he wished her debt to grow. Was that how it had been for her father?

She stepped out of the breeches before she tripped. She rolled down the wool socks and stashed all the clothes, including the shoes, in the back of her wardrobe. She quickly laced herself into the blue day dress she had been wearing before she'd gone pickpocketing.

Her braid was messy. She brushed it out and pulled her hair back into a simple style. She went downstairs.

Sarah and Lady Baldwin were in what the family called the front room. Her Ladyship sat on the settee while Sarah was in one of several chairs in front of a cold hearth. The room was small enough that with blankets and heavy clothing, Sarah and Char found themselves comfortable without the expense of a fire.

Lady Baldwin was almost as wide as she was tall, a sturdy woman who adored colorful prints and patterns that she used together in a style that suited her. She also enjoyed bold hats teeming with feathers. Almost everything about her spoke of a bygone era. She still powdered her hair and painted her face.

She had been Julie's godmother and it was Lady Baldwin who had tracked down Sarah and had warned her of Char's plight with her uncle Davies.

"I would take you in myself," Lady Baldwin had told Char. "But you know my circumstances."

The late Lord Baldwin had been one of the

king's most respected advisors. However, now few remembered his name and he had not left his widow in good circumstances. His heir rarely spoke to her and her daughter thought her an embarrassment. She lived with that daughter, a dour son-in-law, and six rowdy children. It was an uncomfortable situation.

"She wishes I would just die," Lady Baldwin had sighed to Char on many an occasion. "But I won't oblige her. I often wonder if I should have just stayed on the stage instead of running off with Bertie. Then where would my haughty daughter be?"

Her Ladyship enjoyed spending the night in the house on Mulberry Street, and Sarah and Char kept a bedroom for her use.

Sarah was refilling the glass Lady Baldwin held out with ratafia, something else their small household kept on hand for Lady Baldwin's enjoyment.

"Charlene, my girl," Lady Baldwin called out in greeting. "Come give me a kiss."

Char dutifully crossed to her and kissed her offered cheek. "Sarah says you have a surprise for me." While she spoke, she noticed her aunt was untying the drawstrings on the money purse.

"Not just a surprise," Lady Baldwin answered. "An opportunity!"

Just as she said those words, Sarah poured the

coins into her lap and Char was distracted. The amount in the purse exceeded the money for the back rent. Here was enough to keep them a good long while. There had to be close to fifty guineas there. No wonder the purse had been so heavy.

Sarah's amazement mirrored Char's. She began counting the coins as she put them back into the purse. "I can't believe this. The randy old roué has honored his debt."

"And just in time," Lady Baldwin said. "We are going to need that money."

"That is true," Sarah agreed.

Money that *Char* had earned. She tried to make sense of the conversation. "I'm sorry, Lady Baldwin, what were you saying?"

"I'm saying that you have the opportunity of this century, my young friend. How would you like to be a duchess?"

"Yes, please, thank you," Char said, matter-of-fact, reaching for the ratafia bottle to pour herself a glass from those on the tray Sarah had placed on a table in front of the settee. "That is, if there is a duke who wants a dowerless bride. Does such a man exist?"

"Yes, he does." Lady Baldwin held up a gilt-edged card with information written in the finest hand. "The Duke of Baynton is on the hunt for a wife. He is wealthy enough for seven dowerless wives and I believe you have a good chance to catch his attention. This is *your* invite to his ball given to me personally by his great-aunt." She threw the invitation down on the drink tray as if playing a trump card.

Char looked at the richness of that single paper and started to laugh. "The idea that I could go to a ball—" She broke off at the preposterousness of the idea. "Or marry a duke? Why, I've never been presented. No one in Society knows me. I'm poor."

"*And* you are uncommonly beautiful," Lady Baldwin countered. "A woman's face is her fortune."

"Not in the real world," Char argued.

"It was for me," Lady Baldwin practically sang, reminding her.

Sarah spoke. "I had the same doubts, Char. But hear Lady Baldwin out. This is your chance to take your proper place in Society, the one that is due to you."

Char could have told her that her proper place was here, with people who loved her. Still . . .

"So why do you believe I could be a duchess?" Char asked Lady Baldwin. "I've heard of the Duke of Baynton. He is one of the most important men in England. He could take any woman for his wife."

"That he could, but he desires someone special—like *you*," Lady Baldwin said with relish.

"He doesn't need a dowry. He has more money than he knows how to spend. What he wants," she said, holding out a green-gloved hand to tick off his expectations, "is breeding, manners, breeding, beauty, and *breeding*. I have this on the best of authority. I am close to his great-aunt. Dame Imogen is a stickler and she is desperate to find the 'right' wife for him."

"And 'right' is about breeding?" Char said, unconvinced.

"It must be," Lady Baldwin answered. "He has an obligation to the title and his descendants to choose a woman from the correct family. Dearne had faults but his bloodlines were impeccable, as were your mother's. Indeed, when I suggested you to Dame Imogen, she grew very excited. She insisted I show you to her. She approves. She approves very much." Lady Baldwin tapped the invitation on the tray for emphasis.

"When did she see me?"

"Three days ago when you and I went for a walk in the park. She was sitting in a sedan chair. I doubt if you noticed."

"Because it was so cold," Char said. She looked to Sarah. "I found it strange Lady Baldwin demanded we take a walk. I thought my nose would freeze."

"If it froze, it was for a good cause," Lady Baldwin declared. "She thought you lovely. You reminded her of your father. She apparently was quite fond of him."

Char did not know what to think.

Seeing her confusion, Sarah asked, "What harm is there in going to a ball? You deserve to go to at least one in your life."

"Will you come?" Char asked.

"That would not be wise," Sarah said. "Actresses are not welcomed in formal ballrooms. However, Lady Baldwin will chaperone you."

"But Lady Baldwin was an actress."

"Who was been made respectable through marriage," Sarah pointed out.

"Besides, you and Sarah are among the very few who know *all* the details about me," Lady Baldwin said. "Dame Imogen is so rigid, if she were aware of my past, she would give me a direct cut. Then again, I'm such an old lady, who cares?" She helped herself to another glass of ratafia. The bottle would be empty shortly.

"So will you do it, Char?" Sarah asked.

"Is it important to you that I do?"

Sarah's eyes softened. "Yes, it is. You were made for a finer life. I would like to see you secure and safe."

"But what of you?"

"If you are the duchess of the wealthiest man in

London, you can take very good care of Sarah . . . and me." Lady Baldwin lifted the glass to the thought. "Why, you would be so rich, you could pay to have Sarah's plays produced. Baynton could even buy the theater. Or build his own!" She was quite taken with the idea.

"We will have to buy you a suitable dress, perhaps some other new clothes as well," Sarah said. She adored to plan. "We have the money now." She indicated the coins in her lap.

"Several new dresses are a must," Lady Baldwin said, giving Char a critical eye. "We will also need to hire a vehicle. And have you thought of taking on a servant? If the duke comes to call, the house is passable but a servant is a must."

"I can be the servant," Sarah said. "I'll wear a costume from the theater. We will let Baynton believe Char lives with you."

"That will do."

"*Wait,*" Char said. She set down her glass. "The duke has never laid eyes on me and the two of you are already planning what to do when he comes calling."

"Because he will come calling, Char," Sarah said. "Even if every woman at that ball is as lovely as you, he will single you out. There is something about you. You aren't jaded like so many young ladies of your class. Or as wool-headed. Baynton will meet you and he won't be able to help falling in love."

"Especially if Dame Imogen has anything to do with it," Lady Baldwin said. "She doesn't like young women today. She calls them too modern but you struck her fancy."

"My bloodlines struck her fancy," Char corrected.

"Same difference in her eyes."

Sarah leaned forward. "Will you do it, Char? Will you take the risk?"

How could Char say no? She didn't believe for one moment that the duke would choose her, but it was obvious the idea of her going to this ball meant a great deal to Sarah. "Of course I will."

Lady Baldwin clapped her hands while Sarah put aside the money purse to jump out of her chair and give Char a hug.

"We have a great deal to do," Sarah warned. "To save money may I suggest we design the dress ourselves. The wardrobe mistress at the Haymarket will help."

"Yes, that will save a bit," Lady Baldwin said, and they put their heads together on what style of dress would look best on Char.

For her part, Char hadn't quite grasped what all this meant. Unbidden, a face rose in her mind. A handsome-in-his-own-way face. A memory that might stay with her, even though he was the last man she should find attractive. The face of the angry American—Whitridge.

She had to put him out of her mind. "Is the duke young?" she asked, hoping the answer was yes. Right now, he might be as ugly as a Sunday pig and she would feel obligated to consider him.

"Baynton?" Lady Baldwin said. "He is thirty-ish, the right age to marry."

Char nodded, and then had to ask, "Is he handsome?"

"I have never seen him," Sarah said. "He doesn't go to the theater, or at least not the Haymarket."

"I have never met him, either," Lady Baldwin said. "But I have heard that he is considered very handsome. They say he is tall and well-spoken."

Whitridge had been tall but Char hadn't liked a word he said. Still, Lady Baldwin's description set her at ease.

"Do you know anything else about him, anything personal?" Char wanted to know. "Is he kind?"

"I'm certain," Lady Baldwin said. "I've heard no complaints about him. He took the title several years ago when his father died. His mother is still alive. He has a brother, Lord Ben, whom I've been told works in the government. Oh yes, and the duke had a twin but he disappeared."

"Disappeared?" Char repeated. Even Sarah's eyes widened at the description.

"Terrible case," Lady Baldwin said, the plumes on her hat waving as she shook her head. "The boy vanished from his bed at Eton."

"How did he vanish?" Char asked, intrigued.

"That is the mystery," Lady Baldwin said. "Some whispered he'd involved himself with rough characters. Other said he ran away, and still there is some speculation that he could have been a suicide and they just haven't found the body yet."

Her words put a chill into Char, and yet they also gave her something in common with the duke. He'd known a family tragedy. He might understand hers.

She picked up the invitation. She'd not read it and she was now curious. Here was the manner in which the *haut ton* summoned each other to events. Here was her one link to the man who might choose her for his wife.

The paper felt heavy. She scanned the request— and then the name jumped out at her. *Whitridge*.

The Duke of Baynton was Gavin Whitridge.

For a second, Char could not breathe.

She forced herself to reason. The man chasing

her through the streets had *not* been a duke. She was certain of it.

The names being the same must be a coincidence. Nothing more—she prayed . . . because listening to Sarah and Lady Baldwin plan, the die had been cast.

Char was going to the ball.

Chapter Three

February 5, 1812

What the devil had Gavin got himself into?

The line to enter the ballroom ran down the hall and out the front door and still they came.

Ceremony with all of its pomp was part of being a duke, as was finding himself the center of attention. However, tonight was beyond anything Gavin Whitridge, Duke of Baynton had ever experienced, and it was his own ball. He'd created this affair when he'd given his great-aunt Imogen permission to find a wife for him.

His mother had tried to warn him. "It will be a crush, my son. There isn't a family in Britain with a marriageable daughter who doesn't want an invitation."

And apparently Imogen had seen that half

the populace had received one. She was also directing the affair, dressed in her favorite color of purple from the turban on her head to the kid leather shoes on her tiny feet. She stood by Gavin and gave him the benefit of her opinion, in loud whispers, on every family and young woman presented to him.

He would have preferred not having such a formal receiving line but *Imogen* insisted this was the only way the invited women would have a few seconds of his undivided attention. "You owe it to yourself to meet them all," she'd said. "They expect it. Anything less would disappoint them." And so, he had assented.

His brother Ben and Ben's wife, Elin, were the beginning of the line. His mother, the Dowager Duchess of Baynton, and her escort, Fyclan Morris, were to Gavin's left. Other various relatives had been tucked into the line where Imogen had deemed fit.

"Wellbourne," Imogen now whispered, her voice still crisp.

She referred to a tall, long-faced man speaking to Ben and Elin at the beginning of the line.

Wellbourne was accompanied his daughter. "Lady Amanda is the earl's only child. His politics are wrong. However, he is loyal and well connected. A possibility."

Gavin had long respected Wellbourne's constancy to his ideals, although he thought him deluded. Could he tolerate being related to the Opposition by marriage?

"Unfortunately," Imogen continued, "Lady Amanda is as horse-faced as her sire. Her breeding is impeccable and she comes with an income of five thousand, but that jaw will show up in your children."

Not for the first time this evening was Gavin uncomfortable with his aunt's bluntness. Hopefully, the musicians in the ballroom covered her more acerbic comments, like the horse-facedness. She had high expectations, and her ability to catalog one proud family after another, including daughters, nieces, and cousins, was truly impressive albeit too much.

He nodded and smiled as Wellbourne presented his daughter to him.

He also began to listen to Imogen with half an ear. The gambit to find him a wife had turned ridiculous.

Peers of the realm, his friends, and many mere acquaintances, all dressed in their finest, kept coming forward. Each touted a flower of English womanhood for his perusal before happily tottering off to drink his punch and devour his food. Henry the butler and the staff hustled to see to the needs of so many. Trays would be carried out piled high and returned to the kitchen empty.

These weren't guests. They were locusts.

Of course, the idea for a ball was not an unsound one, Gavin thought as he smiled, nodded, bowed, and offered his hand. He was a busy man. There were affairs of state that needed his immediate attention. Britain was at war with France, a conflict that extended to almost every corner of the world. Meanwhile, domestic issues threatened to erupt into violence if not finessed soon. And, as if Gavin didn't have enough on his table, the prime minister insisted on his guidance with an American delegation that had made an appearance and now pestered everyone to hear their list of grievances.

Gawd, the Americans. The damn upstarts thought to bully Britain out of her holdings. They wanted all of North America and would settle for nothing less than their dictated terms. They were like puppies who had shown their teeth once and won and thought to do so again. Gavin detested negotiating with them. They said one thing out of the left side of their mouths and something completely different out of the right. A more confused group of people did not exist in politics.

Meanwhile, what he really needed was a wife. It was time. He was thirty-two years of age. He was ready.

In fact, *past* ready.

While other men had indulged themselves in wildly wicked ways, Gavin had been the dutiful heir to a dukedom. He'd not *wenched*. He had *morals*. He was known for his *character*. No bastards would muddy his line for the simple reason that he had yet to give in to base impulses and "know" a woman, as the theologians were wont to say.

But he wanted to. He wanted to very much.

However, first he must survive this travesty and Imogen's strong judgments.

If a young woman had the right connections and bloodlines, Imogen would dismiss her for looks.

"Unsuitable," Imogen asserted in Gavin's ear when Miss Vivian Dorchester was presented to him.

"Because she is petite?"

"Because you are tall."

"But the last one was tall and you rejected her."

"Ah, because she was *too* tall," Imogen argued. "The portraits of the two of you together would look odd."

"I'm choosing my wife for how she will look in portraits?" Gavin replied in disbelief, annoyed beyond reason.

His aunt smiled her complete conviction. "The portraits will outlast both of your lives. Do you wish future generations to mock your images?"

To worry about what his descendants thought long after he was gone sounded outlandish to Gavin, until he remembered the numerous quips and jibes he and his brothers had made about the ancestors already hanging on Menheim's walls.

"You definitely don't want a petite wife," his aunt informed him. "Yes, they are attractive bits, but you run a danger of breeding runts. And is that what you want for your sons?"

Gavin could have replied he just wanted to breed . . . but in truth, he was as picky as his aunt, well, when it came to looks or figure. Imogen was more a stickler for the family bloodlines. The Duke of Marlborough's niece was not good enough for her. However, the Most Reverend Berk's family could be traced back to the Conqueror so his oldest daughter had possibilities in Imogen's eyes. Gavin tried not to stare at her mustache.

Money was also of little consequence to either of them. Gavin was a very wealthy man.

Of course, if he could have his choice . . .

Gavin's jealous gaze drifted to where his brother Ben stood with Elin. They were very happy in their love. Elin was to have been Gavin's, even though they hadn't really known each other. The betrothal had been arranged by their parents more than two decades ago.

However, Elin had wanted more. She'd wanted

a man who loved her with Ben's devotion and Gavin had reluctantly let her go.

Now, he found himself on the hunt for—what? Love? What the devil was that?

His fate was to marry out of obligation and duty, hence Aunt Imogen's whispered opinions of each young woman's assets without respect to their, hmmmm, well, what Gavin and any other male in the room would consider *assets*.

At the same time, Gavin had a sense he, like Elin, wanted more. The word "kissable" came to mind, as did the thought of companionship. He longed for a helpmate. Ducal responsibilities wore a man down. Gavin could only bear so much alone—

A prickling of awareness tickled the hairs at the nape of his neck. He looked to the door and his gaze centered upon a young woman waiting her turn in the receiving line.

Woman?

Goddess was a better description.

She was not too tall and not too petite but exactly right.

Her eyes were a sparkling blue, as clear as pieces of cut glass. Her hair was so blond it was close to white, speaking to some Viking forebearer, and her brows were dark, expressive. They added character to a face that would have been otherwise bland in its perfection. Her gown was a silvery white. The cut simply, but effectively, emphasized the womanly curves of some of the best *assets* Gavin had ever seen.

She was also undeniably kissable. Her lips were full and pink and, he was certain, very sweet.

Gavin's mouth went dry. His knees turned weak and every male part of him came to attention.

For the first time in his life, he had the urge to toss aside all veneer of civilization, throw this woman over his shoulder, and carry her off to his bed.

Aunt Imogen noticed the direction of his interest and her voice purred with satisfaction as she confided, "*She* is the one I wanted you to particularly meet. The late Lord Dearne's only child, Lady Charlene."

"Dearne? The profligate?"

"And buried years ago for his sins. His wife quickly followed him into death. They left her a penniless orphan. However, her bloodlines are the purest in the realm. Her stock is hardy. Look at the hips on that child. She will bear many sons."

Gavin couldn't stop staring at her hips or any other part of her. "And the portraits?"

"Will be spectacular," Imogen promised.

And then Lady Charlene stood in front of him.

His aunt introduced them as if he wasn't ready to fall into her arms and beg her to kiss him. The tops of her breasts swelled against her bodice with the graceful movement of her curtsy, and Gavin could barely stifle the rush of desire.

He heard his aunt introduce him to Lady Charlene's chaperone. He wasn't interested in her. His focus was on the beauty before him.

Lady Charlene—even her name was lush and full. He took her gloved hand and helped her rise.

She appraised him with the promise of a good intelligence and he realized she was waiting for him to speak. Everyone was waiting for him.

On the morrow, he was certain the papers and anyone witnessing this meeting between them would claim he'd been smitten—and they would be right.

"Welcome to my home," he managed to say.

"Thank you, Your Grace. It is an honor."

Her voice surprised him. There was a huskiness to it, a unique, melodic timbre.

Out of the corner of his eye, he caught his aunt exchange a knowing glance with his mother. They approved. *He* approved.

He was cognizant that they were holding up the receiving line. He didn't care. He couldn't even let go of her hand.

In fact, he was done with this nonsense. He'd

found *his* woman. Let the dancing begin and let him stake his claim by leading her first onto the dance floor. "My lady, will you give me the honor of the first dance?"

She blushed prettily. "I would be honored, Your Grace."

Gavin looked for Henry to signal the receiving line was officially at an end. The waiting guests could meander their own way in. He who only danced if he must was ready to run to the dance floor.

However, the always present Henry was missing from his post where Gavin could see him.

Instead, the sound of stern words and the sight of footmen moving toward the front entrance indicated that there was a disturbance.

Gavin stepped forward, placing himself between the door and the ladies even as Henry burst through the knot of footmen and waiting guests. He strode to Gavin's side. "Your Grace, there is a difficulty," he said in a low voice.

"With whom?"

"The head of the American delegation has arrived and wishes to present himself to you."

"I have no time for thorny Americans." He was done with duty and obligation. He desired to spend an evening basking in the company of a woman. He did not want to discuss negotiations, or business, or favors. "Tell him to present himself to my secretary on the morrow. Talbert will schedule a meeting."

But Henry didn't bow and obey. He leaned close to Gavin. "With all due respect, Your Grace, you may wish to meet this man."

"*Not* tonight," Gavin repeated, his tone alone making it clear he was in no mood for argument.

He turned to Lady Charlene, who had not stayed safely behind him but had moved to his side, obviously curious about the disruption. He offered his gloved hand. "Our dance, my lady?"

But before she could respond, the American literally muscled his way through the hallway door, several footmen gingerly holding on to his arms as if both determined and uncertain about holding him back—and in the blink of an eye, Gavin understood why.

Of course this man would not wait in any line, any more than Gavin himself would.

Lady Charlene vanished from Gavin's mind. The spectators in the crowded front hall all faded from his view, as did the humming of voices in the ballroom and the strains of music.

Instead, he was transported back in time, to his years in boarding school and the largest scandal his family had ever faced.

The "American" was tall and dressed in plain

clothing. His jacket was one that had been worn many times before but he filled it well. His overlong dark hair touched his collar in contrary to any style on either side of the Atlantic.

He gave the impression of being headstrong and proud, something Gavin knew to be true because he understood this man well. He even knew his name before it could be announced.

Gavin and Jack Whitridge were not identical twins, but enough alike in appearance that people would immediately recognize them as brothers— even now, over fifteen years after Jack had vanished without fanfare from his bed at school.

His disappearance had been the great mystery of that year. Their father had hired men to search for him and they'd found not a trace of his whereabouts or even a clue as to why he would go off in the middle of the night.

Bones had been found during that time in a shallow grave not far from the school. Some believed they were Jack's. Experts their father had hired to evaluate them could not reach a consensus.

But Gavin had known. In his heart of hearts, he'd always believed his twin was alive.

No one knew Jack better than Gavin. They had shared the same womb and the same mother's beating heart. In their childhood, there had always been just the two of them, in spite of their brother Ben's birth eight years later.

And now here they were, face-to-face.

At last.

There were no hellos, no outstretched hands or brotherly hugs. Instead, they squared off, stoic men, men much like their sire.

In a voice as familiar to Gavin as his own, Jack proudly said what Gavin already knew, "Your Grace, let me present myself to you. I am the leader of the American delegation."

Behind him, the dowager stepped forward. "Jack," she whispered. *"My son."* She then fainted, falling into Gavin's arms, and the ball was at an end.

Chapter Four

Menheim, his family's London home, had not changed, Jack reflected as he cooled his heels in the wood-paneled library that the footmen had hustled him to while his brother had seen to his guests and brought a gracious end to his ball. The Duke of Baynton must always be the consummate host, in spite of the appearance of a brother he hadn't seen for over fifteen years.

However, Gavin was not allowing any chance for Jack to leave again. Two of the footmen stood guard outside the door. Jack had nothing to do save cool his heels. Such was the diplomat's lot.

The library had been his father's private domain. Apparently it served as his twin's as well although there was little sign of Gavin's presence here. The books appeared to be arranged in the same order on the shelves as they had been years ago, without any additions or subtractions. The chair behind the ornate desk was still well used, the leather molded to the bodies of two dukes. Even the India carpet on the floor was the same. It didn't even look more worn.

Certainly for the number of times his father had forced Jack to stand for hours in front of his desk, there should be bare patches in the imprint of his shoes.

He took a deep breath, trying to release the tightness in his chest. Memories roiled inside him. Good ones and bad ones.

Jack had not wanted to return to England. He had not wanted to meet his brother . . . not this way.

Call upon your family, Governor-elect of Massachusetts Caleb Strong had begged Jack. He was dead set against all the talk coming out of Congress about war with Britain, as was Jack.

It was a heady thing for a young lawyer to have the ear of such an influential man. And Strong knew what he was doing. Jack had no desire to return to London but the governor-elect had appealed to Jack's vanity.

You are the only one who can help us, Strong had told him. *We are standing on the brink of disaster. I am convinced the British have no idea how reckless certain members of Congress are. You can help peace. Your brother has the power to change attitudes, and only you can persuade him. The future of this country is in your hands.*

Only you, he'd said and Jack had been powerless to resist.

Of course, the question was persuasion, the crux of the matter, and the fact Jack had not left his family on good terms. Or spoken to them since. He hadn't even known if they believed him alive.

He had been reluctant to tell Strong the truth. He'd some hollow idea in the back of his mind that he could be an effective diplomat *without* Gavin's help.

However, he had been in England for two weeks now and had accomplished nothing. He had presented his letters of introduction to all the proper persons and had not managed one productive interview. No one wanted to talk to the Americans, a situation that had given Silas Lawrence great satisfaction since his purpose for being on the trip seemed to be to thwart Jack's efforts.

And Matthew Rice? Jack had no idea why he'd come along, except to make a fool of himself.

Now, as Jack stood in this room that had served generations of dukes, he could almost hear his ancestors laughing at him, his father's voice rang loudest of all—

The door to the library opened. Jack faced it as if he expected a hundred swordsmen to come flying at him.

Instead, just his twin entered. Baynton was still in evening dress, his expression one of annoyance.

He shut the door without looking at Jack. "Could you have chosen a more dramatic way to let us know you have returned?" He walked over to the cabinet holding the whisky decanter. He poured himself a generous measure. "Do you want one?"

"No."

With a lift of one brow, an expression so reminiscent of their father Jack had endeavored never to use it, Gavin set the decanter down. He took his glass but didn't drink.

Silence stretched between them.

Jack broke it. "How is Mother?"

"Shocked."

"I'd like to see her." Years ago when he'd left, he'd not given a thought to what she would think or feel. His goal had been to escape.

Even when he'd walked into the house this evening he'd been more focused on Gavin than on the woman who had given birth to him—until she'd fainted. Then he'd noticed. Then he'd started to gain some idea of what his disappearance had cost her.

She'd aged. The fact had surprised him and it shouldn't have. After all, *he* was no longer fifteen. Why could he not have anticipated his mother would advance in years as well?

Still, he had not expected her wrinkles or the silver in her hair. He'd pictured her the way she'd been when he'd left. She had once been very important to him, but he'd callously tossed her aside.

Doubt was an uncomfortable emotion.

"So," Gavin said, "are you going to tell me?"

"Why I have presented myself to you?"

"Why you *left*." Gavin set his drink down on his desk without having taken a taste. "You walked into this house this evening as if we'd only seen you yesterday. It has been almost seventeen years. Where the bloody hell have you been?"

Jack had always assumed that someday there would be an accounting. The knowledge did not make this any easier.

However, Gavin was not waiting for a response. Instead, in typical style, he charged ahead. "We searched for you for years. Father hired the very best men. They combed England, the face of the earth. *They said you were dead.*"

The raw emotion in his brother's voice caught Jack off guard. "And how did you feel about that, Gavin? My being dead?"

For a second, his brother's stare hardened as if he could not believe what he'd just heard . . . and then he spoke. "Devastated."

The word rose in the air to take shape in the form of tiny daggers, a willing betrayal.

Jack had his reasons for leaving, reasons that now, he realized, years later, had been foolish—or had they? What sort of man would he have been if he stayed?

And yet, in the face of Gavin's honesty, he owed his twin something. "I had to leave," he said.

"By all that is holy, why?"

"Because."

Again, his brother's brows came together. He leaned back as if rejecting what he'd heard, and then suddenly he began laughing. He laughed loud, hard. He sounded half mad.

Jack saw nothing funny, and then he noticed the tears in his twin's eyes. He took a step toward him, uncertain of what he could say. This reaction was not expected—

A knock on the door interrupted them. "Your Grace, it is Ben." Ben, their brother.

Gavin underwent a transformation. His shoulders straightened. Had there been tears? Jack could see no sign of them.

"Come in," Gavin said. He reached for his drink.

Ben entered the room. He had the broad shoulders and strong nose of the Whitridges. However, he was a few inches taller than both Jack and Gavin and leaner in build.

Eight years separated the ages of the brothers. Jack barely knew Ben. He'd been off to school when Ben was born and had rarely returned home afterward. The more he stayed away from their father, the happier Jack was.

He now held out his hand to Ben. "We have not seen each other in a good while."

Before Ben could respond, Gavin said, "You offer your hand to Ben and for me, you had nothing?"

Ben shut the door as if he didn't want Gavin to be overheard.

Letting his hand fall, Jack said to his twin, "There was a time we knew each other so well, we could read one another's thoughts. Did I need to explain?"

Gavin took a sip of his drink and frowned as if it tasted bitter. "Yes, I believe I am owed an explanation. Perhaps even an apology. I would dare to suggest you owe both to all of us."

God, he sounded the very image of their father.

A wildness that had always been inside Jack reared its ugly head. For the past several years, he'd tamped it down but now here it was—his pride, his independent spirit, *all* the things their father had attempted to beat out of him.

"Mother is the one who deserves an apology but I don't think I owe you anything, Your Grace. You seem to have fared well without me."

"Perhaps the two of you wish to pound this out alone?" Ben suggested, placing his hand on the door handle.

"*Don't* think of going anywhere," Gavin answered Ben. "The days of my knowing what my twin is thinking are long past. We are barely acquaintances now. Tell me, Jack, how *has* your life been?"

Jack had set off this evening aware that presenting himself to his family would not be easy. Hard questions would be asked and he was certain they would not like the answers. However, right now, he could just as happily rip off his twin's head. If he could have accomplished his mission to his chosen country without him, he would have walked out the door.

Instead, he forced back his anger. "My life has been good," Jack answered. "And yours?"

The corners of Gavin's mouth tightened. "Father died."

"I had heard."

"Did you? *When?*"

Ben stood to the side, his body tense as if he wished he were anywhere else but here. However, now he, too, leveled his gaze on Jack.

Here was one of the answers that would damn him. "In 1808. He must have been dead for a year by then. A friend told me."

The lines of Gavin's face deepened, and then he walked behind his desk, setting his glass on the blotter in front of him. He sat, taking on the air of a judge ready to weigh evidence. He did not speak.

Ben shifted his weight. Was it Jack's imagination, or did this younger brother that he barely knew seem to have some commiseration for him?

The truth. Clear the air and speak the truth. The voice inside Jack, that voice that had prodded him to run, to escape, now urged him to not flinch from this moment. Indeed, Gavin deserved to know Jack's feelings . . . even if he would not like them.

"I felt no grief," he admitted. "Our father was a tyrant. You might not recognize that fact. After all, *you* were the chosen one."

Gavin did not move, not even an eyelash.

Ben bowed his head, and yet Jack sensed again that his younger brother knew of what he spoke.

"I was second best, Gavin, and according to Father, a serious disappointment."

"Therefore you ran away? Let all of us think you were dead?" There was no heat in Gavin's voice but his words were tense.

The anger, the frustration, the bloody fear his fifteen-year-old self had harbored that *this* would be all his life held welled inside Jack. "I needed to be free." He paused and then confessed, "I meant to come back. I thought I'd be gone a month, maybe two." He looked to Ben, to the sympathetic one. "Catering to Father's demands, his expectations, and knowing I had no role other than as a backup in case something happened to the first born ate at my soul. I wanted more. I *deserved* more. I certainly didn't want to be compared to you, Gavin. You were everything Father expected, all that a duke should be. Studies were effortless for you. You had the ability to spend hours inside poring over the most boring books when such endeavors were misery for me. I could think of nothing but escaping the library. You did everything well, Gavin. This role, being duke, was the reason you were the first out of the womb. I had no talent for it."

As Jack spoke, his twin had brought the full force of his attention upon him. He leaned forward, his hands on the arms of the chair as if he would rise. "No one expected you to be anything other than what you were—my brother."

"From your perspective," Jack answered. "From mine, I felt trapped. Bloody trapped."

"And so you bolted? You abandoned your family?"

Jack did not answer. He stood on a tinderbox.

"And you present yourself this evening," Gavin continued, "in front of all my company, as a delegation from another country? You would deny your nationality, the very essence of who you are? *Father was a bastard—*"

Gavin sounded as if the statement had been dragged from the depths of his being, as if he'd *never* spoken such words before, and there was a chance he hadn't. Jack had never heard him say such a thing. When they were lads together, Gavin had always defended their sire's decisions. Even Ben dropped his jaw in surprise.

"However," Gavin continued, suppressed anger behind every word, "*what* gave you the license to treat *us*, who loved you, as if we were *nothing*?" He leaned on the desk. "We believed you murdered or worse. And you were merely playing devil-may-care—?"

Jack rooted his feet to the ground. "I had reasons for not returning."

"What were they?"

The rebellion that was a strong part of Jack's nature bristled at his brother's tone. When he was younger, he would have told him to sod off and be done with him.

However, he was wiser now and he had a mission to accomplish. An important mission. The future of his adopted country was at stake.

Besides, his family was owed an explanation, as much as it galled Jack to be forced in the matter.

"Do you remember the acting troupe that came to Windsor the week before I left?"

Gavin frowned and shrugged.

"Of course you don't," Jack agreed. "You were so busy studying that you seemed indifferent to girls—"

"I was not."

"You gave that impression."

"If one can't act on the desire, why allow it?"

"I'm not that stoic, Gavin. Back then, women were always on my mind. In that acting troupe there was a particular young lady I took a fancy to and she liked me as well. I decided to go with them when they moved on."

Gavin held up a hand for understanding. "You left school to pursue an actress? Was that a mature action?"

"It wasn't my maturity doing the thinking."

Jack's comment startled a snort out of Ben, one he quickly stifled after a glare from the duke.

But Jack was not put off by Gavin's disapproval. "You wanted the story. I'm giving it to you. I traveled with them to Portsmouth. The troupe was playing in a fair and I found myself cast in a role. I rather liked acting and I certainly enjoyed the lass, so, if someone was searching for me—and on my word of honor, I was not aware of any search—then, no, I did not want to be found. Unfortunately, my life took a bad turn. I was taken by an impress gang."

"You were impressed?" Ben repeated.

"Aye. I served on His Majesty's ship the *Hornet*. They needed a crew for the Indies since most of theirs had succumbed to fever on the last run, and they chose me."

"Did you tell them who you were?" Gavin demanded.

"So often it earned me a lashing," Jack assured him. "They had no desire to hear me claim to be a duke's son, especially to a man as important as Father. It would have been far easier for them to toss me overboard than reckon with the Duke of Baynton."

"That was not right of them," Ben said.

"True, but I found I liked the roving life. I've seen Bombay. I've sailed around the Horn and enjoyed my time in the West Indies. I became the *Hornet*'s storekeeper. However, the first chance I had, I jumped ship."

"And you didn't think to come home?" Some of the anger had left Gavin's tone.

"I would be a wanted man," Jack explained. "The Crown does not look kindly upon deserters."

"We would have taken care of that misunderstanding for you," Gavin said.

"Aye, but after four years of living by my own wits, I'd come to like it. I was in an American port, Charleston, and I started walking until I couldn't see the ocean."

"Then what did you do?" Ben asked.

"I trapped, traveled around, married." He said the last evenly as if it was of no consequence, but it was—and, of course, Gavin caught it.

"You are married?"

"I was." Jack glanced over to the cabinet with the whisky decanter and moved toward it. He needed a drink. He could be calm, reasoned . . . until he let himself remember. He poured himself a healthy amount and took a swallow, letting the smoke of very good whisky ease a hated memory.

"Childbed fever took her." Jack drained his glass in one gulp. "It was a difficult birth. My son was stillborn."

For a moment there was silence, and then Ben said, "I am sorry."

"As am I," Gavin agreed.

A hard lump formed in Jack's throat the way it always did when he let himself remember too much. "She has been gone seven years."

"What was her name?" Gavin asked.

"Hope."

"What was your son's name?"

Jack paused a long moment and then said, "Daniel, after her father."

"I'm sorry," Ben said.

Gavin picked up his own glass and swallowed before saying, "As I am as well."

Jack set his glass on the cabinet. He now turned it thoughtfully as he finished his tale. "I had a farm at the time. There was nothing left for me there so I sold it and decided, ironically, to return to school. I attended Harvard College, studied law, and apprenticed under a man I admire, Caleb Strong. I started my practice in Boston. After so much time in the wilderness, the city suits me." He took a step away from the cabinet. "So there is my story. That is where I've been. And now I'm here because our two countries are dangerously close to going to war."

Gavin made a restless movement as if the change of subject to Jack's purpose annoyed him.

"And this is why you have finally returned? To persuade us to do what? Give you Canada?"

"There is a list of grievances I wish to share with you—"

"Bah!" Gavin said, rising and moving out from behind his desk on the side away from Jack. "I don't want to prattle about that nonsense now."

"Then when?"

Before Gavin could answer, the door opened. A lovely dark-headed woman came in holding the seemingly frail arm of their mother. Marcella, the dowager duchess, wore a dressing robe, and the pins had been removed from her hair so that it fell in silver locks around her shoulders.

Gavin was by her side immediately. "Mother, I thought Mr. Higley suggested you rest?"

She waved him away while she moved toward Jack. She stopped in front of him and placed her hands on his arms above the elbows. Tears formed in her eyes. "I had to see him again, to feel him. I needed to be certain I wasn't dreaming." She leaned close and Jack felt his arms go around her in the same manner that she had once hugged him when he was half his size.

His mother seemed impossibly small in his arms.

She drew in a deep breath. "Yes, you are my Jack. You have the scent I always remembered about you."

"What? Flowers and roses?" Gavin suggested.

"Dirty potatoes," their mother said, straightening and smiling up at Jack. "Welcome home, my son. Welcome."

Jack hugged her tighter then, the sting of his own tears in his eyes. He blinked them back. Men did not cry. He'd cried over Hope and the son he'd lost. He'd mourned for them for years. However, now he had heavy responsibilities. He could not let sentimentality cloud his vision.

His mother stepped back and urged the young woman to come forward. "Here, do you remember Elin?"

"Elin Morris?" Jack said. "Ah, you were betrothed to Gavin." Their father had betrothed him to Elin when she was little more than a babe. "Certainly, you are his duchess now?"

A becoming color swept her cheeks. It was Ben who answered. "Actually, she is *my* wife."

If someone had punched him in the face, Jack could not have been more surprised. The old duke had prided himself upon the Morris alliance and it stood to reason that Gavin, who had always jumped to their father's bidding, would have married whom he'd chosen.

Except he hadn't.

Jack now saw his twin with new eyes.

"You are a lucky man, Ben," Jack said and he meant the words. Elin had an air of both grace and good intelligence.

Again, she blushed as a modest young wife should. "I am also pleased to make your acquaintance. It is good to see that our worst fears for you had not happened."

"Tactfully spoken, my lady," Jack said, bowing again.

His mother wrapped her arms around his as if he were a mooring anchor. "You will stay here," she said.

Jack wanted to please, but he couldn't. "It would not be wise—"

"Why not?" she demanded.

Words failed him. He looked down into her eyes and did not want to tell her the truth.

Gavin did it for him. "He is an American now, Mother. He is negotiating for his new country."

"But that doesn't mean he is not *my* son," she informed the duke. "I want him under my roof. We have been apart for too long. What would people say if my lost son did not stay at Menheim?"

Jack looked at Gavin. His face had become a mask. Jack remembered how their father would retreat in that manner. No one knew his feelings or how he would react.

"I can't stay," Jack said gently to his mother. "There will be negotiations that could be compromised—"

"Nonsense," Gavin cut in. "In fact, if you wish my support in opening negotiations, then your wisest course is to please Mother."

"It is a conflict of interest for me to stay here," Jack insisted.

"Then return to Boston," Gavin answered. The negotiations had begun. To win the Duke of Baynton's cooperation, one must do as the duke wished.

And Jack wanted to refuse him, to exert his own authority, but he was a man now and the stakes at play were high. This was no time to indulge in old grudges.

"Then, yes, Mother, I will stay," Jack heard himself say, and prayed he was making the right decision.

Chapter Five

Sarah was sitting in the front room at her desk, writing away under the flickering light of a brace of candles, when Char and Lady Baldwin walked into the house on Mulberry Street. She set aside her pen and placed the cap on the ink bottle.

"How was the ball?" she asked. "You are home early, earlier than I had anticipated."

"We have quite a story," Lady Baldwin said before taking a moment to place a coin in the palm of the driver of the hired chaise that had carried them to the duke's ball and then home again.

The man did not want to leave. Hungry eyes on Char, he said, "If you ever need me again, ask for Lewis. I'm happy to be at your beck and call." He was young and handsome in a rawboned way and quite obviously taken with her.

"Yes, well, that is enough for tonight," Lady

Baldwin assured him and all but slammed the door on him to make him leave. She looked to Char. "I always receive the best service when I'm with you. However, sometimes, it is a bit too much."

"*He* was," Char agreed. She was tired, exhausted. She hadn't realized how wound up she'd been about this evening until now that it was over. She helped Lady Baldwin out of her velvet cape and took off her own cloak, hanging them both on the row of pegs in the hall.

Char had thought herself quite presentable for the evening until she'd arrived at the duke's house, handed over the wool cloak she'd borrowed from Sarah, and had seen it against the furs and embroidered outerwear of the other female guests. The poor wool had appeared quite shabby. It had been a humbling moment for Char, one of many.

Sarah knew something was wrong. "What happened? You weren't refused at the door, were you?" she asked as if she had feared the invitation was a hoax.

"Oh no, nothing like that," Lady Baldwin assured her, walking past her into the front room. "Something worse."

"Worse?" Sarah repeated.

"Yes, worse," Lady Baldwin declared, practically falling into a chair, the green and yellow feathers of her turban slightly askew. "Charlene, a glass of something, *please*."

"I need one as well," Char murmured. "And so will you, Sarah." She started for the kitchen but Sarah stopped her.

"I have it in here. I set up a tray for us to celebrate. Now tell me, what happened?"

"You will need a glass of something first," Lady Baldwin said.

Sarah began pouring from the sherry bottle on the tray. She handed a glass to Lady Baldwin. "Did she meet the duke?" she demanded.

"I met him," Char said.

Sarah handed her a glass. "Did he not like you? Oh no, he must. What did he say? Did you talk to him very long? Did he appear interested? Did you dance with him?"

"Oh, he was *very* interested," Lady Baldwin assured her. "I have never seen a man more taken with a woman than the Duke of Baynton was with our Charlene. One look and it was as if everyone in the ballroom—and it was packed, mind you. There were lovely girls and not so lovely ones with hopeful parents covering every inch of it. Packed to the rafters they were—"

"Will you finish your sentence?" Sarah said with no small amount of exasperation. "Everyone in the ballroom *what*?"

Chastened, Lady Baldwin said, "Why, it was as if everyone in the ballroom disappeared. He only had eyes for Charlene. He couldn't look hard enough at her. Dame Imogen was right by his side. She gave me a smile and a little nod of her head—" She demonstrated the barest of movements. "I took it as a sign that he had not had this reaction to any other young woman."

"He *liked* you," Sarah said to Charlene. "But then I knew he would. How could he not? This is wonderful, exactly what we'd hoped for. But then, why are the two of you so crestfallen? Why are you not happy?" Sarah's face had gone pale and Char knew what her aunt was thinking. They had spent almost all the money from the stolen purse. The rent had been paid for the month but everything else had gone toward preparing for this one evening.

And it had all been for naught—because of the appearance of *one* man.

"The duke's brother arrived," Lady Baldwin said. She drained her glass.

"And?" Sarah prodded.

"Apparently, he's been missing *for years*," Char explained, and of course, Whitridge would show up when she least needed him. She had not told anyone about her confrontation with him, not even Lady Baldwin. He had been her secret.

"Yes, everyone thought him dead," Lady Baldwin explained. "I remember when he first vanished. They said he had been sleeping in his bed at Eton and then—*poof!* He was gone. And then decides to show up on this one night, just as Charlene has been presented to the duke." She began acting out the moment. "The duke had asked her to dance. He looked around as if to signal that he was done with the receiving line, that he had found the woman he wanted."

"Oh my," Sarah said.

"But then the duke's brother broke in, *uninvited*, to the ball and ruined it all. The duke was not happy to see him and he seemed to forget our Charlene. She was pushed back out of the way while the two brothers had this reunion that they could have had tomorrow or the next day or the next one. I pushed her forward, Sarah. I wanted to remind him of her presence. By the by, Charlene was *not* help with that," she added as an aside. "I pushed forward; she kept trying to hide behind me."

Charlene had been trying to elude Whitridge's attention. Fortunately, he was so focused on his brother and the drama of the moment, he hadn't noticed her . . . which was good . . . except it had stung her vanity, which was odd because Whitridge was definitely someone she should avoid. She'd been very lucky to escape his notice and risk being labeled a thief in front of the duke and all the world.

And yet she found herself piqued about how oblivious he had been to her.

"Then the dowager duchess fainted," Lady Baldwin continued, "and the ball was called to a halt." She poured herself another glass of sherry.

Sarah reached for a glass as well and filled it to the brim. She looked to Char. "I don't suppose there was any chance the duke might remember you?"

Char shrugged and then admitted, "Not even a remote one. The ball came to an end then. We were practically pushed out the door by the footmen."

"Well." The word was a sentence in and of itself. Sarah looked into her overfull glass a moment and then lifted it in the air. "We tried. We took a risk and you can now say you have attended a ball."

"Or part of one," Lady Baldwin corrected. She tipped her own glass. "To our Charlene. Baynton is a fool to lose you."

Char could agree to that and raised her glass. "And to my lovely aunt and caring friend. You are my family and all I need to be happy."

They drank, the moment mellowing their disappointment over the evening.

Sarah spoke. "So, what did you think of Baynton when you met him? Is he as handsome as they say?"

"I couldn't quibble over his looks," she admitted. "He is tall with deep blue eyes and dark curling hair. If the Haymarket had him playing the lead roles, Colman would sell out every night."

"That handsome?" Sarah said, impressed.

"Aye, he has looks," Char returned.

Then again, the man who had caught her attention—and not just because he could denounce her—had been Whitridge.

She found herself thinking about him at odd moments, and not just because he had almost caught her. His looks were rougher than the duke's. He was far from being as polished. However, there was an air of confidence, an assurance about him.

Tonight, he had walked into their glittering company in tall boots and a plain jacket, and she knew there wasn't a female in the room who hadn't noticed him. Almost immediately, fans had started fluttering and there had been an air of restless interest.

And that had not set well with Char, either.

How contrary she was being. She should want to stay away from Whitridge.

Instead, she was not pleased that he had caught the eye of other women.

"Char, are you all right?" Sarah asked.

Her aunt's concerned question startled her. "Yes, of course. Why?"

"For a moment, your mind seemed miles away."

"I was thinking about the ball. You were right. I am glad I went. I will never forget it."

"I'm sorry it didn't turn out the way I had hoped," Sarah said. "My imagination had penned a whole new life for you. Baynton would sweep the penniless orphan up in his arms and make her his lovely duchess. There would be no worry, no doubt, and only happiness in your future."

"And stuffed goose every Sunday for dinner," Char added lightly.

"Oh, a stuffed goose would only be the beginning of the Sunday feasts in the ducal mansion," Sarah assured her.

"For my tastes, I would want a rib roast," Lady Baldwin said. "My daughter had one served last Sunday, but they sent a plate of chicken to my room. They had guests," she explained.

"That was rude," Char said. "What did your daughter say when you informed her that you were attending the Duke of Baynton's ball this evening? Was she surprised? Humbled?"

"She doesn't know I went and I don't know if I

will tell her. I said I was going out and she didn't bother to ask where. And look at me—I'm in all my finery . . ."

Lady Baldwin fell into a sad silence before almost ruefully saying, "Last week, I let my granddaughter Verity play in my clothes. She is only six. Lovely girl. Reminds me of my daughter at that age. Margaret used to enjoy dressing up with my things when she was that age. However, when I sent Verity to show her mother how pretty she looked in my feathers and scarves, Margaret laughed and asked her if she was trying to be a clown like her grandmother. She didn't know I was listening."

Sarah reached over to give Lady Baldwin's hand a squeeze. "Did you tell her what you heard?" Char asked.

"No, not that she would care." Lady Baldwin finished her glass and added, "I had some thought that after our Charlene was a great success, I would tell Margaret of the part I'd played. I would be the close friend of a duchess and not just *any* duchess, but the Duchess of Baynton. Now it is not to be. Silly of me to want to dream that way."

"My lady, I am so sorry—" Char started but Lady Baldwin shushed her.

"It isn't your worry, my girl."

"But you should come live with us," Sarah said.

"And add to your already many burdens? I think not. Besides, I value our friendship. If I lived with you all the time, you might not be so pleased with me. Margaret certainly isn't."

"Margaret is a prig," Char said loyally, and her friend smiled, an expression that didn't quite reach her eyes.

Before any more could be said, a knock sounded on the door.

"Who would be calling at this hour of the night?" Sarah asked, rising to go to the window and glance outside at the step before answering— and then she raced to the door.

"Who is it?" Char asked, coming to her feet.

In answer, Sarah stepped back, inviting two liveried and bewigged footmen into the house. Between them they carried an arrangement of red hothouse roses so large it was half the size of Char.

One of them bowed to Sarah. "Lady Charlene?"

She pointed toward Char, before covering her lips with both her hands as if to contain her excitement.

The servants gravely bowed before Char. "My lady," one said, "the Duke of Baynton bid us deliver these flowers to you."

"In the middle of the night?" Char said, dumbfounded.

"His Grace ordered it be done with all haste."

And when the Duke of Baynton spoke, his servants apparently jumped to his bidding.

"Where would you like us to place them, my lady? They are a bit heavy."

"On the desk," Char said as Sarah rushed to clear her writing from the surface.

The glorious bouquet took over the top of the desk. The servants were careful of the vase. It was swirled glass and a tribute to a glassblower's art.

"How could he arrange for this in the middle of the night?" Char said in wonder.

A footman answered, "The Duke of Baynton may do anything he wishes, my lady."

The scent of roses filled the air.

"His Grace also bid me deliver this letter." The footman presented to Char an envelope in the same heavy, gilded vellum that had been used for the ball invitation. "He directed me to wait for your response."

Char shot a look at Sarah and Lady Baldwin who gestured for her to hurry and open the envelope. The sealing wax was imprinted with a crest featuring a stag and a crown. Carefully prying it from the paper so that she could save it to examine later, she pulled out the card inside.

I regret we did not have our dance this evening. However, with your permission, I would call on you on the morrow.

The signature at the bottom was "Baynton," carelessly scrawled as if he wrote his name a hundred times a day.

She looked up at Sarah and Lady Baldwin. "He wants to call on me." She could scarce believe she was saying such a thing.

Fear of Whitridge vanished.

There wasn't a marriageable young woman in London who wouldn't have sold her soul for this request. *Char had been chosen*.

It was only then she realized that she had not actually believed it had been possible. Yes, Lady Baldwin and Sarah had predicted he could not help but notice her, but Char had not been convinced. After all who was she? The penniless daughter of a disgraced earl. A poor, pitiful relation.

And *she* had captured the attention of the most important duke in Britain. A handsome duke. A thoughtful one.

Her gaze went to the flowers. They were such a fulsome gesture. He wanted her to know he was serious in his intent.

Why, if a man could spend the money for hothouse flowers in February, he would be able to sponsor one of Sarah's plays or help Char provide for her aunt and her friend Lady Baldwin.

She'd even have five guineas to pay off the Seven and live a life free of petty larceny.

And she was glad now that Whitridge had not recognized her. He'd been standing practically next to her and had not realized who she was. Perhaps he had put her from his mind? Or had not registered her features as completely as she had the ability to recall his?

Sarah cleared her throat, a reminder to Char that the footman awaited an answer.

This marriage could change the futures for all of them. Would Char be her father's daughter if she didn't take a chance?

"Yes, I would like His Grace to call. I would like that very much," Char said.

The servants bowed and left. Sarah closed the door behind them. She walked forward as if entering the presence of greatness. She threw her arms about Char and swung her around the room. Lady Baldwin did her own jig, the half-empty sherry bottle held high.

"You did it," Sarah said. "You did it, you did it, *you* did it. Oh, sweetie—" She used a pet name for Char. "Our luck has changed."

Char prayed she was right.

Chapter Six

Jack woke the next morning in one of Menheim's very comfortable beds and his first thought was of the lovely pickpocket.

After their confrontation, he'd gone out of his way to walk that particular section of the city, looking for a slender lad hiding hair kissed by the moon under an overlarge hat.

Of course he didn't find her. She was clever enough to avoid him. And he had more important matters to consider than a petty criminal, even a lovely one.

He'd forced her out of his mind. He was singular of purpose and focused on what he needed to do . . . until this morning, and he wasn't certain why he thought of her now.

Something had prompted his curiosity about her and Jack couldn't fathom what it was.

Gavin had sent footmen the night before to the Horse and Horn for his belongings. Jack now dressed himself and, seeing the time, left his room bound for a meeting of his delegation at the inn.

Menheim was quiet when he went out the door, which was not unusual considering the ball the night before. Not even Henry, their ever-present butler, guarded the front door.

"I hear you created a stir last night," Silas Lawrence commented in greeting as Jack sat down at his table in the public room. The Horse and Horn was a busy posting inn and accessible to wherever one might wish to go in London, or in England.

The room charges were also reasonable. Jonathan Russell, the United States chargé d'affaires to the Court of St. James, had recommended it to Jack's delegation. He'd also warned that the United States government was notoriously slow with paying travel vouchers. Matthew Rice might have enough money to lose his purse and replace it, but Jack didn't. He wasn't certain about Silas's financial standing, but the man had offered no protest at the choice of residence.

"And you heard this where?" Jack said.

"The papers." Lawrence spread his hands over the paper he had been reading. "They are full of stories about your brother's ball last evening. I didn't realize you had gone missing and had been believed dead."

"I am more resilient than most consider me," Jack returned.

Lawrence gave him one of his tight smiles. "Apparently. I knew you were well connected but I didn't realize there was so much family spectacle involved. You are all anyone can talk about. I've been sitting here for an hour and your name is on everyone's lips."

"I am not here to discuss my family history. Where is Matthew?" Jack nodded as the serving girl, a buxom lass with more swagger to her hips than a sailor, gestured to see if he wished a tankard. He pointed to whatever Silas was drinking. "I sent word we should all meet at this hour."

"And I am here." Lawrence began folding the paper. "I did notice you didn't return last night."

"I'll be staying with my family."

"Ah." Lawrence had a way of making that one syllable sound a condemnation. "Well, our young friend may not be joining us. He is sleeping it off."

"Sleeping *what* off?"

"Relax, Whitridge. Matthew is young. He took in too many of the sights, if you understand my meaning." His gaze lingered appreciatively on the serving girl as she placed a pewter mug in front of Jack.

Leaning forward to block his view, Jack said, "We are not here for enjoyment. I know you are a war hawk." He referred to the faction in Congress that seemed always anxious and ready to declare war on Britain. "I expect you to do all you can to ruin any good I can accomplish, but let's keep Matthew away from the whores."

"And spoil his enjoyment of the city?" Lawrence asked as Jack took a drink of his mug and then almost choked in surprise.

"Rum? This early?"

"It is beneficial to my constitution."

"So when we finally have our meeting with Whitehall, I have on my side a rum swiller and a green lad who wants to make a name for himself not in diplomacy but by poking every wench he sees."

"I don't swill all the time," Lawrence answered. "However, it is good of us to finally have this conversation instead of our usual polite coldness."

"Glad you feel so obliged."

"Oh come now. If the powers-that-be—and that does not include either you or me, but most certainly your mentor Governor Strong and my good friend, Speaker of the House Mr. Clay—wished to negotiate with all the goodwill of our United States, then they wouldn't have sent us.

Some of the most noble of our statesmen have already done exactly what we plan to do, lay out the American grievances, and they failed to earn any interest from our current hosts. If nothing has been accomplished since the Chesapeake-Leopard Affair"—he referred to a naval incident where the HMS *Leopard* had attacked and boarded the American ship looking for supposed British deserters among the ship's complement—"then there is little *we* can do. We've been here two weeks, Whitridge, and we can't find anyone to accept even our letters of introduction. Another sign, if you ask me, of Britain's complete disregard for our country. War is inevitable."

Jack took a more circumspect sip of his rum. It was not good quality. "We could be crushed."

"With the English fighting the French and Lord knows whom else? Their forces are spread too thin. I plan on assuring Mr. Clay that *now* is the hour to strike."

"Look around you, Lawrence. The very world is represented in this inn. People are here from every continent, merchants from all corners, visitors anxious to trade with the mighty. Don't believe for one second that Britain doesn't have the power to defend her holdings. Especially at sea."

"So you are not up for the fight? Or perhaps seeing your family has changed your allegiances?"

Jack could have grabbed Lawrence by his bagwig and pounded his face on the table.

He didn't. He'd given up those sorts of actions once he'd decided to become a gentleman. That didn't mean he didn't have the thoughts.

"I've touched a nerve," Lawrence observed, reading Jack's expression accurately.

"You have questioned my loyalty. We may have a difference of opinion but we both want what is best for our country."

"*Our* country? The papers are stating you were welcomed home with open arms."

"You can't believe the scribblers here any more than you can at home. I know my own mind and I know what happened last night." Jack leaned forward. "The only reason I presented myself to my brother is because we were not making headway. Our reception should be different today."

"My, the Duke of Baynton is powerful indeed if that is the case," Lawrence said mockingly.

"He has more than power, he is respected," Jack returned.

Lawrence laughed his response. "Very well, tell me what you wish of me. However, let me assure you that Madison and his war hawks have decided upon war. A delegation comprised of something other than a newly minted lawyer, a rum-soaked scholar, and our wenching friend Matthew will not deter their decision."

There was truth in that statement.

"My advice," Lawrence continued, picking up his paper, "which I am certain you won't heed, is that we enjoy ourselves while we are here in London and keep our expectations low. For all we know, war may already have been declared."

Jack refused to accept this. There were good men willing to do all that they must to avoid such a happening. "I'm not one to avoid a challenge—"

"You are in the minority, my friend."

"At least we know where each other stands." Jack stood.

"Returning to the family?" Lawrence's manner was so offhand and mild, they could have been speaking of the weather instead of the future of a nation that Jack had come to value.

"I was sent to do what I could. I shall carry on."

"Let me know how your request for the Canadian provinces is received."

Jack could have taken the man's head off. "You may mock me, Lawrence, but you will not deter me. Warn Matthew of the clap. His future wife, Ruth, would not be pleased with such a surprise. And as for yourself, stay the bloody hell out of my way."

With those words, he turned away, and that was when he noticed the seemingly nondescript man sitting on a bench by the door. His hat was pulled low over his eyes as if he was taking a snooze. Here was the perfect target for the Jack's frustration with his American compatriots.

Leaning over the table, supposedly for the purpose of pouring the contents of his almost full mug into Lawrence's now empty one, Jack said, "Do you see that man on the bench with his hat low over his head?"

"I do."

"When you have the chance, mark his face. Tell me or send a message immediately if you see him or anyone like him following you or Matthew."

"Who is he?"

Jack smiled grimly and did not answer. Instead, he walked over to the man and kicked his boots before sitting on the bench beside him. The man sat up and Jack had a good look at his face.

He did not know him, although he knew his hunch about the man was correct. "My father, the old duke, used to have a gent who dogged my every step when I was a lad. He was not successful, as you know. I still managed to elude him many a time, and I can do the same with you."

To his credit, the man did not disavow Jack's suspicions. He stretched and sat up, tilting his hat on his head. "I am merely doing what is asked, Lord Jack." He had even features but bland ones. Brown eyes, brown hair; he could stand in front of someone and, if he was surrounded by a crowd, they would not see him.

The title needled Jack. He was not comfortable with it. He held out his hand. "Call me Whitridge. Or Jack. I answer to both."

The man hesitated and then shook his hand. "I'm Perkins."

"I imagine my brother has charged you with following me around."

Perkins did not answer.

Jack shrugged. "So much like Father." He stood. "Very well, Perkins. I'm off to Whitehall. You can either follow me or walk beside me."

His brother's man stood. "Which would you prefer?"

"Walk with me," and on those words, Jack left the Horse and Horn. Perkins followed a step behind.

It was a sunny day for February in London. Jack made good time on his way to Whitehall, the section of buildings housing the government. He had traveled this way every day for the past week and a half. No one had been particularly interested in what he had to say.

However, matters might be different now that

he had revealed his connection to the Duke of Baynton.

He'd gone to his brother last night because he'd finally come to realize he must swallow his pride and use his connections. He'd struggled with his rebellious streak. He had wanted to do this himself. Still, it was more important to him that he make his mark on an issue that mattered.

And then, perhaps, he would stop believing himself a failure.

He wasn't certain when the shadow of doubt had first fallen across him. He'd not lied to Gavin when he'd said he'd enjoyed his years sailing. It had been an adventurous life and a hard one. He'd been a smart sailor and he'd basked in the relative independence of being able to do as he pleased without his father's constant criticism and disapproval.

Jack had even considered himself wise when he'd taken leave of his ship. Here was true freedom. He'd roamed the American wilderness, working for his food whether by trapping, trading, or manual labor. He'd enjoyed those days. He'd met enough characters to tell stories over a lifetime. He liked Americans. He liked being one of them.

Of course, his free-spirited rambling changed when he'd met Hope. Lovely women like Hope had been scarce in the wilderness, and at three and twenty, Jack had been more than ready to take a wife.

His days of wandering may have come to an end. However, his ambition had not. He'd needed to prove himself. He must. It was the lesson his father had drummed into him. Farming and working the trading post with his wife's family had not been enough. He'd always wanted more.

Then, after Hope's death, he found he needed a complete change from what he had been doing. The law became his calling. He'd discovered he actually liked studying. Gavin would laugh if he heard that. Jack had never been a good student before.

Now, as he walked past the statue of the first King Charles in Charing Cross, the thought struck Jack that he was becoming more his father's son than ever before. *That* idea stopped him dead in his tracks.

Perkins came to a halt as well and looked questioningly at him.

Jack stood where he was, taking in the sights and sounds where the Strand ran into Whitehall road. The traffic was busy. The coaches, riders, and sedan chairs of the powerful intermingled with drays and hundreds if not thousands of pedestrians from every walk of life. They were intent on their personal interests, weaving their way around other people's busyness, going about their lives.

And he was—what?

Oh, he had purpose. His legal practice in Boston gave him great satisfaction. He was determined to bring the list of American grievances to the attention of Prime Minister Perceval's government.

He'd lost much already in his life, including a wife whom he'd adored, but he had no complaints at this moment—except, he realized, he was looking for *her* again. He searched for hair so blond it appeared white. Or startled blue eyes.

"Is something the matter?" Perkins asked.

"Ah, no. Just thinking," Jack answered. "Every once in a while, a memory forces me to pause."

Perkins accepted the excuse, nodding as if he understood, but Jack knew he didn't. It was insanity to keep thinking of the pickpocket. Jack's days of being ruled by his small head were long past.

Or should be.

Jack made himself walk toward the rows of government offices in front of him.

Perkins went so far as to accompany Jack on his rounds of the different offices inside. Jack had already visited each of them numerous times. He had asked for an audience with different representatives of each department. He'd been rebuffed.

However, today he anticipated matters to be

different. As Silas Lawrence had pointed out, the papers were full of the very public family reunion. The civil servants who had been so disdainfully cold to him should be more temperate in their reception of him and his mission.

They were not.

Indeed, they were actually more condescending.

So much so, Perkins started to take pity on him. "That was a rude fellow," he said of the third assistant to the assistant secretary for colonial affairs.

Jack didn't answer. He was too angry.

And then he saw his brother Ben. Ben had just stepped out of a room with a group of men. He carried several ledgers and appeared to have his own assistant to the assistant.

His younger brother stopped at the sight of Jack. The men he was with looked on with more than polite interest. Ben said something to them and then started walking toward Jack.

"Hallo, brother," he said as if he and Jack were on the friendliest terms.

Aware that they were being observed by the curious, Jack held out his hand. "Good to see you."

While shaking Jack's hand, Ben nodded to Perkins. "Baynton has you back at work, I see."

Perkins shrugged. "It is always my honor to work for His Grace."

"Give him a wild chase," Ben advised Jack. "Perkins becomes bored if we don't do something to liven his dull existence."

There was humor in his comment but a touch of anger as well. So Jack wasn't the only one Gavin had unleashed Perkins on.

"What are you doing here?" Jack asked his brother.

A guarded expression came to Ben's eyes. He glanced at the gentlemen waiting for him. They actually *all* had the look of assistants—and they waited for Ben.

His brother looked down at the floor as if uncertain of what he was about to say before admitting, "I work for Liverpool."

Elation and relief flood Jack's veins. "How fortunate. I didn't know." Ben could have told him this last night, but Jack dismissed the idea. The meeting with his family had been an emotional one and, while he was always ready to advance the cause of his adopted country, he could understand there was a time and place for such discussions. Like now.

"Let me have a moment of your time," Jack said. "Perhaps you can listen to what I have to say and between us we can chart the best course."

Ben glanced again at the men waiting, a signal to Jack that he did not have time. "Have you talked to Russell?" he suggested. Jonathan Russell had been named chargé d'affaires when Ambassador William Pinckney had been recalled by President Madison.

"I have done more than talk to him. He has made the rounds with me and is as frustrated as myself over the implied slights we have received. Ben, I have yet to present my letters of introduction to anyone of importance. Even to those who are *un*important. I am continually put off—"

"It is difficult, Jack. We have more pressing concerns with Napoleon eating up the Continent—"

"You are going to have two battlefronts if I can't find someone willing to listen. Our grievances with Britain can be resolved. However, we need your government to sit with us in good faith."

Ben took a step back. "With us?"

"With us Americans," Jack clarified, although he thought it was obvious.

His brother now moved closer. "Everyone knows that you are the head of the American delegation but you *are* British."

"I was born in England," Jack agreed slowly. "However, I've taken up residence in America."

"But you are *British*."

"I don't consider myself so."

"And that is the problem. Once an Englishman, always an Englishman, Jack. Of course many of the gentlemen in this building remember you calling on them numerous times before last night. However now that they know you are Baynton's missing twin, well, the mood is not welcoming. They think you disloyal."

"I'm not being disloyal to *my* country."

"That isn't how they see the matter." Ben sounded almost regretful, until he added, "I understand their concerns. You are English, Jack. *I'm* English, and we have the same parents. You come across as a—" He caught himself from finishing the sentence, but Jack was not going to let him slip away so easily.

"A what, Ben? A traitor?"

His brother frowned as if not liking the sound of the word and then said in a low voice, "Somewhat."

"Somewhat like yes? Or somewhat like no?" Jack was pushing him, but he was quickly moving past caring.

"You were *born* English," Ben insisted doggedly.

Jack could have roared his irritation. "Regardless of *which* country I am from, or which country I choose, I would *like* to believe *any* of us would wish to avert *a war*. To me, that is the larger question. Does that not make sense?"

"My government is not concerned about American grievances right now, Jack. We have more pressing issues."

"More pressing than *war*?"

"We are already at war."

Now it was Jack who took a step away from his brother. Their conversation was going in circles. Ben would not see reason. He would not help him. Meanwhile, gentlemen had come out of their offices to witness the confrontation. Perhaps one of them would have heard his case and realized the grave concerns at stake.

Or Jack might find himself the topic of more articles in the papers on the morrow.

That thought gave him pause.

He struggled with his temper. Creating a scene, especially with his brother, would not help his cause. "Very well," he said quietly. "But there must be someone who is willing to listen. Someone who has the power to make your government do what is honorable and right."

"You know who that person is," Ben said.

Of course, Jack did—Baynton. His twin. There was so much between them. Too much.

"Where is he now?" he asked Ben.

"At the time of the day, he can be a number of

places. However, I happen to know that his intention was to go courting."

"Courting?"

"Yes, Jack, our brother is in the market for a wife. The purpose of the ball last night was to introduce him to eligible young women."

This information tickled Jack's interest. "Did he meet anyone he liked?"

"Well, the ball came to an abrupt end," Ben reminded Jack. "However, I believe he was introduced to someone of interest. Lady Charlene Blanchard," he said as if needing to share the information. "He is calling on her this afternoon. Elin and I also spent the night at Menheim and when I saw him this morning, he was—well, how to describe it? Afloat. He was cheerfully afloat."

Jack gave his brother a look of disbelief. "Gavin is never cheerful in the morning, unless the years have worked a miracle in him."

"They haven't. He still is not his best in the morning. However, *this* morning, he was afloat. I even heard him humming."

"*Our* brother?"

Ben nodded.

"So what you are saying is that if I want to speak to Baynton right this minute, I need to find this young lady?"

"Well, if you want him *right* this minute," Ben

agreed. "But I wouldn't. Baynton will not be pleased."

Jack didn't care. "I have been complacent, Ben. I have been polite and I have been diplomatic. The time has come to shake the tree a bit, starting with the one man who has the power to help me."

"Don't tell Gavin I was the one who gave you the information."

"You needn't worry. Our brother will be so annoyed to see me, he won't ask. Come along, Perkins."

And with that Jack set out to track down his twin.

Chapter Seven

$\mathscr{G}$avin was courting.

He stood on the front step of the address on Mulberry Street and took deep breaths to calm his nerves. Dukes could not fear anything. They lived to lead, and confidence was vital to that process.

However, from the first moment he'd received word Lady Charlene would be honored if he called, his initial elation had quickly turned to a cold sweat. Gavin had never wooed a woman before. He'd never even paid a call on one.

For most of his life, he'd been promised to Elin Morris in a betrothal his father had arranged back when they were children. His father had explained that having a wife chosen for him freed Gavin to prepare to be the duke he should become. His father had high expectations. He'd wanted his heir to focus on becoming a man of importance, a man of history.

Nor had Gavin balked at following his father's dictates, not like Jack had. Jack had always been surly over their father's demands.

In contrast, Gavin had actually enjoyed the challenge of meeting his father's standards and often bettering them. He'd come to gain confidence in *every* facet of his life from the political to the social . . . except for one area.

Women.

They were a mystery to him. Because he had Elin, he'd shied away from forming any attachments to them other than his female relatives. And those women seemed a bit capricious to him, even his mother. He was never certain what they were going to think or do. It was only logical to assume the rest of womankind would share this trait, one that served no purpose to his way of thinking: Facts were facts. A schedule was set and to be followed. Black could not be white.

Elin should have been his wife . . . but her heart had taken a different direction, something Gavin wasn't certain he understood. He was never comfortable with talk of emotions.

However, he'd had the good sense to realize that she belonged with his brother Ben.

Now he had to find another woman to take to wife. He could do this. He knew he had looks that attracted them, even if his title hadn't. Even Jack had managed to marry.

His twin's admission had rattled Gavin a bit. He and Jack had once been very competitive. That Jack had achieved matrimony and he hadn't, well, the thought gnawed at Gavin a bit.

And he wasn't going to win a wife unless he knocked on Lady Charlene's door. He lifted his hand and rapped smartly.

The weather door opened immediately, which told him Lady Charlene's household knew he'd been standing there. Perhaps they had noticed his phaeton pulled by smart grays that his tiger was walking while he paid his addresses. Perhaps they had been aware of him standing on their stoop and had wondered *when* he would knock.

The maid, her hair hidden under a huge mobcap, lowered her eyes modestly and curtsied. "Welcome, Your Grace," she murmured in a strangely subdued voice. "Please, come in."

He offered his coat and hat to her. As he did, he caught a glimpse of her eyes—cat eyes. Green ones. Quite unusual.

Something else bothered him as well. The

maid seemed to be playing at being subservient. He sensed, and it was an odd notion, that she was anything but dutiful.

He looked around the cramped hallway. The house was exactly what he expected for this neighborhood. The appointments were modest and yet the energy was good, as if the occupants liked each other.

Gavin had learned to detect the moods of a place early in his youth. He'd used the skill to divine his father's often mercurial tempers.

He looked into the front room of the house and all thoughts of maids, fear, nerves, and father were banished by the sight of Lady Charlene standing demurely in front of the hearth, waiting for him.

There had been times, over the hours since he'd last seen her, that Gavin had questioned if she was as lovely as he remembered. His feverish yearnings had pictured her as perfect, exquisite. His common sense warned that he might have just been caught up in the intent of the ball. Everyone had been dressed their best. In everyday life, there would be flaws, imperfections . . . but if there was a blemish anywhere on Lady Charlene's person, he did not find it.

Her very presence lit up the winter afternoon.

She was glorious, a Viking goddess come to life dressed in rose-hued muslin. Her eyes were the color of cornflowers, her skin as lustrous as the Scots pearls that were the pride of his family— and would be his bride's gift to the woman he would choose.

Lust was a new and intriguing emotion. Gavin had never felt it as sharply as he did now. And certainly, the fire in his blood was encouraged by the way the fire in the hearth behind her illuminated the shadow of her shapely legs beneath her skirts.

He walked into the room and bowed. "Lady Charlene."

She curtsied. "Your Grace." She gave him a tentative smile that was charming in its shyness. "You do remember my chaperone, Lady Baldwin?"

No, Gavin hadn't a memory of anyone but her. Beautiful, luscious, delectable her.

Dame Imogen had been correct. The sort of children he should breed was an important consideration and their children would be magnificent. In fact, he was ready to breed right now.

It was a struggle for him to tear his attention away from Lady Charlene and bow over the hand of the older woman with a lace cap covered with cherry-red ribbons over her powdered hair. She had risen from her seat on the settee. "Lady Baldwin," he managed.

"Your Grace." She gave a small curtsy. "You honor us with your presence."

"The honor is mine," he dutifully answered.

"Please, sit," Lady Baldwin said, perching her own ample self on the settee and spreading her orange and red striped skirts over the cushions.

Gavin waited for Lady Charlene to delicately sit on one of the two chairs before the hearth while he took the other. Usually, he was impatient during these sorts of formal calls. However, he would do anything to please Lady Charlene.

"We have tea," Lady Charlene said, indicating a tray on a side table next to her chair, "and some sandwiches. Would you care for refreshment?"

"Tea would be nice," he answered, and watched with approval as she poured just the right amount in a cup and lifted the creamer to see if he wished any. She was grace personified.

For the first time, he was glad, no, overjoyed, that he had not married Elin Morris.

"No cream," he said to her unanswered question. "I'm surprised you had the tray ready," he managed. He found himself surprisingly tongue-tied, another first.

She smiled and handed him his cup. "There is always a hot kettle in our kitchen and we had time to prepare for you."

"You knew what time I was coming?" he said, flattered at the thought they had been poised at any moment to receive him.

"You were out on our front step for a bit of time," she said, the most charming light in her eyes. "Would you care for a sandwich?"

At her mention of how long it had taken him to gather his courage to knock on her door, Gavin felt a dull heat creep up his neck. In another time or place, he would have laughingly tossed out some witticism about having important matters on his mind. After all, he was a duke.

However, with her, he seemed struck mute.

With a shake of his head, he declined the sandwich and she turned her attention to preparing tea for Lady Baldwin and herself.

He watched her every move, marveling at her perfection. He was also aware that the maid had entered the room. She stood by the door, and he had the uncomfortable sense that instead of being properly servile, she was taking in all that was happening as if weighing him for her own opinion.

Gavin tried to block out her presence, but she had a thorniness that was hard for him to ignore.

Lady Charlene did not seem to notice her servant. Instead, she offered Lady Baldwin a cup of tea and then saw to her own. She liked her tea with cream and a sweet. She stirred the cup and smiled at him. "We enjoyed your ball last night," she said.

"Yes, Your Grace, it was excellent," Lady Baldwin agreed.

"The evening ended far too early," he admitted, and then dared to add, "Before we could have the dance you promised me."

A blush rose to her cheek. Lady Charlene smiled. Her dark lashes lowered shyly against her cheek as she confessed, "It was probably just as well. I'm a terrible dancer. I always step on someone's feet."

Gavin could have promised she was free to tromp on his feet all she liked. "I shall keep that in mind when we do have that dance," he answered, and she laughed, the sound as light and musical as angel wings.

And then they fell into silence.

And Gavin, usually able to make conversation in any other circumstance, did not know how to break it.

He didn't dare say or do anything that might possibly make her disapprove of him, and consequently was paralyzed. He looked around the room, noticed the gigantic arrangement of roses that he'd sent to her. It was a wonder he hadn't noticed them immediately. Their scent owned the air.

The arrangement was really too ostentatious and he experienced a stab of panic. No wonder she was quiet. The flowers were exactly the wrong gift. They were over the top. She probably thought him a braggart.

* * *

Charlene was uncomfortable in the silence.

She felt she should say something but what does one say to a person one doesn't know? Especially if the person is the Duke of Baynton.

It was one thing to have met him in his home with all the trappings, but to have him here? On Mulberry Street? Char was certain he must think them several steps below him.

She glanced at Sarah, who stood like a humble maid waiting orders. As Char had hoped, Sarah knew she was in over her head. Sarah helped her out. *Horses*, she mouthed.

Oh yes, every man liked to talk about horses. "Tell me about your horses," Char said.

The duke jumped at the topic. He was proud of his grays and had bred them himself. He carried the conversation, and all Char had to do was appear interested. She was so relieved.

Lady Baldwin acted thankful as well. Apparently she had been equally stumped for a topic.

Of course, after the first few minutes, Char's good intentions began to lag. She knew very little about horses, having never been around them much. Her attention began to wander. She also wondered what subject she would choose next once he'd run dry on this one.

She also noticed that the duke did not ask her anything about herself.

Perhaps being a duke, no one else was as important as he was . . . ?

Such an observation would not serve her well. She was determined to marry him for the security that the marriage would provide for herself and Sarah and Lady Baldwin. She must learn to like him—although she did not *dis*like him.

Char wasn't quite certain what she felt.

She did believe the duke was handsome. She could understand why eligible young ladies had flocked to his ball. However, she found herself looking for signs of his twin in the duke's perfectly groomed person. It was almost as if the two men were shadow, not mirror, images of each other.

Was it wrong to possibly prefer Whitridge to the duke?

She was certain Sarah would think so.

"Well," the duke said, bringing her attention back to him, "I need to take my leave. There are matters I must attend."

Char smiled, relieved. "Thank you, Your Grace, for making time for me during your busy day." She and Sarah had practiced this statement and Char thought she had delivered it rather well.

He seemed pleased. He stood. Bowed over her hand and murmured, "I would that I had nothing to do but bask in your presence."

That was an alarming statement. Char didn't know if she could manage the agony of the silence she had suffered before she'd asked about horses. She would go half mad.

Fortunately, dutiful Sarah-the-maid had fetched His Grace's coat and hat. She held it for him by the front door. Seeing her, he bowed to Lady Baldwin and started from the room.

Prompted by a look from Sarah, Char rose and trailed after him, feeling a bit like a lost puppy.

Sarah helped him with his coat. He took his hat and then faced Char. "I must admit something."

That statement lifted Char's interest. Sarah's as well, she noted.

"This is the first time I have paid a courting call."

The news surprised her. She would have supposed a gentleman like him had wooed countless women. For the first time, she truly looked at him. His eyes were kind.

"This is the first time I've ever had one as well," she answered.

"So, we are both celebrating firsts."

"Is that why we both were a bit stiff?"

"Stiff? Or wary?"

She blinked at the choice of words and the insight into his character they offered. She frowned. "Stiff. I'm not wary of you."

The smile he gave her transformed his face. He could make any woman light-headed when he looked at her like that instead of the intent scrutiny he'd given her while she'd poured tea. It had made her feel awkwardly aware of him.

However, now, she found she could breathe.

"I've discovered that 'firsts' are always difficult," he said. "I look forward to bettering our acquaintance. My hope is to see much of you over the next several weeks."

The smile Char gave him was genuine. "Nothing would please me more, Your Grace."

He released his breath as if he'd been holding it against her answer. "That's good. *Very* good. Until the morrow then. And be ready," he warned, "I have a feeling you will soon receive a stream of invitations. They will be for events that are on my calendar. I hope you accept them. Wherever you are, I shall look for you." He took her hand. "As you come to know me better, you may feel you can relax around me and we won't have to talk about horses."

His comment, that he had been aware of her boredom, sparked a laugh. Yes, he was a *good* man. One she could respect, and perhaps even grow to love.

Love. It was such a funny word. Her mother had loved her father so much that after the miserable

Cathy Maxwell

life he'd given her, she'd followed him in death. Char had never thought she could trust love. But Baynton was different. He had the resources to provide a good life.

But would he slay a dragon for her?

A heavy knock sounded on the door. A pounding actually, because the wood slats of the door jumped with each blow.

Startled, and since she was standing closest to the handle, Char opened the door, and then stepped back in shock.

Whitridge stood there. He seemed full of himself as if he had news to impart.

"I am looking for the Duke of Baynton—" he started, and then stopped, his jaw dropping for one long, endless second. "*You?*" he whispered, recognizing her.

Char slammed the door in his face before he could say more.

Chapter Eight

Jack stared at the door. He'd barely pulled back before having his nose smashed.

It was she. The girl. The pickpocket.

The lass who for some reason had been nesting in his mind.

She was here at Lady Charlene Blanchard's house. She was right on the other side of the door.

And of course he had to knock again. He would bloody damn well hammer the door down. It was that sort of day for him. She owed him Matthew's purse, and an explanation.

He also wanted another very good look at her. She was a beauty in breeches, but in a dress, well, she had no equal—

The door opened to his knock but instead of

his thief, his brother came out, looking ducally perturbed. He set his hat on his head. "What the blast are you doing here?"

"Knocking on a door. Looking for you. Who is the girl that answered?" He tried to catch a look around his brother.

Gavin shouldered him away, closing the door. He brushed by Jack.

For a second, Jack was caught between his desire to chase the lovely thief and his duty to talk to his brother. Honor won out, barely.

Gavin was already in the seat of his phaeton; his tiger, a small man in Baynton livery, jumped to stand on the step behind the driver. In a second he would be gone.

The thiefess would have to wait.

Gavin was turning the phaeton around, a tricky maneuver in such tight quarters as this narrow street. It took little effort on Jack's part to step up beside the tiger. He offered the man a coin. "I wish to speak to my brother alone."

Gavin looked back at him, frowned. He had his hands full backing and turning the horses. He nodded for the servant to leave. The tiger jumped down to make his own way home.

Jack climbed over the seat of the moving vehicle

to sit beside his brother. It was a narrow seat with only a ledge for one's feet.

Jack reset his hat on his head. "Nice horses," he said.

His twin did not respond. His jaw had gone rock-hard. Jack smiled. If he'd wanted his brother's attention, he had it.

"Father always preferred bays," Jack continued as if making conversation. "However, like you, I'm partial to grays. Do you think it is one of those ways we are alike, but we don't think we are—?"

"I have no idea." Gavin didn't even bother to look in his direction.

Jack leaned back in the seat, rather enjoying the ride although the traffic at the corner was a mess. Two dogs in separate dogcarts had taken a dislike to each other and were snarling and yapping. One had overturned his cart.

"Listen to them," he said to Gavin. "We could sound much the same if we had a mind to."

Gavin frowned in the direction of the dogs, but he didn't speak.

"To be honest, I have no desire to be at odds with you. You're my brother. My twin. Perhaps we are not close, but that doesn't mean we don't have things in common."

"What do you want, Jack?"

"You know what I want, Baynton."

"My support for your 'negotiations'?" He shook his head. "I don't have time for the matter. Talk to Ben. He is the one you should tap."

"I saw Ben today. He said that no one wants to deal with the American grievances or take time to discuss what is considered undiscussable." He pretended to laugh. "Russell warned me that the Court of St. James is rude to the point of being disdainful, but I want to think better of the English. Ben said the only person who could force the matter is you."

"And so you tracked me down?"

"It wasn't difficult."

"Did Talbert tell you were I was?" His tone had gone silky. He was not pleased.

"Your secretary is as tight-lipped as they come. I asked around the stables. Your tiger had requested directions to Mulberry Street. By the way, we left Perkins back there. I suppose he needn't follow me if I am with you."

Gavin grunted his response.

Jack was not afraid of poking the lion in the eye. "So why were you there? Were you 'calling' on Lady Charlene Blanchard?"

Gavin moved the horses down a side street, attempting to avoid the snarl of traffic.

"Ben said you had gone courting," Jack continued.

His twin's eyes narrowed, but he did not speak.

Jack sat forward. "Do you know, this silent treatment that you are attempting has never worked with me? Do you not remember? You would be all bluster like Father and then decide you would have nothing to do with me or my mates, and give me this cold shoulder. Never bothered me. However, one thing we have in common is our persistence, Gav. I don't give an inch any more than you do. For the record, let me remind you, I did come to you last night. You insisted I stay at Menheim, I have. Now, I believe it is *your* turn to give a bit."

"I told you to stay at Menheim for Mother. *I* don't care where you sleep."

"Ah, brotherly love." Jack hitched an arm on the back of the seat beside his twin, making himself comfortable. He moved the conversation to what he was truly interested in. "Was Lady Charlene Blanchard the one opening the door or was that a relative? Or a servant?" Jack was intensely curious about the answer.

"It happened to be Lady Charlene."

Jack sat in stunned silence. His brother was courting the pickpocket. Then again, what sort of gentlewoman picked pockets?

An intriguing one . . .

Jack also found himself reevaluating his opinion of his twin. The Gavin he had known had strived to be morally superior to the rest of his sex. He could not know what she was about. Or could he?

The traffic had begun to move again and Gavin weaved his team around other drivers wanting to move. As he drove, Gavin chided, "What? Have you no witticism to toss at me? No mocking words?"

"Not one," Jack admitted honestly. "I'm actually a bit stunned. Damn, Gavin, you are human like the rest of us."

"And that means?"

"That you are as ruled by your little head as any other man around."

Gavin's response was to stare, glower actually, ahead.

Jack was unperturbed. He had come here with the purpose of shaking up his brother. He had now found his way.

"Good family?" he asked.

With a haughty lift of his noble chin, Gavin said, "The best. Dame Imogen has approved her bloodlines. Lady Charlene is aligned with some of the noblest families in England."

"You would not be able to tell that by where she lives."

"There is no dishonor in being without funds."

"I'm not saying there is," Jack was quick to answer. "I've lived by my wits and eaten hardtack."

"Although you needn't. You had a family to take you in."

Jack decided not to argue that point. Besides, his curiosity was about Lady Charlene. "She doesn't? Not one of her stellar relatives would open their doors?"

"Did you ever hear of Dearne?"

Jack shook his head.

"He was a miserable gambler. Drink ruined his brain. They pulled him out of the Thames. He left his wife and child with nothing. A few years later and the wife died. Lady Charlene is their orphan."

"Tragic."

"More than that—Father gambled with Dearne. I don't know if you remember but Father won the Scots pearls off of him and whatever else he could take. He found it great sport although it was much like blind robbery."

Jack sat up. "Are *you* criticizing Father?" He made a pretense of looking around. "Am I in London? Is this truly *my* brother?"

The look Gavin gave him would have skewered him if it had been a sword. "I am aware Father had faults. I wasn't blind, Jack."

Jack had thought so. He'd never imagined his brother would question their father. Certainly not in the way Jack had. "I admit I am surprised to hear you say this."

"You must think me a dunderhead."

"It may not be wise to say."

Gavin ignored the barb. "I learned after Father died that what he did and what he had expected from me were two different things."

This was news. "Such as?" Jack asked.

"Father had been bleeding the estates dry gambling on bad investments. I am certain he meant to recoup his losses but he died before he could."

"Had he lost that much money?"

"Most of it."

"What did you do?"

"I went to Fyclan Morris. You remember him?"

Jack nodded. "Of course. Elin's father. He was standing by Mother last night."

"Morris's wife died a year or so ago. He and Mother have been keeping each other company."

That was another interesting tidbit of news.

"Morris helped me put most of the fortune back together. It was a harrowing adventure. Father had invested in the wildest of schemes."

"Such as?"

"He favored inventions, many of which were the handiwork of charlatans and if it included electricity, he would double the amount he invested. Then there were risky expeditions. A few came through but not with the riches Father had anticipated. I learned the important lesson that what people see on the outside isn't always true on the inside."

He was right. "And how are you now?"

"Better than I should be. Morris is a genius when it comes to money and I've been very lucky."

"Or shrewd," Jack said with admiration. He had assumed that all had been easy for his twin. Instead, Gavin had been trapped in his own little box. Granted their sire had built it for him, but it had been his choice to stay and fight and he had. "I give you credit. That must have been a challenge."

Gavin nodded.

"And now you are looking for a wife. This is all good."

His twin glanced at him. "Are you mocking me?"

Jack held up a hand. "I am not. I'm happy to see you becoming your own man. In fact, I owe you an apology. I have been guilty of misjudging you."

Again, Gavin sent him a doubtful look.

"My word of honor," Jack promised. "And to be honest, I have no quarrel with you. Yes, I had assumptions but I've changed—for the better, I believe. Why would you have not changed as well?"

Gavin pulled the phaeton over to the side of the

road and set the brake. "Do you mean that? Or are you just interested in manipulating me into advancing your negotiations?"

"Both," Jack said. "I mean what I say and, yes, I would very much like your help because a meeting between our two governments might not happen without you. I have heard that I am now labeled a turncoat because I consider myself an American."

"Aren't you? You are quite literally rejecting your heritage."

"But not my family. Gavin, I've never had a pretension to the title. Oh, when I was younger I believed it unfair that because you had made it out of the womb before I did, you should be Baynton. The truth is, I would have been a miserable duke. If I had discovered that Father had wasted a fortune, I would have been bloody angry."

"I was. However, anger doesn't solve problems."

"You should have told me that years ago. Perhaps it would have saved me some time learning it."

His admission drew a reluctant smile from his brother. Gavin shook his head. "I'd forgotten how blunt you could be . . ." His voice trailed off as if he was considering something new.

Jack waited, curious about what was on the ducal mind.

Gavin sat up. "I need help. It seems only right that if I help you, you help me."

"What can I do for you?"

"Did your wife love you?"

This was not a change of topic Jack could have anticipated. "Yes, she did. Surprising, isn't it? However, she could never have loved me as much as I loved her."

"I want Lady Charlene to fall in love with me."

"And you need me because?"

"I don't know how to go about it. I sent flowers to her last night but they were the wrong thing. I realized when I called on her today. She was gracious, but there was a moment when the silence was awkward, uneasy."

"Those things happen," Jack said with a shrug. "I also don't believe you need to worry about winning the lady. You are a duke—"

"I don't want her to love me for my title. I watch Ben and Elin and she has such care for him, I'm jealous. Did your wife think that highly of you?"

"I believe so. I also understand what you mean. Hope liked me. No matter how arrogant or ridiculous or headstrong I was, she cared. And often would bring me back to a sense of myself. She could say what others couldn't."

"Yes, that is what I see in Ben and Elin. I want that." He asked, "Do you see yourself marrying again?"

Jack nodded. "Sooner or later, but I won't settle for just anyone. Hope taught how me good it can be between a man and a woman. I confess, I want what I had. Someday I hope to find love again."

"I want Lady Charlene. I *want* her."

There was that little head again—and yet was there ever a man who married without feeling lust deep in his gut?

"Then do what you did today," Jack said. "Call on her. Take time to know her."

"Time is the one commodity I don't have."

"You will have to find it. There is no other way to woo a woman that doesn't include giving her your undivided attention."

Gavin sat on that a moment. "All right, I will. I told her today that I wished to see her as much as I could—"

"Good."

"I have instructed Talbert to see that she is invited to all the events I attend."

"Somewhat good."

"What is wrong with that?"

"Time, *time.* If you meet her at balls and routs,

you must plant yourself right by her side. You mustn't move because *that* girl is lovely. There will be a dozen other gentlemen, maybe more, who will note your interest and be willing to swoop her up from you just for the fun of the chase."

"Bastards."

"Men. We are what we are."

Again, Gavin nodded. However, he made no move to pick up the reins.

"Is there something else?" Jack asked.

His brother looked out over the street a moment, watching the passing traffic, although Jack doubted if he saw anything. Instead, his mind appeared furiously at work.

And then Gavin said, his voice so low Jack had to lean toward him, "I've never been with a woman."

Jack took in his words. "Never been with . . . such as sleeping with one?"

Gavin kept his sight focused on something only he could see. There was a long beat of silence and then he confirmed, "No, I've never slept with one."

Jack sat back. "You are a virgin?"

Gavin started as if Jack had punched him. He looked around as if to see if anyone had over-heard.

No one could have. Jack had not spoken *that* loudly and the people on the street were more interested in finding their homes than in what secrets the twins shared.

"Well?" Jack pressed.

Gavin gave a terse nod. "I know it sounds odd," he said. "Or religious. I'm soon to be three-and-thirty."

Jack shrugged. "Damn it all, Gavin, it isn't a crime. I am surprised. What have you been doing with yourself?"

"Working."

"Working? Even in your bed?"

"When were *you* first with a woman?" Gavin asked.

"That night I left my bed in Eton," he assured his twin. "And every night after that one until they hauled me off and threw me on a ship. That lass was magic."

His memories did not help his brother. If anything, Gavin appeared more stoic.

Jack sought to raise his spirits. "Come on, man. You can always find out what it is like. A man with your wealth? Your position? I'm surprised the women haven't propositioned you."

"They have. There are those who are very forward."

"Yes, well, if they dangle bait in front of you, bite."

"I'm not that sort of man," Gavin protested.

Jack felt the ice grow thinner beneath his feet. "Are you saying you don't like the ladies?"

That garnered a reaction from his brother. "*Of course* I like women. I just don't throw my seed here and there. I have responsibilities to the title. I don't want to breed bastards. Furthermore, the woman I marry must be a virgin. How else will I know that the child she carries is mine? Why should she not expect the same from me?"

Jack hummed his thoughts. "That statement sounds like Father."

"He was giving me good advice. Just the other day, my friend Rovington confided in me that he is having some difficulty with his 'private parts.' He has a good wife but he has been pursuing some actress. He says he can't have enough of her. Now he worries he has too much of her. Father warned me that those things could happen. A man could lose his peter."

"He warned me as well, but it hasn't happened to me. I mean, I was never one to poke everything that came along, beyond that girl when I was fifteen. I learned it is good to be discerning. You have to find a clean woman, Gavin. You just don't"—he searched for the right word—"go at one with scurvy or sores. But there are women who are as cautious as we are."

"And then what?" his brother asked.

Whoa. Jack didn't think he would need to explain this much. "You have an understanding of anatomy, the differences between us?"

"Of course I do," came the testy reply.

Jack wasn't so certain he did. However, he knew it was wisest to be careful of insulting his twin. The ducal pride was an entity unto itself. "Well then you have at it," Jack explained. "Let nature take its course. Enjoy the moment."

"But how do I reach that moment? I can't pounce on the woman. I don't want to do anything that shows how green I am. I take it from listening to others that a measure of clumsiness is accepted when we are young and brash, but at my age, well, it is assumed I know what I am doing. I mean, my friends assume I've done it, albeit I'm very private about personal matters."

"As we all should be. Gavin, you *will* know what you are doing when the time is right," Jack assured him. "Bed play is not like studying for exams and worrying about marks. It is gift from God and meant to be fun."

"Fun?" Gavin repeated.

Perhaps his twin did not know what fun was? Considering all he'd been through over the years since their father had died, that was quite possible.

"Yes," Jack answered. "It is also the most blessed act between two people in love. Don't fear it or make it complicated. We are supposed to enjoy our bodies, Gavin. And your friends like Rovington and my compatriot Rice, who are indiscriminate in their sexual lives, well, they aren't you. Let yourself fall in love. Court your lady and learn her heart. Then when you consummate your marriage, you'll have the right spirit between the two of you. By the way, there isn't a man on the face of the earth who didn't wonder if he knew what he was doing the first time, but we all gain the hang of it."

"I don't know if I can wait for courtship. When I am around her, I feel ready to burst. Does that sound terrible?"

"No, but it does sound like how I felt for Mary Swanson when I was fifteen."

"Oh gawd."

Jack laughed and his twin joined him. Gavin picked up the reins but before he moved the horses, he said, "Thank you."

"For?"

"I don't have anyone I can trust. We were always at odds even as boys but you have always understood me in a way others haven't."

"I do. You must learn to silence Father's voice in your head. It will take time. It took me years. You are a good man, Gavin. An honorable one."

"As you are, which is amazing. When you were

fifteen, I would not have thought you would be a lawyer."

"I'm a good one."

"I don't doubt it." Gavin looked at the reins in his gloved hands and then said, "It hurt when you left. I was angry for a long time."

"You are still angry."

"Perhaps. I missed you."

"And I missed you as well," Jack agreed. "Until the next argument."

Gavin laughingly conceded the truth of his statement. He flicked the reins. The horses moved forward.

They rode in companionable silence until they were in sight of Menheim and then Gavin said, "I dine with Lord and Lady Hurst this evening. Join us. He is on the Committee for Colonial Affairs in Lords."

"He is exactly whom I wish to meet."

"They set a good table and are generous hosts. I'll send a note letting them know you are coming."

What could Jack say? "Thank you."

"I'll also have Talbert set the meeting you have requested. It will take some time to arrange."

"I am happy to wait and completely at your disposal."

Gavin gave him a thin smile. "You will need to be seen with the family as often as possible. At

the balls, musicales, whatever. We want to overcome the impression that you do not value your
heritage."

"Understood. Thank you."

"Well, it is our bargain. You help me win my
ladylove and I shall give you your meeting."

"I would like to believe you want to arrange the
meeting to avert a war between two countries,"
Jack insisted mildly.

"That as well." He pulled the horses to a halt at
Menheim's front door.

The tiger was waiting for them. Both Jack and
Gavin jumped down, and the servant took the
reins to drive the horses to the stable.

Together, the twins entered the house. Their
mother was happy to hear Jack would be joining
the company for dinner and he was pleased he
had agreed.

Later that evening, over port and after the ladies
had excused themselves to leave the men to their
business, Hurst and the other gentlemen around
the table listened reluctantly to Jack's overview of
American concerns. Encouraged by Gavin, some
asked good questions.

The duke also received a quizzing by both men
and women about Lady Charlene. Apparently the
papers had noted Gavin's interest and gossips had
been busy at work.

Jack would wager they would be even busier on the morrow after the ladies around the table went calling. He'd even overheard mention of Elin's name and realized that among outsiders of the family, the consensus was that she had jilted the duke.

For that reason, the next day, Jack decided it was time he had a talk with Lady Charlene about her lifting of purses. It was clear Gavin was more than infatuated. If the lady was a brazen criminal, Gavin needed to know now so that he didn't find himself made a laughingstock. Or worse, married to a woman who practiced avarice.

Considering the sharing of confidences, and all that Gavin was doing to help his mission, Jack believed he must do what he could to protect his twin.

After a meeting with Russell to discuss the dinner with Lord Hurst, Jack took off for Mulberry Street. It was late afternoon. The day was overcast but cold and dry.

Quickly covering the distance, he was close to his destination when he noticed a familiar character walking in the opposite direction from where he was heading.

He also realized that, now that he knew what to

look for, Lady Charlene's shapely legs were hard to disguise in breeches. Nor was she traveling alone. Two street lads flanked her. They appeared a rough-and-tumble crew.

What the devil was she up to? More criminal work?

He followed to find out.

Chapter Nine

"Leo wants to see you."

Charlene had stared at Danny standing on her back step as if she could make him disappear.

"I'm not alone," she had warned. Lady Baldwin was in the front room, snoring so loudly she could be heard in the kitchen.

"The other woman who lives here is gone," Danny had answered. "And you have left before when the old lady in feathers is here."

How did they know? Were they watching her? Probably.

"My aunt might be back," Charlene had answered.

Danny had shrugged. "Leo means for you to come now."

Char had known she must be careful, especially now that the duke was apparently involved in her life.

Lady Baldwin had sworn that he was enamored of her. "He is yours," she had predicted. "He wants you."

Sarah had agreed. "He is hooked, you lucky girl. A marriage to him will give you security for the rest of your life."

"Did your marriage give you security?" Char had countered.

"There is no comparison between Roland Pettijohn and Baynton." Sarah rarely mentioned her husband by name.

"But did you marry him for security or love?" Char had wanted to know.

"Both . . . and I was sorely disappointed," Sarah had answered. "I wasn't even sad when he left and the day I received word he had died, I danced on a table. The duke may be a bit starchy but he seems an honest and good man. You must admit he is easy on the eyes."

However, Char wasn't about to count on a marriage to the duke, not after she'd seen Whitridge on the step. It was a mystery to her why he hadn't immediately charged into the house and denounced her. She'd spent all of last evening and a good portion of this day waiting to be exposed. Every time there had been a knock on the door, she'd expected it to be the Watch to take her away.

Instead, it had been one invitation after another

to social occasions from people she had never heard of.

Lady Baldwin had, though, and she had exclaimed over the names on every card Char opened. "Why, these are all the finest families. Charlene, we will be socializing with the very best. My daughter will eat herself up with envy. I can't wait to tell her where I shall be tomorrow evening." She had held up an invite and waved it in the air.

Sarah had been busy penning acceptances while fretting how they would be able to afford dresses for the affairs. She'd left early for the theater, hoping for help from the Haymarket's wardrobe mistress.

The last thing Char had anticipated was a summons from Leo.

"This isn't a convenient time," Charlene had informed Danny.

"You owe the Seven money."

"I know, and I am trying to pay you back as quickly I can. However, I shouldn't leave the house at this moment."

She would have shut the door but Danny had blocked her action with his arm. "*Now*, or there will be others who will come."

That had sounded ominous.

After all, any of the Seven could see her to

prison as easily as Whitridge and everyone knew there was no honor among thieves.

Of which she was one.

The thought no longer thrilled her.

"I need to change into my disguise," Char had said. Heaven forbid she be recognized with the likes of the Seven.

"Good idea" had been Danny's answer.

Checking on Lady Baldwin, who slept on the settee with her feet on the floor, her chin on her chest, Char had debated leaving a note but had decided against it. Anticipating the possibility of a call from the duke, Sarah had let them set a fire in the grate, a luxury for them on a chilly afternoon. Char had lifted the lady's feet upon a footstool, covered her with a lap blanket, and then left to change.

She had quickly pulled on her breeches and shirt, and had used pins to put up her hair. She had then plopped her hat over her head and shrugged on her coat. She hadn't bothered with a neck cloth. Grubby boys didn't always pay attention to them.

Char had gone out in the garden, put her hands in some dirt, and then rubbed it on her face. Danny had been waiting for her at the gate. He had not been alone. Another one of the Seven, a boy around Danny's age named Hal, had joined them.

Together they had set off to see Leo. Char prayed the interview would not take long.

"So, what is going on?" she asked Danny as they walked. She noticed that another of the Seven had fallen into step behind her. Simon was his name. He was one of the younger boys.

He, too, was solemn and he followed with intent ceremony.

Char reminded herself that they were, after all, just boys, but they were serious, grim. Almost dangerous.

And they were not interested in answering any of her questions.

She did wonder what they would do if she refused to take a step farther or ran back to Mulberry Street, and then feared the answer.

As she was being marched, she could miserably understand a bit of the desperation her father had felt.

Char had never confided to Lady Baldwin about Leo's "tribute." She knew that her friend would be horrified to know what had started off as a bit of lark had taken such a sinister turn. And she certainly did not want Sarah to learn of this. Her aunt would be disappointed in not only the thievery, the debt, and Char's bad choices, but also that Charlene had not confided in her. Sarah worked very hard to provide for them and she would interpret the situation as *her* mistake.

Tension built between her shoulder blades as they moved closer to the Seven's lair.

And then they were there. Hal looked left and right before ducking down the narrow alley. Danny prodded her to go forward.

In the courtyard on the other end, Leo threw back the flap of his dwelling and came out as they approached. He placed his *chapeau bras* on his head. The other members of the Seven material-ized out of their hidey-holes and makeshift structures. They formed a ring around Charlene.

She faced Leo, her shoulders back and her lips pressed together firmly for strength.

"Hello, Lady Charlene," Leo said. He swept his hat off his head and bowed, before replacing it.

"Hello, Leo," she answered.

"Do you know why you are here?"

"You think I owe you money—"

Leo held up a finger as if to warn her. "I *know* you owe us money."

"I can give you your money, but not until the month is over." She said this with perfect convic-tion. Her father would have been proud.

"I don't believe you," Leo answered. "You told us two weeks ago that you had failed to snatch a purse on Threadneedle Street, even though our allies in that territory saw differently."

"They were wrong." She was beginning to sound convincing . . . she thought.

"Were they? Tall Adam and his lot claim they saw you pinch the man's purse. When he came to me for his share and I told him what you'd said, he was very angry. He wanted to do you harm. The lads and I talked him out of it."

She looked around the circle at the faces that were too old for their young years. "I told the truth."

"I doubt that," Leo answered.

She was tempted to lie again, so she said nothing.

Leo approached her. He was about her height but wiry and strong. "I also don't believe you have the money any longer, my lady because you spent it."

"I can't spend what I don't have," she dared to counter.

"*Stop* it. You are not a good liar, my lady. Nor is it wise to believe I can't read the papers," Leo answered. "They have a school in Newgate, just for lads like myself that need moral guidance. The reformers set it up. They taught me to read. I've been interested in what I've read about you and what I hear on the streets."

"And what would that be?" she wondered.

"That you might become a duchess." Leo grinned in anticipation. "Why, all the papers are full of the Duke of B. being on the hunt for a wife. He had a huge ball so that he could look at all the prime stock in London. Duke of B. Silly, ain't it? Everyone knows who *he* is. And they say he is taken with a Lady C. Well, I don't know who Lady C. is but since Tall Adam came to me complaining, the Seven have been watching your house. We have an investment in you now, my lady. We saw the Duke of B. call on you yesterday. We even watched over a week ago when you went shopping. Had a day of it, you did. You spent more than five guineas."

"That was my aunt's money."

The sly smile left Leo's face. "We don't care whose money it is. You pay us first."

"I didn't know that," Char answered. "You didn't give me terms when last we spoke—"

"*Then* let me give you new terms. The price has gone up."

"*Why?*"

"Because you need to learn a lesson, and we have an idea."

Char did not want to play this game any longer. "What is it?"

"Five guineas will not cover your debt any longer."

"How much do you want?"

"It is *what* we want that matters. I have people I answer to as well. You want money, we want money, they want money—it goes round and round. The new terms are a hundred pounds."

Char almost fell backward. "A hundred pounds? There is no way I will have that sort of money."

"You could. You do have a talent for filching a purse—"

"I'm done with it. I never want to do it again—"

"Or you can pay us when you marry your duke. There will be interest, of course."

"This is outrageous."

"Aye, but it is too late now. You have done it. We are partners whether you like it or not. If you want our silence, you will be paying for it, Duchess."

He was right and it broke her heart.

She thought of Sarah. Her aunt would be horrified to learn of the turn Charlene had taken. "What if I don't?"

"Then you will be in Newgate prison. Pity you already know how to read. They have good tutors."

"No one will believe that I'm a pickpocket," Char said, trying to brazen it out.

"The papers will. There are always those interested in bits of scandal and they don't much care if it is true or not. And the Duke of B., if he is wise, and they say he is, he'll run."

He would.

"But this won't be the end, will it?" she suggested. "You will always come to me for money."

"You have the reputation to protect, my lady. We don't."

Char's hands curled into fists at her side. She looked around at the faces of the Seven. They watched her with the expressions of cats who have trapped a mouse, and it was all her own fault. This was the desperation her father had experienced. There was no way to be free of them.

She also noticed something she had not paid particular attention to before; none of these lads showed the signs that they were keeping their money. Their clothes were threadbare, the soles of their shoes thin. Even Leo did not appear wealthy in spite of his cocky *chapeau bras*. The money they made went to criminals higher up the chain of authority from them. They didn't even look as if they ate decently.

"May I leave now?" Char asked.

Leo nodded to Danny. "See her out. The rest of

you, we have an hour until dark. Be busy." The boys scattered, many leaving through the alley passageway.

"This way, my lady," Danny said, and led her away.

Char felt as if her feet had been turned to weights. A part of her refused to believe any of this was real, including Leo's threats.

The sane part of her knew it was all too true.

They came out onto the street. The pedestrians were thinning and there were more men out and about. Groups of them. A few sailors, some lads looking for trouble, men hurrying to wherever they had to go.

Char pulled her hat lower over her head and followed Danny. She was anxious to return home and prayed Lady Baldwin had not woken from her nap because Char's feeble brain was growing tired of all the lies she'd told. She also needed to put together what would undoubtedly be a cold supper. A bit of the chicken left from last night's meal, some cheese, bread, and apples.

Indeed, this task, making a meal and taking care of the house on Mulberry Street, now seemed the most longed for experience in her life—

Whitridge's tall, commanding figure stepped

out from around a corner, blocking her path. Danny took one look at the angry blue eyes and firm jaw and took off running.

Char wished she could run, too, but she wouldn't. The time had come for a reckoning.

"Go ahead," she dared. "Send me to Newgate."

And then she burst into tears.

Chapter Ten

Jack had envisioned surprising the audacious Lady Charlene. He had hoped coming out of the shadows would frighten her, therefore scaring the truth out of her before he decided whether he should help his brother win her or warn him off. Jack wasn't aware of all her sins but he knew the criminal element when he saw it. The lads she'd been with were bad news.

What he had not expected was for her to break down weeping, and he had absolutely no idea of what to do. He'd never been good with female tears. He avoided them as much as possible.

She stood on the street, dressed like a young buck, her head bowed, and sobbed. The sounds grew stronger with each passing second until she was hiccupping.

Worse, she was gaining the attention of passersby.

Jack tried to quiet her. "My lady—" he started, and then realized he did not want to give away her sex. Not with a band of unruly sailors standing by a public house's door, tossing back one ale after another.

"*Laddie*," he amended lamely. "Now, laddie."

His words caused her to cry louder. It was as if once started, she didn't want to stop.

The sailors now craned their necks, elbowing each other to look in Jack's direction. One yelled something that Jack did not want to hear. Strangers passing began to slow their steps. Crude and knowing glances were sent their way.

"Come, let's leave here," he ordered, putting a sheltering arm around her shoulder, and then realizing his mistake.

The men of the sea were on it immediately. Catcalls and hoots were sent up.

Jack immediately dropped his arm and instead picked her up by the scruff of the neck, using his other hand to keep her hat on her head.

"Come," he ordered, anxious to escape the scrutiny of the street, and marched her around the corner.

This street was quieter than the other. There

was a small tavern close at hand and he directed her in there. She was down to sniveling now, her eyes and nose red.

Considering what a stunning beauty she was normally, Jack rather liked the fact that crying brought her down a notch, humanizing her.

The tavern was very dark, which was perfect for Jack's purposes. The front room was crowded with patrons but, taking her sleeve, he pulled her through them and found tables in a back room. No one was there so he went to the farthest corner and plopped her down, bouncing his hand on her hat to make certain it stayed there.

He looked for a tavern maid. She'd caught sight of him coming in and hurried over. "Ale," Jack said. He threw some coins down on the table.

"Two?" she questioned.

"No, an ale, and a cider," he decided, not knowing what ladyish drink to order. Cider should do. Lady Charlene was calming down but he needed her spirits bolstered before he questioned her.

The maid left. Lady Charlene sat in the chair with her hands at her sides. She was beaten, done for it. Jack didn't know if he liked her this way.

Slowly she looked up and around as if she hadn't been aware of her surroundings.

And she wasn't. "Where are we?"

"Around the corner from where I met you."

She nodded as if remembering and then rubbed the tears from her face with the sleeve of her coat, an honest gesture, one unhampered by anything coy or crafty. "I didn't mean to carry on that way. I lost all sense of self. This has been a very trying day."

"It must be."

"I don't usually cry," she informed him with a hint of defiance. "It never solves anything."

"And what were you trying to solve?"

Now that he knew her sex, he marveled he could have ever mistaken her for a boy. Her lashes were dark and long and right now spiky from her tears. Even the line of her jaw had a feminine tilt.

Before she could answer his question, the serving maid returned with their drinks in tankards. Raucous laughter followed her out of the main room and her attention was, fortunately, on it instead of a man and a weepy lad. She set down the drinks, picked up the money, and hurried back to her more interesting customers.

Lady Charlene looked at the cider. "Is this for me?"

"I ordered for you."

"You are giving me one last drink before you call the Watch?"

"Do you believe I'm here to call the Watch?"

"If you do, it will be the end of me and everything I hold dear. Then again, I'm ruined as it is."

"That is an interesting statement. Would you care to enlighten me?"

"I don't know."

Her voice had trembled, but she held her tears at bay. Instead, she took a drink of the cider and pulled a face at the taste. She set down the tankard and pushed it away with one finger that she kept held against the pewter side as if wanting to contemplate her nail against the metal rather than the man sitting across the table from her.

However, Jack was not going anywhere. He drained half of his ale in one gulp. He leaned back in his chair, waiting.

She knew he expected her story.

The question was, would she give him one? Or the truth?

He could see the decision of whether to trust him weighed heavy in her mind. Little did she know he probably had the knowledge that would solve any and all of her problems—Gavin wanted her. She would be a duchess . . . depending on what she said in the next few minutes.

She raised eyes dark with worry to him. "May I trust you?"

With a lift of his hand, Jack indicated she could, if she wished.

She wasn't completely sure. She tapped the side of the mug, then sat up and leaned across the table toward him.

"I am in a sorry plight," she confessed.

"Obviously."

"You've heard of my father?"

He shook his head, wanting to hear the tale from her.

"My father did not have a head for money. He was a very good man and the best father, except when he drank. Ale, whisky, even small beer, it all went to his head and then he lost all sense of what he could and what he couldn't do, and people took advantage of his weakness."

"He gambled when he drank."

"Yes, and lost."

"That is what happens."

"He always believed he was going to win. Mother used to beg the gentlemen in the set my father favored to please watch out for him, to pull him away before he did something foolish, but they never could."

"They probably ate him alive."

"Some tried to be honest friends but I'm certain forcing him to do what was best for him was difficult. My father eventually wagered away anything of value we owned. But he was good man."

"Well, you are lucky in that respect. My father wasn't."

"I know."

"You do?" Jack frowned. "How did you know this? His reputation is sterling. He had power, prestige . . . the ear of the king." He could hear the cynicism in his voice but was incapable of changing it. His bitterness toward his sire was always right beneath the surface.

"Your father took advantage of mine during a game of cards. By all accounts, Father was in no condition to be sitting at that table. Others, more honorable men left. They refused to play, but not the duke. He won a set of pearls that was the pride of my family. We called them Scots pearls. Your mother was wearing them the other night at the ball."

"I'm not going to justify my father's behavior. I don't question your story. However, when a man sits down to play, drunk or sober, he can lose."

"Mine took his life. Everyone said it was an accident but I remember my mother crying and hearing people whisper when they thought they could not be overheard." She took another swallow of her cider and then added quietly, "I once asked my mother for the truth and she said we must lie because what Father did was unspeakable. I believe what *your* father did was unspeakable."

Jack opened his mouth, and then shut it. What could he say?

"My mother died a few years after Father. She never recovered from his death. She loved him," she said as if the possibility was somehow odd. "He did everything wrong and yet she always made excuses for him."

"She was loyal."

Lady Charlene nodded absently. "I lived with my uncle Davies who is the most miserly, pious prig ever to be found in England. I was miserable. Everyone in his family resented me. They blamed me for the lack of any funds in the estate. My uncle inherited an empty title, a widow, and her child. He was not pleased."

"I don't imagine so."

"At Mother's funeral, her godmother, Lady Baldwin, asked me a number of questions about Uncle Davies. I don't believe she liked him. I didn't understand why back then but I now know his reputation is not one of the best around women. There were times even with Mother when I was nervous. The day after I talked to Lady Baldwin, Sarah came into my life. She took me away from him."

"Who is Sarah?"

"She is my mother's half sister. Her mother was an actress and my grandfather's mistress. She is much younger than my mother and there was a time when she needed help. My mother and father took her in and then later sent her to a school. Sarah said she never forgot their kindness. Coming for me was her way of repaying them for what they did."

Lady Charlene took another sip of the cider. Her voice stronger now, she said, "Uncle Davies was afraid of Sarah. She can be quite formidable. She made him promise to pay my expenses and he did until last September. Then he stopped. No explanation, no excuses . . . just no money. Sarah and I both wrote him and I've tried to visit him but he has shut us out."

"So you needed money."

"Of course. We were behind on the rent and Sarah was not receiving the acting parts she had when she was younger. What she really wishes is to be a playwright."

"A woman?"

"Why not? The managers at the Haymarket have been using her to add polish to their plays. However, she wants to see her own work on the stage. I've read her plays and they are wonderful."

Jack placed his arms on the table. "So why are you picking pockets?"

A world-weary sigh escaped Lady Charlene. "Two reasons. The first, of course, is for the money. I want you to know that I have offered to find work. I could be a governess or sew. I'm good with a needle. Sarah won't let me. I keep the house for her. We can't afford a maid. When His Grace called, Sarah put on a costume and pretended to be the maid."

"So you both enjoy playacting."

She had the good grace to blush. "We do what we must. Can you understand that?"

"All too well. What is the second reason?" Jack asked.

"I thought it would be an adventure."

He had not expected that answer. "Has it been?"

"It was in the beginning," she said. "The first time I earned just enough to cover the rent. It felt good to be taking action for myself."

Jack could understand the feeling. "How did you explain the money to your aunt?"

"I told her Uncle Davies sent it. She was so relieved. Apparently the landlord was about to toss us into the street and Sarah has been worried about what would become of us. She has been taking on as many jobs as she could at the theater, but it is never enough. So, you see, I had to do something."

"Where did you pick up this skill?"

"Lady Baldwin. She, too, was an actress before she met Lord Baldwin. I believe she had a rather wild reputation. She is the one who suggested I might try my hand at it. She knew the ways of it and helped with my costume. No one ever suspected I was a woman. Not even you."

That was true.

"And before you think I was just a thief, I'll have you know I had standards."

"You do?"

"I tried to only take from those who could afford it."

"How did you determine my colleague Rice was a pigeon to pluck?"

"That day on Threadneedle Street. I wish I'd never been there."

"Come on, tell me." Jack caught the eye of the serving wench and signaled for more drink. He threw more coins on the table.

Lady Charlene followed the gleaming silver with her eyes before swinging them back up to him. "I didn't know if he had money to spare," she confessed. "But usually those who have are not careful about it. He kept tossing his heavy purse into the air. He was also a visitor to London so that if he put up a cry, few would listen to him. And he was easily distracted. Any time he saw a woman, well, his attention would wander."

Jack laughed. "You read him right. He didn't stand a chance against you."

"I am rather good," she admitted.

The serving wench brought their drinks. They waited until she left.

"Where does my brother fit into your schemes?"

"He doesn't. Lady Baldwin managed to secure an invitation for me to his ball. She and my aunt hoped that he would notice me but I didn't really think there was a possibility. I was doing it to please them and because I'd never been to a ball before. Sarah believes strongly that I should do what I must to regain my station in life."

"What is your opinion?" Jack asked, curious.

"I don't know. It would be good to be able to take care of my aunt the way she has me. If I was to become a duchess I could see her plays were performed . . . couldn't I?"

"Mayhap." Jack didn't know. He had never heard of a female playwright. He also didn't want to speculate whether his brother would endorse one. "Then again, you would need to put your days of petty thievery behind you. Can you do so?"

"I don't know." The tears threatened again. She took a sip from her cider and then whispered, "I am in so much trouble."

"Go on, tell me," Jack said.

She glanced to the front of the tavern as if afraid of being overheard. Then, lowering her voice, she confided, "I ran afoul of this gang called the Seven. They patrol and pick pockets and other small thefts in this area of London. Did you know the criminals have the city divided into territories?"

"I would not be surprised."

"Well, I was. Furthermore, the Seven may just be boys but there is something sinister about them."

"They are boys who have grown up quickly."

"And not well," she agreed. "They took me aside and informed me I had to pay a 'tribute' to them to be in their territory. They said I already owed them a half a guinea but the price keeps rising. And they know everything. They know that I was receiving invitations today to all the best houses and parties. Their leader, Leo, threatened to see me ruined. He wants a hundred pounds from me now. I don't even have five let alone a hundred. He says he'll wait until I'm a duchess. But I know what will happen. He'll demand more for his silence. It will never end. And if Sarah discovers what I've done, she will be angry. I fear telling her because she has given up so much to help me."

Her shame was genuine. She could meet his eye but she was deeply embarrassed.

He sat for a moment, taking her measure. What she had done had been harebrained. He would like a strong conversation with this Lady Baldwin who had pushed Lady Charlene into the scheme.

However, there had been times when he had been desperate in his life. He'd done things of which he was not proud. Leaving his family without a word of warning was possibly one of them.

She placed her elbows on the table and lowered her head into her hands. The action brushed her hat back and Jack could see the white gold of her hair. "I owe so much money. I'm no different than my father." She looked up at him. "I now understand how inconsolable he must have felt. I feel foolish and backed into a corner. I am the last person who should become a duchess."

"You have been unwise," Jack agreed. "The question is are you going to do what the Seven want you to do."

"No, I can't. It is impossible. And I don't know what will happen."

Jack came to a decision. He liked Charlene Blanchard. He believed she told him the truth. It had called for courage to try to take her life into her own hands. She was fortunate that something worse hadn't befallen her.

"Take me to meet this Seven," Jack said. "I would talk to Leo."

"I won't. Then you will be involved in this."

"I already am. My brother's intentions toward you are serious. You do have a chance of becoming a duchess and you might make a good one." He would not tell her about the bargain he had struck with his twin. She did not need to know he was motivated by his need for the duke's help.

"If I don't steal for the Seven, they will see me to Newgate."

"They will not feel that way after I have talked to them."

"It isn't just them. Leo answers to those ranked higher than himself."

"Who are still criminals," Jack reminded her. "If they threaten you, we can threaten right back. I do know this—if you do what they want and steal for them, sooner or later they will abandon you to your fate."

"So I should take my punishment now?" she asked in a small voice.

"No, you should take me to them now. Come." He pushed back his chair and stood.

Her eyes worried, she joined him.

"Lead the way," he said.

The crowd of men had grown larger in the tap-room. He was amused by the way Lady Charlene pushed her way through with the same boldness of any lad.

Outside, the day was quickly passing. Lady Charlene led him back from where he came to one of those alleys throughout London where it was difficult for a man his size to travel, but Jack managed. They came out on a courtyard with wood stacked against the walls, broken chairs, and the other rubbish.

All was quiet.

"Leo," Lady Charlene called.

There was no answer.

Jack poked around in some of the barrels and moved the wood around.

"They were here," she told him. "I've talked to Leo twice here. They may be watching us." She took a step toward him. "Please, you must believe me."

"I do. I saw them escorting you away from your home. But also, look here." He pointed out the shoeprints. "One has lost the heel to his shoe. You can track his movements. And here is a bit of hair." He pulled the strand from a barrel. "Those prints are fresh. Someone was here not that long ago. This may be one of several places they use to gather. They will be back." He turned away. "Let me take you home."

"Oh," she said as if remembering. "I've been gone way too long." She started for the alley.

"Is your aunt home?"

"No, but I left Lady Baldwin sleeping in the front room. I need to fix a supper for us and I hope she hasn't woken and started searching for me."

They hurried then. His stride was long and she managed to keep up with him. They did not run into street boys on the way to Mulberry Street. The Seven were like an Indian tribe with London as their forest. They knew how to blend in.

Catching them would give Jack great pleasure.

When they were close to her home, she stopped at an alley. "I am fine on my own from here." She paused and then said, "Thank you for your help. I was quite lost back there." Again, she hesitated, this time thoughtfully, and then added, "I feel I owe the duke the truth. He should know I don't make wise decisions."

"Few of us do all the time," Jack said. "Including him. No, I advise you to not say a word to him. Let me see what I can do first."

Even as he spoke, he wondered why he was making such a suggestion. Gavin deserved honesty about a woman he believed he wanted to marry. But would Gavin understand *why* people were pressed to make desperate choices? And Jack did believe she'd not only found herself in over her head, but was truly repentant. He could not act as her judge.

A slow, rueful smile curved her lips. "And you will save us all?"

"That is my intention."

She didn't believe him. Right now, he sensed she was certain no one could save her from her foolishness. He would just have to prove her wrong.

And she seemed to understand that was exactly what he planned to do. "Be careful, Whitridge, and thank you."

On those words, she ducked her head and hurried down the alley before Jack could answer.

Chapter Eleven

$\mathcal{L}$ady Baldwin was still asleep when Char entered the house and checked on her. She tiptoed up the stairs and changed her clothes, marveling that in spite of all that had happened, no one knew she'd been gone.

Well, *someone* knew—Whitridge.

And he'd given her hope that he could sort out the terrible mess she had made of her life.

Trust was not easy for her. Trust made a person vulnerable and Char did not like feeling defenseless. Of course, it had been her pride and her fear that had led her into the difficult position she found herself in now.

Char prepared their supper, setting aside a plate for Sarah and covering it with a towel. She woke Lady Baldwin and the two of them had an easy evening.

The next morning, Lady Baldwin took herself to her daughter's house. Her intent was to return that evening and chaperone Char to Lord Vetter's ball. The duke had sent word he would pick them up in his coach.

After she left, Sarah reported that for a reasonable price the wardrobe mistress would help them with another two dresses. "We shall change the trims and they will look like new. They will be in the Greek style, and a stitch here, some ribbon there, and no one will know they are the same dress."

"How much will it cost?" Char asked.

"Enough," Sarah said. "We will be spending the last of the money your uncle Davies sent, but it is for a good cause. Besides, he has more than made up for what he owed us. Now that he has decided to honor his commitment to you, he shall continue to do so again next month. Our letters to him were not all for naught."

Char heard Sarah's wishful thinking, her planning. Here was the chance to tell her aunt the truth.

She didn't, and Char felt remarkably guilty.

The duke sent a lovely bouquet later that afternoon. This time, the arrangement of pink roses was a bit more circumspect than the red roses that still took up Sarah's desk. He'd sent a card with it but all it said was that the duke would arrive for her and Lady Baldwin at half past eight.

"It will be a late night," Sarah predicted. "Perhaps you should see if you can nap a bit."

Char was happy to escape to her room. Her conscience was heavy around Sarah. She surprised herself when she lay down and did sleep, although her sleep was restless. She dreamed that she was being chased by the Seven. They yelled at her for money and threw vibrant blue butterflies at her, only the butterflies did not fly away. Instead, they fell to the ground and lay dead, their lovely wings wide open.

She woke disoriented and a bit edgy . . . and for whatever reason, her first thought went to Whitridge. She wondered if she would see him this evening.

When it came time to prepare, Char wore the dress she had worn to Baynton's ball. They had reasoned that few would remember her in it since the ball had ended abruptly.

While Char had napped, Sarah had braided silver ribbons together and added the trim under the bodice and around the neckline. Sarah then styled Char's hair, just as she had the night of the first ball, sweeping it up and threading silver ribbon through it as well.

"You shall remind of him of Artemis," Sarah said.

Char nodded. She did look well and wondered what Whitridge would say. He'd probably make a quip about her not being in breeches. Well, it was time he saw her as a woman—

Sarah gave Charlene's shoulders a small hug bringing her back to the moment. She whispered, "You are lovely. Don't ever doubt yourself. The man will be smitten."

Char stood, suddenly nervous. Apprehensive.

Placing a hand on Char's arm, Sarah said, "Here I thought you might appreciate this." She was dressed in her maid's costume and pulled a small vial from the pocket of her apron. "It is perfume. I purchased it years ago and I've nurtured it over time. Toilette water is fine but for tonight, you deserve the finest." She opened the stopper. Char took a sniff.

"That is lovely. What is it?"

"The oil of roses and apricots. George had cast me as Cleopatra. It was my first lead role and I believed I deserved a treat. I adore the scent." She dabbed a touch on the inside of Charlene's wrists and on her neck right beneath her ears. "Your body heat will add to the scent."

"Thank you," Char said, pleased. She took Sarah's hand. "I wish you were going with me tonight."

"No, you don't. With our luck we would walk into Lord Vetter's and there would be that trio of lords I told you about when I was in the bawdy melodrama. They would recognize me, start making crude comments, and the duke would run. At this time in your courtship, it is not wise to raise any concerns, such as a bastard actress for an aunt—"

Char stopped her by pressing her fingers to Sarah's lips. "Do not put yourself down. I love you. I love all that you have done for me. You've sacrificed so much. I will make it up to you someday."

"I don't expect that."

"I know, but I wish to do so. Can you understand?"

"I do. However, you have your own life to live. Do not worry about me. I've survived this long."

"You have set a good example to me," Char confessed. "Every time I thought to break down in self-pity, I would think of you and endeavor to be as brave as you."

Sarah placed her hand against Char's cheeks. "Those are the kindest words anyone has ever said to me. Now, go capture the heart of a duke." Char gave her aunt a good, strong hug.

Just as they went downstairs, Lady Baldwin arrived wearing what she referred to as her peacock colors. She was all blues and greens with actual peacock feathers sticking out of her pert chapeau.

"My daughter isn't speaking to me," she said with great excitement. "She is so jealous I am going to this ball, she cannot utter one word. Not even to criticize my dress."

They heard the sound of horses. Lady Baldwin pulled aside the closed curtains in the front room. "It's him. Oh my. Oh. My."

"What?" Char demanded.

"You shall see," was Lady Baldwin's giddy reply. "Come in here." She waved Char toward her. "We don't want him to enter the house and find us all crowded around the door."

Char didn't see what difference it made but she deferred to the older woman.

A knock sounded.

Sarah had taken her mobcap from where she'd tucked it into her apron sash. She pulled it over her bold red hair, nodded to Char and Lady Baldwin—and then she opened the door.

The Duke of Baynton stepped into the hall on a wave of February air and, for a moment, all Char could do was stare in awe. He was a handsome man at all times but black evening dress took his good looks to a new level, especially with a wool cloak draped over his shoulders.

His presence, his air of command, filled the house. But there was something else about him that caught Char's attention—he smelled of winter and sandalwood. A potent combination.

Even Sarah was impressed. Char had never seen her aunt taken aback by a gentleman.

However, his gaze was on Char. She curtsied.

He bowed.

They both smiled their appreciation. He reached for her hand. "You are lovely."

"Thank you, Your Grace. You are quite handsome as well."

Her compliment startled a laugh out of him.

"Did I say something amusing?" she asked, confused.

He took both of her gloved hands. "You said nothing wrong. It is that you are candid and open. I can't remember a time when a woman complimented me."

"They have complimented you, Your Grace. They may not have done it to your face but they noticed."

"And tonight, everyone will notice both of us. Let me help you with your cloak." He took the garment from Sarah and put it on Char's shoulders. "My mother will be riding with us. I hope you don't mind."

"It will be an honor," she said, while past his shoulder she caught the sight of Sarah pantomiming her happiness.

Fortunately, Sarah changed back to dutiful maid when the duke turned for Lady Baldwin's cloak. Lady Baldwin made happy chortling sounds as he helped her with the velvet cape.

He gallantly opened the door, and Char and

Lady Baldwin walked to the coach where a footman waited. Lady Baldwin climbed in first and then Char, presumably so that she could sit next to the duke.

Marcella, Dowager Duchess of Baynton, was everything a duchess should be. She had her sons' presence, only the air of authority was coupled with one of serenity. Char found herself studying her features and decided Whitridge favored her more than the duke did.

She was a tall woman with snowy white hair. Her dress was deep marine blue. She did not wear the Scots pearls this evening. Instead, she wore garnets. Their blood red set off the blue and sparkled in the light from the coach lamp.

"Lady Charlene, I am pleased to make your acquaintance."

"I am honored, Your Grace." She was. The woman was welcoming and warm-spirited.

In spite of it all, Char was aware that there was one person missing. Whitridge.

She wondered what he was doing, but was wise enough not to ask.

The row of coaches waiting to release their passengers on Lord Vetter's front step seemed to stretch for a good quarter of a mile; however, the Duke of Baynton did not have to wait. They went right to the front of the line.

The duke helped all the ladies out of the coach. He offered his mother his arm, as he should, but she waved him away. "I shall walk in with Lady Baldwin. You escort Lady Charlene."

This was a tremendous honor.

The night of Baynton's ball, Charlene had been too filled with apprehension to notice very much. However, now servants rushed forward to open doors and announce him. Lord Vetter left his own receiving line to personally welcome the duke. He bowed deeply over Char's hand.

"The reports of your beauty were not exaggerated, my lady."

Heat rose to her cheeks and she could picture herself a princess in one of the stories her father had told her. The night was just that magical.

The house and the ballroom were not as grand as Menheim's, although the company was as glittering.

Mothers who had obviously been lingering by the door on the lookout for Baynton were visibly disappointed when they saw Charlene on his arm. He made certain that she was included in all introductions, and although he was completely proper, there was a possessiveness about him. Char was certain all sensed that he had staked his claim.

Furthermore, his mother went out of her way to

include Char. "Let me introduce you to my friend Mr. Fyclan Morris," the dowager said.

Fyclan was a handsome older gentleman that others treated with great respect. He and the duchess appeared to have a close relationship.

The dowager started to ask Char a question but Baynton stepped in between them. "I'm sorry, Mother, but they are preparing for the first dance and I must take Lady Charlene away from you. She owes me a dance."

He offered his arm and led her to the dance floor where couples were already gathering. "I have not forgotten your promise to step on my toes," he said.

"You should be careful what you wish for, Your Grace," she answered, and he laughed.

"Here, Baynton," one gentleman called, and Char found herself being introduced to Lord and Lady Rovington. They were a merry twosome and had places in their set for the duke and Char. Lord Rovington and the duke spoke to each other as old friends.

Lady Rovington quickly attempted to put Char at ease by saying, "Please call me Jane." She leaned close. "He likes you. This is good. We all worried over him after—you know."

"I don't know."

"You must know," Jane said.

"I wish I did know," Char answered. "I think?" she added, confused about what Jane meant.

"About his being jilted," Jane prodded. "He was supposed to marry Elin Morris but his brother *stole* her from him."

Char had met the duke's brother and his wife in the receiving line at the Menheim ball. They had appeared happy, and apparently the duke had no quarrel with them or else he would not have invited them. She didn't know what to make of this "friend" trading in gossip.

"Oh" was all she could manage to say and it must have been enough because Jane started commenting on the dress the woman behind Char was wearing.

"She wore the same dress last week," Jane said.

Char almost said she, too, was wearing a dress twice but caught herself. She could hear Sarah advising her that there was no reason to ask for trouble.

Fortunately, the dancing started.

She and Baynton managed to not step on each other's toes. He was actually an excellent dancer, light on his feet and confident in his movements. Slowly, the tension ebbed from her body. She relaxed, and by the time the music came to an end, she felt she had acquitted herself very well.

Afterward, he escorted her over to where his

mother was talking to friends. Lady Baldwin appeared happily ensconced with the matrons by the punch bowl.

The circle around Baynton began to grow. The duke was very popular, as was Mr. Morris. Men and women flocked to Baynton. He tried to keep Char close but there was almost too much going on and the conversation was not light. There was a discussion on a farm bill they needed to pass and speculation about the Continent.

If she hadn't known Baynton was important before, she would have gained the idea listening to those around him.

The evening began to feel as if it was happening to someone else. She was an observer, a distant bystander. She could even see herself in her pale, silvery blue gown. She saw that she was poised with a pleasant smile on her face and knew that for some mysterious reason, she wanted to run.

It wasn't that she felt out of place. The duke was doing everything he could to shepherd her . . . but *her*, the *real* her, didn't belong here. She would rather be home reading a book.

She was asked to dance by several gentlemen. Well, they asked her but they looked to the duke for approval. Char found that annoying. She wondered what they would do if she grabbed them by both ears and made them face her—

Her thoughts came to a halt.

The small hairs on her neck tingled with awareness. The false her that smiled politely and didn't grab ears joined with her real personality and she became *present. Aware.*

She knew he was here.

Glancing over her shoulder to the main doorway, she discovered her senses had not lied.

Whitridge appeared as handsome as his ducal brother in the black evening dress. His hair was still overlong. Considering how impeccably presented the duke was, Char could speculate that there must have been some mention during one of their conversations that Whitridge needed his hair cut.

She could also easily imagine him telling his twin he'd not submit to barber's shears. He was that sort of man. He did as he wished, and she was jealous.

Someone was talking to her. A gentlewoman complimented her on the lovely braiding design on her dress. Char brought her mind to where it belonged. "Thank you," she said, and smiled because that was all anyone really wanted her to do.

And then Whitridge was at the edge of the group surrounding them.

The duke saw him. "Jack, here are some people I wish you to meet."

Jack. Jack Whitridge. Char liked the sound of his name. It was bold and self-assured, just as he was.

Whitridge worked his way through the knot of people around the duke. He took a moment to kiss his mother's hand and to comment to Mr. Morris. He turned to his brother.

Baynton said, "The first person I wish you to meet is Lady Charlene Blanchard. My lady, this is my unredeemable twin."

Everyone around them laughed at the duke's jest. Whitridge smiled but it was quick, polite, as pat as her own responses were to their gossip and quips.

"It is a pleasure, my lord," she said.

"My honor, my lady," he answered. They could have been perfect strangers.

The conversation took up around them again.

Baynton leaned to speak in his twin's ear. Whitridge nodded. The duke turned to her. "My lady, I must excuse myself for a moment. There is a group of gentlemen here who wish to discuss a matter of some importance. I will return to you as swiftly as possible. In the meantime, my brother will see to your needs."

He was handing her over to Whitridge?

Part of Char was elated; another part was somewhat offended.

"I hope you do not mind?" the duke said, reaching for her hand and giving it a squeeze. "I will return in time to escort you to the supper room."

"I don't mind," Char mumbled, and that was all she needed to say. Baynton clapped his brother on the shoulder as he started moving toward the door. Five or so of the other gentlemen in their group went with him.

The wives pouted. So did the dowager, since Mr. Morris had also left for their private discussion. She made an annoyed sound and then began talking to her friends around her.

Whitridge and Char were side by side.

He appeared to be a bit irked with the task his brother had assigned him, but she was pleased. Very pleased.

At last, someone she could talk to.

"You don't have to be my minder," she told him. "I can join Lady Baldwin."

He knew exactly why she had said what she did. "Please do not think I am annoyed with you. I told my brother that if he was wise he needed to stay by your side. Apparently, he has decided I'm his placeholder."

"You don't need to be."

Whitridge looked down at her, studying her for a moment. He and the duke had the same eyes, or were Whitridge's sharper? More intelligent?

"Skirts become you." His voice was low, for her ears only.

"But there is little freedom in a dress," she countered.

"There is enough to dance, is there not?"

He was asking her to dance.

Char's heart slammed against her chest. She swallowed, a bit unnerved.

He offered his hand. "Will you join me? If I am going to be standing in for my twin, we should at least enjoy ourselves."

Oh yes, she thought, and she was very aware and very present in this moment. The sounds around her became clearer, the lights overhead brighter.

"I would like that," she managed, her voice calm, slightly detached.

He smiled, the expression rueful, as if he had a sense of regret. His gaze did not meet hers but focused on where he offered his hand. She placed hers in his.

His gloved fingers started to close over her fingers and then paused, loosened. She understood. He was being carefully correct.

But as he led her to the dance floor, every fiber of her body was singing.

Chapter Twelve

$\mathcal{A}$sking Lady Charlene to dance was not prudent, and yet what other choice did Jack have? His brother had figuratively thrust her into his arms. He must do what was polite . . . shouldn't he?

He shouldn't.

If he were wise, if he kept in mind his purpose for being in London, he would give a wide berth to her. He was far too attracted to the lady than was prudent, especially with his twin's trust in the balance.

And yet, he could not help himself. He'd watched her dance with one partner after another and he'd been jealous.

His desire had become a primal thing, and he realized it had started building inside him from the moment he'd caught her in that alley and her hat had tumbled off her head. He'd understood all too well what Gavin had meant when he'd declared he "wanted" her.

Yes, she was lovely, undeniably the most beautiful woman in the room. Her youth, her coloring, the evenness of her features, combined with a hint of naiveté, would have stood her in good stead anywhere.

But he knew something else about her, something no one else knew—she was a survivor. It was a rare and valuable trait and explained her resilience, her resourcefulness, her willingness to carry her own weight. Perhaps the quality was not valued in the smoothly civilized society of London but from where Jack had just come, such a woman was worth more than gold.

Jack had never been on a London dance floor, but he hadn't imagined it would be too difficult. He danced. His mother had insisted that all her sons receive lessons from an early age. He had enjoyed the raucous jigs and quadrilles of frontier society.

However, as he took his place in line across from Lady Charlene, he had his first inkling that this might not have been the wisest idea. First, he had no idea what dance they were about to do, and there was no caller.

Second, it put him in the position of being given a cut direct. The men on either side of him made a point of offering him their backs. The one on his left, ostensibly to speak to others. But the man on his right was very pointed in his actions.

Jack had suffered this particular cut several times this evening. He'd overheard whispers and words like "turncoat"—which he preferred over the more common "fool."

Now he smiled at Lady Charlene, wishing to pretend all was fine and sincerely hoping the hostility of small minds did not influence or impact her.

She smiled back, squaring her shoulders, her arms held gracefully as all the other women held them. Her eyes were vibrant with anticipation and, looking in them, Jack could forget where he was . . . to the point that when the music started, he not only had *still* not gleaned what dance they were doing—a minuet—but he started on the wrong foot.

One foot tripped over the other in his haste to right a wrong. Jack stumbled, his clumsiness disrupting the line of dancers. Eyebrows lifted in disapproval or confusion. The hand he'd used for balance accidentally hit the man in front of him, the man who had been the rudest, no less, and sent him off balance and into the man ahead of him in the line.

Quick as a deer, Lady Charlene leaped forward, hooked her arm in his, and circled, effortlessly directing him to where he should be. She laughed at her success, the sound so infectious that, for a moment, it seemed to him that even the musicians stopped to listen.

Other couples around them laughed as well and, to Jack's surprise copied the movement. Up and down the line of the dancers, couples broke ranks and circled each other. Yes, there were those watching who censored them with their gazes, but these couples on the dance floor didn't care. They were young and full of Lord Vetter's punch. Jack had a moment to reclaim his equilibrium.

The musicians caught the spirit of the thing and the slow, sedate minuet was quickly whipped into a quadrille. The dance took on a life of its own. Even the gentleman on Jack's right began stomping his feet. When the steps called for him and Jack to pass each other in order to regain their partners, the man actually looked him in the eye and smiled.

And in that moment, Jack experienced a miracle. For the span of the dance, he was part of the people in this room. He was not a stranger. Her gift had been to see him included and he was humbled to realize that he wanted that.

He needed it.

In a moment of self-realization, Jack understood that, yes, there were those who considered him a traitor of sorts for adopting another country. However, he had been wearing his decision a bit like an armored breastplate. He had come to London to tell them a thing or two, and they, quite wisely, resented it.

Too soon the dance was over.

The gentlemen bowed to their partners and the ladies curtsied. Jack had only held Lady Charlene's hand a time or two during the dance.

He wanted more.

She raised blue eyes up to him and he sensed the connection, the desire, the kindred thought to his own.

Neither moved. They stood as if rooted to the floor, Jack almost afraid to breathe lest he destroy the moment—

His brother's hand clapping his shoulder brought Jack back to where he was.

Gavin smiled. "The two of you were the most remarkable couple on the floor."

Lady Charlene's gaze swept down away from Jack as if she, too, had been startled back to reality. "You were watching us, Your Grace?"

"I could not tear my eyes away from you," Gavin answered, looking intently at her.

She blushed and the rush of molten jealousy that poured into Jack's being was dangerous. He had no right to feel this way. Women were not his purpose for being in London.

Gavin looked to Jack. "Thank you for taking such good care of my lady while I was called away, my brother, my twin."

The double name. Was Gavin attuned to Jack's attraction to Lady Charlene?

Certainly his smile appeared without guile. Jealousy made a man a miserable person, and Jack did not quite know how to cope since he'd rarely experienced it.

Gavin leaned close. "While you have been enjoying yourself on the dance floor, I have been busy on your behalf."

"Yes?"

"Vetter's library is down the far hall on the left. Charles Mouton—do you remember him? The Earl of Wellsden? We were in school with him—is waiting for you. He is anxious to discuss the American concerns. He would be instrumental in setting a meeting."

Now Jack felt like a damn fool. "Thank you," he said, meaning the words, and silently vowing he would keep his distance from Lady Charlene.

"You still have to sell him but I've opened a door. Go on, man. Be the diplomat." Gavin turned from him and offered his arm to Lady Charlene. "I believe the supper room is open. May I escort you in?"

"Yes, of course," she said.

Jack watched as his brother and Lady Charlene walked away. *Think with your big head*, he ordered himself, and went in search of Wellsden.

He remembered Charles the moment he opened the library room door. Wellsden was a short, sandy-haired man whose nose and cheeks had always been ruddy red and were still so today.

Wellsden was sitting before the fire, his feet on a footstool, a glass of brandy in his hand. He waved Jack in. "Lawd, Whitridge, you've actually grown bigger. I remember you as a giant back in Eton. I say, don't they have barbers in America?"

"They do, but I manage to avoid them."

The earl laughed. "Come in, come in. It is quiet in here and the ladies don't pester you to dance. Pour yourself a drink and then talk about why Americans shouldn't be willing to allow our sea captains to search for deserters on your ships? Of course, I will put forth that your captains should willingly turn the buggers over to us. However, Baynton says I should listen to you explain and so I shall."

This was not the most promising beginning, but Jack believed in the strength of his cause. He did not bother with the drink but sat beside Wellsden and stated his case.

* * *

The duke was a considerate escort. He seated Char at a table, offering to prepare a plate for her.

"That would be nice," she said, uncertain. But then she noticed that other gentlemen were also serving their ladies. Apparently it was the thing to do.

She could feel people watching. She tried to pretend she didn't notice.

His Grace returned to the table with a glass of iced wine, silverware, and a plate with several different selections from the sideboard. He sat across from her. The table was so petite, their knees could touch.

"What of you?" she asked. "Are you not going to eat?"

"I prefer watching you," he said, picking up the fork and offering it to her.

"I can't eat with you watching. Here, let us share."

"A good compromise." He motioned for a servant to fetch another fork and glass of wine.

Char moved the plate toward him. "What is this?" she asked, pointing to a white meat.

"Lobster. You have never tried it?"

She shook her head. "My aunt and I set a simple table," she told him.

"Try the lobster. Let me know what you think. I drizzled some melted butter over it. That is the way I like it served."

She tasted. It was rich, sweet. "I might grow fond of this."

"I wish that you would," he said, taking a bite for himself. "It is one of my favorites. I always enjoy Vetter's table. His cook is one of the best in the city."

"We cook our own food," she had to say, sampling the thinly sliced roast beef. "Oh, this is good."

He cut a bit and tasted it to see if she was right. "So if I was coming to your house for dinner, what would you prepare for me?"

Char laughed. "I like that question, although I don't know if you will like the answer."

"I'm waiting."

"Very well, I make chicken stew and Sarah and Lady Baldwin both agree that I have a knack for it, or else they just want me to make dinner."

"Who is Sarah?" he asked, spearing a boiled baby potato and popping it in his mouth.

Too late, Char realized what she'd done, and then she decided to tell the truth. "Sarah is my aunt, on my mother's side."

"And Lady Baldwin is related to which side of your family?"

What did they say about liars being caught in their own snares? Char tried to remain calm. "She is a good family friend." That was the truth.

"And you live with her? But not your aunt?"

Char smiled brightly, while her mind scrambled for an answer. "No, Lady Baldwin lives with her daughter although she stays with me—when my aunt is out of town." Now a lie.

"Why is she out of town?"

This was painful. Char could not meet his eye. She looked down at the plate and moved a pickle around with her fork as if it was of intense interest. "She . . . has a friend who is not feeling well and she has gone to stay with her."

"How kind of her."

"She is a very kind person," Char agreed. She smiled at him.

He smiled back. "Where does her friend live?"

Char was beginning to hate this conversation. She reached for her wine. "Manchester. Her friend is in Manchester."

"That is a good distance away. I'm surprised that when your aunt is out of town you don't stay with your uncle, Lord Dearne."

"*That* will never happen," Char answered. Here, she could be honest.

"I don't know him well."

"You are wise."

He sat back as if stunned by her bluntness. She feared she had broken one of those unwritten rules of Society Lady Baldwin nattered on about, that he was offended. If he was, that would be too bad. She would not apologize for disliking her selfish uncle.

And then the duke surprised her by laughing. It was a full, rich sound. Masculine and strong, and it filled the air. The others dining in the room with them all stared in their direction as if they had never heard him laugh before. Knowing smiles came to their faces.

Oblivious to the attention around him, Baynton leaned toward her. "I enjoy candor. Please, always speak your mind to me. I respect honesty. That and loyalty are the two virtues I demand from those around me."

Oh dear.

"Tell me, Your Grace, how are your horses?" She'd grabbed that subject that Sarah had advised. The one it seemed all men were happy to discuss. And even though they had talked horses the other day, His Grace seemed to take delight in talking more about them. He spoke of the stables at his country estate, promising to invite her there.

"I would like that," she said, because it was expected, and his smile said he was pleased.

She wasn't. Their conversation in the supper room was stretching her nerves. He valued honesty.

If he continued pursuing her, well, sooner or later he might learn some truths that he would not appreciate, even without confessing the pick-pocketing.

The duke was now talking about his family. She pretended to listen, her mind racked with guilt until he mentioned his twin.

Char looked up, unaware until that moment that she had been studying the pattern in the tablecloth. "Are you enjoying having him back in London?" she asked.

He tilted his empty wineglass. "Of course." He didn't sound happy. There was a pause. He set the glass aside, pinned her with his eyes. "My twin and I are very different men."

"In what way?" Char had to ask.

"Almost every. His life had been the opposite of mine. He has even married."

Whatever he said after that, and he did continue talking, Char did not hear. *Whitridge was married*.

She should not be upset by that information, but she was.

He'd not mentioned it to her. Then again, why should he? *I caught you picking pockets and, by the way, I'm married*.

No, that conversation would not have taken place, although she did believe that at some point Whitridge should have mentioned a wife. It was the decent thing to do . . . unless he was not and had never been interested in her.

While she had found him very interesting.

The music had started again. People began leaving the supper room to return to the dancing. Char wanted to go home.

Her enjoyment of the evening had vanished. She had the need to retreat to her bedroom, her sanctuary, to mull over the news about Whitridge. She tried not to let the duke see that anything was wrong. She was relieved when he suggested they return to the ballroom.

They had just gone out the door when a gentleman came up to them. "Your Grace, here you are. We've been looking for you." He leaned close to the duke's ear but Char could overhear him say, "Perceval wishes to talk with you in the library."

Baynton drew a deep breath as if annoyed and yet could not say no. He said to Char, "I must step away for a bit. Let me take you to Lady Baldwin."

She nodded, even though she was ready to leave. She was not accustomed to late nights or disappointing news. She prided herself on not complaining.

He delivered her to the dowager. Lady Baldwin was nowhere to be seen. She had probably gone to the card room.

With a promise that he would hurry back, the duke left to meet with the prime minister.

Her Grace was in a deep conversation with two women whom she introduced as old friends. The set for the dancing had already started. Several men looked her way as if interested in asking her for the next set, but Char avoided their eyes. She was not in the mood to dance. She needed to clear her head. She needed air—especially when she saw Whitridge on the dance floor. She wondered if his partner, a buxom lass, knew he was married.

Char whispered to the dowager that she was going in search of the necessary room set aside for the ladies' use. The dowager nodded and Char slipped away, moving instead toward a door leading to the portico outside.

There was no one out there. It was too cold but the air felt good to Char. It made her think of something else other than her own disappointment.

Whitridge was married. It should not bother her. Everyone wanted her to marry his brother, the one with the money and the title.

However, she'd formed a bit of affection for Whitridge. He'd been kind to her yesterday. He'd believed her story.

How she had spun that into his having personal interest in her, even an attraction, was a bit unsettling. Char had prided herself on being sensible. Sarah had warned her a woman must be to survive in this world—

"What are you doing out here alone?" Whitridge asked from the door behind her.

Char moved away from him and the light coming from the windows, toward the shadows. "I needed air."

"It is cold out here. You need a coat."

She nodded. Her teeth might start chattering soon, but she did not go inside.

"Something is the matter," he said. A statement, as if he knew her—and he didn't. Not any more than she knew him.

Char faced him. "You are married."

"I am widowed."

That was not the answer she expected. "I did not know. I'm sorry. That's terrible."

He came up beside her and leaned a hip against the stone balustrade. "It is," he agreed, "although my wife died seven years ago."

"That is sad."

"Yes, I loved her. Very much."

Was it possible to be jealous of a dead woman?

To want to believe Whitridge could say that of her?

"Who told you?" he asked.

"The duke mentioned it."

"Ah," Whitridge answered as if he had expected it. "He said I was married. In the present?"

"I took it that way," she said. "I may have jumped to a conclusion. I—" She broke off, feeling culpable and silly.

He looked out over Lord Vetter's night dark garden. She placed her hand on the balustrade, pressing her fingers into the rough stone . . . having a feeling for what he was about to say, and not wanting to hear it.

"My brother is a good man, my lady. An excellent man. You could do no better."

Her chest grew heavy. She had to concentrate on breathing.

Whitridge pushed away from the railing. "That is what I have to say. I—" Now he stopped.

"You what?" she prodded.

He lowered his voice and said not unkindly, "I didn't come to England for a wife."

"I know." She gathered herself. "We barely know each other."

"True."

She tried to smile.

He didn't. Instead, he reached out and lightly caressed her check with the backs of his fingers and then he pulled away as if touching her scalded. "We need to return inside."

Before anyone noticed they were gone.

Before *the duke* noticed they were gone.

Char did not wait for him but lifted her skirts and rushed to the door.

Inside, all seemed exactly as she'd left it, and yet, everything was different.

The duke had returned. He scanned the crowd, looking for her. He wanted her.

She waved, a small gesture, catching his attention. He smiled and came for her.

And from the portico, she knew Whitridge watched.

During her second dance of the evening with the duke, an act that shouted louder than words that he was staking a claim to her, Whitridge left the assembly. She knew.

She watched him go.

Not once since she had returned to the ballroom had he looked at her, and he didn't look as he left, either.

On the step of the house on Mulberry Street, the duke asked her to call him Gavin, "When we in private, like we are now."

Lady Baldwin, who had imbibed a bit too much at the ball, had already hurried inside out of the cold.

Char was anxious to go in herself but felt one of them needed to soberly thank the duke for his many kindnesses over the evening. The dowager had taken a ride with her friends.

She nodded, not trusting herself to speak.

He took her gloved hand, lifted it to his lips, and turning the wrist, placed his kiss there.

Char could feel the heat of his breath through the thin leather. *My brother is a good man. An excellent man. You could do no better.*

"Thank you . . . Gavin." Her brain treated his name like a foreign word. A very personal word.

He released her hand. "Until the morrow."

"Yes, that would be nice." She stepped into the doorway, his signal to leave.

"Gavin" backed away as if not wanting to take his eyes off her. His footman held open the door. "Gavin" swung himself into the coach.

Char shut the door, and feared she would collapse. Only then did she feel free to finally relax the smile that had begun to seem plastered to her face.

"Are you all right?" Sarah asked, coming from the front room.

"Oh yes," she lied.

"How was the evening?"

"Good."

Sarah tilted her head. "The way he lingered on the step, I would think it was more than just 'good'?"

Char knew she should say more, but if she did, she had the strange suspicion that she might burst into tears.

And one wasn't expected to cry . . . especially when—what? She had a handsome, important, wealthy man interested in her?

Whitridge was nothing to her except a man who had been kind. She didn't know why she was so disappointed or had expected something more. "I'm tired. I believe I shall go to bed."

"Of course," Sarah answered, sounding slightly deflated. "Lady Baldwin has already gone up."

"I shall tell you all in the morning," Char promised, even as she was starting up the stairs.

Inside her room, she could barely undress herself before falling into the bed. Both brain and body were exhausted; however, sleep eluded.

No, she curled up with her pillow and thought of Whitridge, remembering each and every detail of their conversation. She tried to reword it in her mind, to change his response or hers . . . and yet, it was done. There would not be a second chance.

The next morning she woke up groggy and out of sorts. It didn't help that Lady Baldwin was cheery. Char found her and Sarah at the kitchen table rehashing the evening over tea and toast.

"She conquered him," Lady Baldwin was saying to Sarah as Char entered the room. "Everyone, *tout le monde*, whispered about them. They were the most handsome couple in the room and the most favored."

"Well done," Sarah said to Char as she sat in a chair, still not ready to face the morning.

"And the papers agree," Lady Baldwin added, tapping the paper in front of her. "They are full of you, Charlene. The 'Fairest of Them All' they call you. Don't you like that?"

"It is a bit nonsensical, isn't it?" Char answered.

"Let me make you a cup of tea," Sarah wisely offered, and Char nodded her head.

She asked Lady Baldwin, "You've already been out and purchased the papers?"

"Oh no," Lady Baldwin said. "Sarah started to go out and buy them. We were certain they would say something about the ball last night and we couldn't wait to read what they wrote. However, these were on the front step. And they were open to the recounts of last night's ball and your stunning success."

"On the step?" Char repeated.

"Yes, isn't that interesting? Opened and folded to the social pages. A neighbor must have thought we should see them."

But Char knew it was no neighbor. Stirring her tea, she knew Leo was keeping track of her.

After all, he'd learned to read in Newgate prison.

Chapter Thirteen

Char's days became filled with the duke. She began to know his servants by name. Ambrose was his coachman, Pomeroy his tiger, Henry his butler, and Talbert—well, Talbert took care of everything. He was the duke's secretary. She learned to distinguish the difference between the duke's handwriting and Talbert's. She could tell when the duke ordered a particular arrangement of flowers for her and when Talbert was just following general orders, which was quite often.

Sarah told her not to quibble. A hundred thousand girls would be glad to have such a problem.

Baynton was always busy and this afforded Char the opportunity to become well acquainted with his mother and other family members, including Elin, his brother Ben's wife. There was no rancor that she could see between the duke and the couple. He treated them with great affection as they did him in return, no matter what the gossips enjoyed whispering.

Whitridge was with their company from time to time. He was polite but formally distant. He was also an outsider. His family included him but even Char could see that a good number of Society didn't. There were always murmurs when he passed. Char had heard some of the names they mentioned.

However, women still found him attractive. Char had also noticed the looks they gave him, but he didn't seem open to their obvious lures.

He was focused on his purpose for being in London, his "meeting," as his family called it, to discuss American interests. A meeting that always seemed to be on the brink of happening and then would be postponed.

She was certain Whitridge was frustrated by the delays. She wondered if his mother and brothers were playing with him a bit. Perhaps they hoped that time with them would give Whitridge a change of heart, that he would realize the error of his ways and denounce his American loyalties.

She could have told them he would not. He was

one of the most honorable men she'd ever met. She mourned losing the right to trust him with her confidences.

What Char did have trouble doing was calling Baynton by his given name in private. She'd forget. He would gently remind her, and she would forget again . . . because it was annoying to have to think all the time if she was in a personal setting or a public one. And because, well, she wasn't certain *exactly* why she seemed unable to consistently honor his one simple request.

Invitations arrived daily.

She and Sarah were becoming adept at taking her meager wardrobe and changing dresses with ribbons and lace so that they looked different. These moments spent tearing off trim and replacing it were good times between them.

Baynton often asked about her aunt. He was anxious to meet Sarah and would wonder when she was returning from Manchester. Sarah was equally anxious to avoid such a meeting.

"It is too soon," she would say. "The duke might reject you because he doesn't want to align himself with an actress."

"He is always polite to Lady Baldwin and, from the stories she tells, she was rather wild."

"She was, but her years on the stage were decades ago. We give the older generation a pass in meeting our standards. It is the way of the world. I'm content playing your maid."

"But if I marry him, he will expect to meet you."

"Not if, *when*. And we'll meet when the time is right."

There was no arguing with her. Secretly, Char wanted to push a meeting between them. She was tired of keeping track of the lies she'd told. She wished to rid herself of all of them. Then her feeble brain would not hurt so much.

Furthermore, if Baynton could not accept her aunt, Char wanted nothing to do with him . . . but then the rent came due on the twentieth of the month.

And there was no money. It had been quickly spent on ribbons and lace.

The landlord called upon them. This was a first. He was also very polite. Another first.

"I understand how difficult it must be for two women alone," he said. "I do not wish to pressure you—"

"We know, Mr. Harris," Sarah interjected. "We just request a bit more time."

"You may have all the time you wish, Mrs. Pettijohn," he answered, his hat in his hand. "I just hope you will mention me to His Grace, the Duke of Baynton. He actually owns a small warehouse close to Canary Wharf that I've had my eye on. If Lady Charlene could put in a good word for me, I would greatly appreciate it."

Her eyes wide in shock, Sarah looked at Char and nodded. "You could, couldn't you?"

"I—" Char started, uncertain, and then nodded. What else was there to do?

"Very good," Mr. Harris said, placing his hat back on his head. "Very good, indeed. We will just consider the rent you owe as a loan to be paid when you have the ability."

Which meant, once Char married the duke.

"I'll only charge three percent interest," he concluded. "Good day to you."

Sarah closed the door. "I'll wager the property he wants will make him more than our measly three percent interest." She leaned back against the door. "Hopefully, Davies's money will arrive soon. Then again, he is always late when he pays." She looked to Char. "You are very quiet."

Char pressed her lips together before asking the question on her mind. "What if I don't marry the duke?"

"What do you mean?"

"What if he doesn't ask?"

Sarah laughed. "Oh, he will ask, and rather soon, I believe. When he calls, he looks at you as if he is ready to throw himself at your feet. I'm surprised he hasn't asked yet."

"Perhaps he is waiting for my aunt?" Char suggested.

Sarah did not like that idea, although she did not comment. She went into the front room and sat at her desk. The manuscript pages of a play Colman wanted her to rewrite were spread upon it.

Char followed her. She sat in a chair by the desk.

Her aunt sorted the papers, trying to bring her attention to where it was before Mr. Harris's call. For a moment, she acted as if she was going to ignore Char, but then she looked up. "I don't want you to feel as if you are selling yourself in this marriage."

"But I am," Char said, her mind not only on rents and livings for people she loved, but also on Leo and the Seven. They watched her. Every once in a while, she'd catch a glimpse of Danny and the young boys. She sensed they were there all the time and letting her see them occasionally so that she would not forget the debt she owed them.

"Do you not like him?" Sarah asked.

"Of course I like Baynton. He is kind and proper—"

"And very handsome."

"Yes."

"Then what is it?"

I think I don't love him. Those words could not pass her lips. Nor would *I believe I love someone else.* Sarah would ask who . . . and not be pleased.

Only good would come from a marriage to the duke. As for Jack Whitridge, the man might not even return her feelings. His emotions might still be tied to the wife he'd lost. Shared confidences given in trust were not love, were they?

"I feel as if I am using the duke's affections for my own purposes."

Sarah considered her words a moment and then said, "We all use each other. He gains something from a marriage to you—a kind and intelligent woman for his wife."

"But I don't believe marriage is that simple," Char insisted. "If it was, then Father would have been happy."

"Your father had a character defect. He was unable to appreciate Julie. Does Baynton drink?"

"Not to excess that I know."

"There, see? There is no comparison."

"Did you marry Roland Pettijohn because of what he could do for you?"

Sarah leaned away from Char, her gaze going out to the street outside the window. She sat still, a line of concern between her eyes, and then faced Char.

"Love. I married him for love. But I want something more for you." She rested her arm on her desk. "You don't belong on Mulberry Street or doing your own marketing, or threading needles. You are finer than that. You were born for better things."

Sarah drew breath, released it, and then added, "And in case you are wondering, Julie married Dearne for love. She told me the family was dead set against him but she would accept no other. Char, I've loved a man and learned I could not live with him. The duke is a man you can live with and you will learn to love him."

"How do you know?"

"Because he is kind and you already, I believe, respect him."

That was true.

"But will he slay dragons for me?" Char whispered.

"Slay dragons?" Sarah shook her head. "No one slays dragons anymore, my love. We just learn to live with them."

Char rose from the chair.

"Are you all right?" Sarah asked.

"I will be," Char answered, but when she went to her room, she lost herself in tears . . . tears that could never solve anything.

* * *

Jack did not understand why Gavin hadn't made an offer for Lady Charlene yet. He was obviously besotted with her. He expected her to be at whatever social events he attended or family dinners. All of London was waiting for an announcement and the odds in the betting books on who Baynton would marry were firmly in Lady Charlene Blanchard's favor.

Nor had he needed any advice from Jack. He appeared to be doing well enough in wooing his ladylove. He rarely asked Jack to be his place-holder and protect her from the interest of other gentlemen. She was obviously his.

Gavin did keep his part of their bargain. He finally confirmed a meeting for the coming Monday. All players, including the possibility of the Secretary of State for War and the Colonies, Lord Liverpool himself, would be in attendance.

The United States chargé d'affaires Russell was impressed. Lawrence, not so much. He had done his best to sabotage everything Jack was attempting to do. When Jack talked to someone of importance about the true issues, Lawrence would follow behind, often with his lapdog Rice, and raise questions on matters that were bound to inflame British opinions.

His favorite was to question whether any true Englishman should listen to someone like Jack who had apparently renounced his citizenship. That did not make Jack friends.

However, the Duke of Baynton was a powerful ally. Gavin had his lawyers research the question and in short order, a caveat was added to Gavin's own *letter patent* that stated any heir to his title must reside in Great Britain. It was unusual but resolved an issue, and generated a great deal of interest in Jack.

Of course, his mother was not happy. She wanted all her sons around her. "I know you will go. I understand you must," she told Jack in a private moment. "However, never forget you have a mother here who loves you. Write her."

"I'm the worst of sons," Jack admitted. "Once I'd left and time had passed, I did not know what impact my turning up would have. Then I heard Father had died and it seemed wrong for me to bother you."

She placed her hand over his. "Then I am thankful for the possibility of war if that is what it took to bring you back to your family. Never again doubt my love for you."

He wouldn't. She was all that was gracious.

She even sensed that something troubled him. She questioned him several times, but he could not confide his feeling for Lady Charlene in her. He could confide in no one.

Instead, he kept himself apart when Charlene was around and remained polite and as distant as he could . . . which was difficult. They often attended the same events.

The more he observed her, the more he found to admire. She had a good heart and the sort of spirit that didn't suffer fools.

She knew Jack avoided her. A time or two, she'd tried to engage him in private conversation. He had not allowed it. There was hurt in her eyes, and yet, he believed she understood.

He did do one thing for her. Routinely he walked by the alley that was the lair of the Seven. There were signs they still visited the place. He knew it was only a matter of time before he met Leo. The trick to successful hunting was patience.

Saturday evening, the duke, Lady Charlene, the dowager, and Jack were together at a dinner party given by Lord Raneleigh. Fyclan Morris was slated to attend but canceled at the last moment. Jack was interested to note that his mother was not offended. Instead, she announced that Jack would be her escort.

"Don't worry," she had assured him. "You may talk politics all you wish."

Gavin felt Raneleigh was a person who could

derail the meeting if he chose. He believed it important for Jack to be present and search for an opportunity to cultivate Raneleigh's support.

Jack knew he had a challenge ahead of him when he saw that he was seated well down the table. His brother, Lady Charlene, and his mother were in places of honor. Jack supposed he would need to bide his time to make an impression at the end of dinner when the ladies withdrew to the sitting room, leaving the gentlemen to enjoy their brandy.

Matters did not work out that way.

The caustic Lady Damian decided to mock Jack and his loyalties right there over the first course. She had a blistering tongue with an arrogance that would have put zealots to shame. She prided herself on being a social keeper of the hallowed *haut ton*.

"Americans are like impertinent puppies," she announced, picking up her soup spoon. "Sharp teeth, no manners, and a need to be routinely paddled. They act as if they have a voice in the world. They don't. And another thing I don't like about Americans, they are cowardly whiners. And yet we accept them." She sniffed her disdain and shot Lady Raneleigh a look as if holding her personally responsible for Jack's offensive presence.

Lady Raneleigh appeared ready to swoon.

A gentleman did not attack a lady. Nor would Jack make a scene at a civilized table, even to defend his country.

However, he did want Raneleigh's support so he was pleased when Gavin spoke up. "I support my twin's decision."

Any man at the table, understanding Gavin's power would have backed down.

Not Her Ladyship. "Because you are clueless. Or undiscerning, Your Grace. I beg your pardon, Your Grace," she said to their mother. "I understand you have no control over your sons. After all, what choice do you have? Family allegiance demands you support the black sheep. The rest of us would prefer to see him on the gallows."

Silence met that statement. Both Gavin and their mother were speechless.

Everyone else at the table either agreed with her or was cowed by her viciousness—except for Lady Charlene.

"I find your comments ridiculous in their naïveté and cruel in their content."

Lady Damian stared at Lady Charlene as if she had never seen her before, and perhaps she hadn't. Jack was fairly certain the sarcastic woman had dismissed Lady Charlene for a pretty face with more hair than wit.

She was wrong. Lady Charlene continued. "If you wish to be rude, then do so to someone who can answer you back in kind without impugning *his* honor. I believe to behave otherwise is cowardly. We must not hide behind our sex if we wish our opinions to matter."

Her rebuke was more than a warning shot across the bow. It was a broadside. The guests, Gavin, and the duchess appeared stunned. Even the servants stopped moving.

And Jack wanted to clap. She was going to be a magnificent duchess.

Lady Damian twitched like a banty hen ready to do battle. Apparently no one had *ever* challenged her before.

For her part, Lady Charlene sat serene.

Lady Damian opened her mouth. There was fire in her eyes, but before she could deliver a blast of whatever spite she had in mind, Lady Charlene smoothly warned, "Be wise, my lady. I'm certain the women around this table have all been subjected to your scorn. However, *we* are not honor-bound to sit silent. If we band together, you may find yourself very uncomfortable."

"And why should *I* feel that?"

"My aunt always says that women need take care of one other. Our power is in our understanding of what is important in this life. I find good manners have a certain grace. I don't think it is right to embarrass guests. It is insult to the host and hostess." Not even one of the patronesses of Almack's could have delivered such a setdown.

Nor did Lady Charlene rest on her laurels. She looked to Jack. "Please tell us, Mr. Whitridge"— he liked that she used a plain "mister" instead of the title "Lord Jack," which seemed alien to him—"what have you found about America that has encouraged you to support it?"

In all the weeks he'd been in England, not one person had asked him that question.

Jack did not hesitate with the answer, knowing that if he was going to keep Lady Damian at bay, confidence was key.

"Opportunity. It is everywhere. If a man is willing to work hard enough, he can accomplish his wildest dreams. And there is no class order. Well, there is, humans being what they are, but it is more fluid. Good ideas and courage are what is valued. My brother is generous and as you all know, a leader in his own right, even without the title. I hope to prove myself of the same mettle. However, as a second son, my only hope to fully be the man I am is if he dies. I love him too much to wish that upon him."

They were listening, Lady Damian with malevolent intent.

Jack forged on. "Britain and the United States have much in common. We speak the same tongue. The shores of Massachusetts where I live, indeed, all up and down the coast, were settled by Englishmen with vision. Our countries share ties that are bound in the blood of family histories. We have more in common than we have in discord. Why should we want war with each other? Our differences are not insurmountable. And the good, the profit, the wealth that we could create by working together and with respect for each other"—he nodded toward Lady Damian—"could surpass any that has been seen by the history of man."

The assembled company had gone still. At the head of the table, deep lines etched Raneleigh's face.

Lady Damian looked at her host's expression and then smiled at Jack as if he was a bloody fool. She opened her mouth to give her opinion but once again, before she could speak, someone else took the turn.

Raneleigh himself said, "Tell me more."

"Where to start?" Jack wondered. "I have traveled the territories. Words fail me to describe the forests or the fish in the rivers and lakes. But the cities like my own Boston are growing at a rapid pace and are on par with any England can boast—save London, of course."

"How is the hunting?" one gentleman asked, and after that, Jack knew he had their interest.

The dinner went well and no one was surprised when Lady Damian excused herself after the last course and went home.

Lady Charlene had slipped into a quiet corner as she was wont to do. Jack approached her there. Gavin had been pulled away by Lord Raneleigh.

"Have you come to guard me again?" she asked.

"What?"

"His Grace told me. He confided that he used you to keep watch so that no one else would take me from him." The suppressed bitterness in her voice caught Jack off guard. "You don't need to worry yourself. No one will intrude on me here." She started to walk away.

Jack stepped in her path. "Now, wait—" He shook his head. "Why would Gavin tell you about that? It was his idea but he hasn't needed me."

"But I have."

For a second, Jack thought his ears played tricks. They hadn't.

In a quiet voice, she said, "I thought we were friends."

He wanted more than friendship. "I believe by now you know you may trust me."

"How? You avoid me."

Jack didn't answer. What could he say? Nothing that would make the situation better.

Instead, he said, "I wanted to thank you for speaking up at the table. That took courage."

"Courage?" She appeared genuinely puzzled.

"I don't believe many take on Lady Damian. Even Mother is impressed."

"I was being fair, Whitridge. It was what was right. Isn't that one of the things you like about your new country?" She paused a moment and then added "I thought you explained yourself well. I wished I could see this land you so obviously admire."

He wished he could take her there. "You started the conversation and it did the trick. Raneleigh was the last person I needed for my meeting on Monday."

"Ah, yes, your meeting." She paused a moment and then said, "Does your conscience bother you that you came to England after being gone so long just to use your brother?"

Damn her sharp tongue. "I came to avert a war," Jack reminded her. "There was some thought that by going through Baynton we would receive a fair hearing."

"Yes, using him."

"I didn't want to," Jack admitted. "I tried without him . . . and it is true I need him. However, what I have received is a reunion with my family. I hadn't realized how much I missed them."

"And what has he received in return?"

You. "He has not asked for anything. He truly is a good man."

She studied him a moment. He could read her every thought in her clear eyes.

What Jack saw was that she understood what he *hadn't* said.

"I pray your meeting is worth the cost," she murmured.

He wanted to step forward, to tell her it wasn't. That letting her go was an almost unbearable price, one he was just beginning to fathom—

"Here you are," Gavin's voice said from behind them. They both turned. He frowned. "Why do the two of you look so serious?"

"I was thanking Lady Charlene for rescuing me from Lady Damian's teeth."

"She was amazing, wasn't she?" Gavin agreed. He looked to Lady Charlene. "And I can't wait to meet your aunt. She sounds forthright. I now know why you are so special. When is she returning? Mother believes we should have her to Menheim for a family dinner."

Jack had heard him mention the aunt before. Was that why he'd not offered marriage yet? He was waiting?

"Soon," Lady Charlene said. "She will return soon."

She did not look happy. Jack sensed immediately something was wrong.

However, Gavin was oblivious to the tension in her. "Come, I ordered the coach. Mother is ready to go and you must be as well."

With those words, he took Lady Charlene away from Jack.

Chapter Fourteen

$\mathcal{T}$he next day, Sunday, the air was chilled but the sky was a brilliant blue in that way it rarely happens in winter. Jack set his hat low over his eyes and pulled on his gloves.

He had some thought of checking with Lawrence and Matthew. There was much to be done for the meeting on the morrow. Last night's successful discussion around Raneleigh's table had given him hope.

He found his reluctant compatriots sharing an early supper. After a list of instructions, all of which Jack was certain they would ignore, he began walking home . . . except his path led to Mulberry Street.

This time he didn't just check the alley, he did something he'd not done before—he paused at the corner to study the house. There was no sign of his brother or Lady Charlene, which was good. Jack did not know how he would explain his loitering in the area. That would certainly raise his twin's suspicions at a time he needed him most.

The streets were relatively quiet for a late Sunday afternoon. Most of the traffic was by foot.

Knowing he had stretched his luck, Jack forced himself to continue past Mulberry Street, and it was at that moment, he noticed a street boy snuggled down behind the rain barrel on the corner. Jack stopped, curious. He glanced back toward the house on Mulberry Street. At this angle, the boy would have a clear view of who was traveling up and down both Mulberry and the connecting street. The lad was small, not more than eight years of age. He could crouch by the barrel and not be seen.

Jack walked up to the boy who had dismissed him earlier as someone of no consequence. He probably had his eye out for the duke or Lady Charlene.

Coming up behind the boy, his steps so quiet the little rascal did not notice, Jack said, "Has Lady Charlene passed this way yet?"

The lad startled and looked up at Jack. He must have seen a resemblance because the boy tried to run but his feet barely scrambled to let him stand before Jack had him by the collar.

"What are you doing?" the boy complained. He twisted and turned trying to free himself.

"What is your name?" Jack asked.

The boy hit out at him. He was a skinny lad with the furtive movements of a weasel wanting to break free of a trap. Jack gave him a shake. "Your name."

"Toady. Not let me go, sir. *Let me go.*" He said this last as a holler as if wishing to attract attention and possible rescue.

Jack held him up so he could look into Toady's grimy face. "No one is interested in a gentleman chastising a street boy."

Toady fell quiet, an acknowledgment of the truth of Jack's statement.

"Now that I have your attention," Jack said, "take me to Leo."

"Who?"

Jack smiled. "If you do not take me to the den of the Seven, they may never see you again."

"And what can you do to me?" Toady had the impudence to ask.

"I can peel the skin off of you from liver to gizzard," Jack assured him. "And then I will take your eyeballs and use them for dice."

Toady was uncertain if Jack was serious. "I don't think you will."

"You are wrong."

The boy let himself hang in the air a moment. "Very well, sir. I will take you to see the Seven."

Jack lowered him to the ground. He released his hold—and as he anticipated, Toady took off at a run. He was fast, Jack would grant him that. He also believed he was outrunning Jack. He shot a triumphant look over his shoulder. He believed he had escaped.

Instead, Jack was gratified to notice the boy was running in the direction of the alley he had been scouting, the one where Lady Charlene had met Leo.

Jack followed, but at his own pace. Toady was actually free to go anywhere in the city, but the Seven reminded Jack of a tribe, and a good tribesman always warned the others of danger. They also had a habit of returning to the same safe campsites.

Reaching the alley, Jack removed his hat and moved stealthily through the narrow passageway. He was halfway along when he heard Toady's excited voice warning the others of the man who had almost captured him. Jack hurried his step and burst into the courtyard.

Leo was exactly what Jack had anticipated. He was a tough creature, a man in a boy's body. His face still had the smoothness of youth but the eyes had seen too much. He wore a jacket, a filthy shirt, and a black neck cloth tied with such flair any dandy would be jealous. He carried a crop in his hands and wore an outrageous *chapeau bras* on his head. The hat made Jack laugh.

The other members of the Seven were more like Toady, wise to the ways of making their own way. They were clever lads and Jack was certain they could be devils if they chose. Several of the lads were older, sixteen or so, like Leo. But unlike him, they were brawny young bulls. They'd used their fists a time or two.

Jack set his hat on his head. "Hello, Leo."

Toady announced, "*That's him.* That's the man who grabbed me. He threatened to use my eyeballs for dice."

"And I still might," Jack assured him.

Leo stepped forward. "You're the one who has been sniffing around here. What do you want?"

"I want you to leave Lady Charlene alone."

"Who is Lady Charlene?" Leo said, his words round with innocence.

"She is the woman who owes you money." He pulled his purse from his pocket and counted the money. Five guineas. He tossed it to Leo. "There, she is acquitted of you. Leave her alone."

Leo made no move to pick up the money that had fallen at his feet. "That is not the amount she owes us."

"It is the only amount you will be paid," Jack assured him. "If you are as intelligent as you wish to pretend, then you know that the Crown frowns on blackmail."

"But not among criminals," Leo said, spreading his hands as if that explained all. "Lady Charlene is not an innocent. She is one of us and we can bear witness."

"Leo," Jack said as if having to explain life to the boy was tiresome, "no one will believe you. All seven of you could line up in front of a judge, standing on stacks of Bibles, and not one of you would be believed."

"The duke will believe us. He won't want to marry a woman who would cause him that much scandal. They say Baynton is a stickler. High and mighty, he is. He won't want to hear what we could tell him."

"And then Lady Charlene won't have *any* money to pay you," Jack agreed. "That solves everything, doesn't it?"

"Are you blind or ignorant of Lady Charlene's obvious charms?" Leo answered. "We will work our money out of her."

That was the wrong thing to say to Jack. "Take what I gave you and leave her alone." There was no longer humor in his voice.

"Or what?" Leo asked.

"Or it will not go well for you."

The leader of the Seven did not like backing down.

Neither did Jack.

"Grab him," Leo said to his crew. "And take his purse."

Immediately the older boys picked up heavy boards from the ground and attacked. So did the younger boys. They came at him head-on, a sign they weren't sophisticated fighters, not like the frontiersmen and sailors Jack had faced in his past.

Yes, the lads lived a hard life, but they'd never had to *battle* for what they wanted. It was easier to steal it or run.

So Jack had no trouble blocking the older boys. He yanked the boards out of their hands and pushed them so they fell into the younger ones.

There was a mad scramble of legs and arms, grunts and curses.

Jack helped by taking the board and giving them whacks. The little ones shouted and threw their hands over their heads as if afraid of more.

The older boys tried to attack again. This time they spread out but Jack was good at hand-to-hand combat. An elbow here, a kick there, and the older boys attempted to make a quick retreat.

He grabbed one by his collar before he could dash away and tossed him into the crowd cowering behind Leo. Leo's hat went flying off his head and bouncing on its triangle-shaped brim across the ground.

"That was as easy as playing ninepins," Jack observed, referring to the bowling game. "Does anyone else wish to continue?"

"Move your arse," Leo ordered his young henchmen, shoving them off him. They weren't trying to rise too fast. Jack was certain they'd had enough of him. He picked up Leo's hat from the ground.

"I'll keep this," he said to Leo. "It will be a sign of your promise to leave Lady Charlene alone. And don't go on about her owing money," he warned as Leo opened his mouth to protest. "As it is, the lot of you have the opportunity to play another day. If I wished, I could see you in prison. Or worse. Let us leave it as it is."

Leo clenched and unclenched his fists. Jack stood patiently but he was ready for another salvo.

And then Leo bent down and picked up the coins that had been scattered about during the scuffle.

"You know, there are those who could harm her," Leo threatened.

"I doubt that," Jack answered. "You don't want to let it be known that I've bested you. Lads like you cannot afford any sign of weakness. You have a territory to protect. And, after all is said and done, I shoot better than I fight. Understand, if anything happens to Lady Charlene, Baynton and I will hunt you down."

Leo snatched his crop up from the ground where it had fallen. He waved it at Jack. "I don't want to see you here again."

Jack bowed his agreement. He turned and walked away. They let him. Thieves preferred easy conquests. He was fairly certain that his lady was safe.

His intent was to return home. That would have been the wise course. It should have been enough that he had freed Lady Charlene from blackmail.

And yet he felt he must do something meaningful with Leo's hat. It was a trophy. A sign that Leo understood he had been beaten.

Of course Jack found himself walking in the direction of Mulberry Street.

The hour was growing late and the shadows long. The temperature had dropped but Jack was too intent on his quest to feel the cold.

Lights burned in the windows of her house. There was a movement in the front window. A woman's slender shape walked back and forth. He knew it had to be her.

Jack pulled the brim of his hat lower over his eyes and strode quickly to the door. He knocked. Footsteps marched toward the door.

A few beats later, the front door was thrown wide open and *she was there*.

For a second, he forgot why he came.

She wore her hair down. Curls framed her face and fell around her shoulders. Her dress was plain, a sensible blue day dress, and yet she made it special.

At the sight of him, her lips parted. She smiled her welcome as if she was truly delighted to see him. She had one hand on the door handle and another on the doorjamb as if opening her arms wide for him.

All he had to do was step forward and he would be in her embrace—

A movement behind her caught his attention. A tall, redheaded woman had followed her into the hall. Her brows were drawn in concern. "Char, who is it?" she asked, and then stopped at the sight of him.

Lady Charlene acted as if she had been as mesmerized by the sight of him as he had been with her. She gave herself a shake and said, "It is Baynton's brother, Mr. Whitridge. Sir, this is my aunt, Mrs. Pettijohn."

"Mrs. Pettijohn," he said with a bow. The aunt. Gavin would approve of her. She was an attractive woman. Now there would be nothing to stop him from asking for Lady Charlene's hand.

"Sir. Are you here on some errand for the duke?" Mrs. Pettijohn asked. "Will you step in?"

How to explain himself? Mrs. Pettijohn did not appear as if she would be patient if he said he was here because . . . well, he had a need to gaze longingly at her niece. To be this close to her, to talk to her, to listen to her breathe.

"I do have a message. However, it is for Lady Charlene's ears alone."

Mrs. Pettijohn wasn't about to let him have a private moment, but Lady Charlene was ahead of her. "Yes, thank you. We shall only be a moment, Sarah. One moment. We will be right on this step."

Without waiting for permission, she came out to Jack, closing the door behind her, holding it shut with her hand. Darkness had fallen but the light flowing from the front windows highlighted her hair, her nose, her eyes.

Raising her voice so that it was loud enough for Mrs. Pettijohn to hear, she said, "What is it the duke wishes me to know?" And then she lowered her voice, "I had hoped to see you this day."

"Why?" He was conscious that he held his breath, as if anxious for her answer.

"The Seven are following me," she said. "I thought I caught sight of one of the youngest spying on me this afternoon."

Her answer deflated his—what? Hopes? He

should not have hopes. Lust? Well, there was that. He had not come to London for Cupid's purpose. And yet, every time he looked at her, all the sharp lines in his world eased and being this close to her felt right.

Jack pulled the hat from inside his coat and gave it to her.

She recognized it immediately. "Leo gave you this?"

"We came to an understanding."

"What sort of understanding?"

"One that has freed you from any obligation to him."

Her face lit with relief. "Are you serious? Oh please, Whitridge, be serious."

"I am," he said, charmed by the way she called him Whitridge. Of course, she could have called him anything and he would have been happy, and in that moment, he knew. He was capable of falling in love with her. He might already *be* in love with her.

"Thank you," she said. And then she reached up and gave him a hug. It was a quick gesture, one of supreme gratitude.

His hand involuntarily went to her waist and for a wild, blessed second, their bodies were pressed against each other, their eyes locked— and he saw the truth.

She loved him.

Jack leaned in. His lips hovered over hers. Dear God, he wanted a taste. He breathed in her breath, her scent, her heat.

This was madness. It could not be. If he kissed her, he would betray all that he was trying to become, including this new reconciliation with his brother, his family.

If she kissed him, then all that a marriage to Gavin promised would be lost. He could not let her make that sacrifice. If anyone deserved to be a duchess, it was Charlene Blanchard.

He stepped back and broke the spell between them.

She lowered her head, nodded as if she had expected him to be the sane one.

Mrs. Pettijohn opened the door. "Char? Is everything all right?"

Lady Charlene faced her aunt. "It is more than all right, Sarah. It is brilliant. Completely brilliant." She did not sound happy.

"Are you going to stand here all night?" Mrs. Pettijohn persisted.

Lady Charlene looked to Jack. "Our business is done here, is it not, Mr. Whitridge?"

"It is." Jack backed down the step. He did not want to take his eyes off her. "I must be going."

"Thank you, sir." She hugged the hat to her

chest. "This is the most noble, magnificent gesture anyone has ever performed for me."

"It was a small thing."

"Not in my eyes."

No blessing could ever be sweeter.

"What did he do?" Mrs. Pettijohn asked.

"He was kind," Lady Charlene answered, but the warmth in her voice made him feel like a knight who had won for his ladylove.

"Good night," Jack said, but he didn't move.

She did not move, either. They took each other in, drinking their fill in silence—because "they" could never be. There was a sadness in her eyes, in the lift of her chin. A regret.

"I pray your meeting goes well on the morrow," she said.

May it be worth the cost, he thought.

He turned and walked briskly away.

Char watched Whitridge until he reached the corner and turned out of sight, swallowed by the ever-present evening fog. She marveled at how a moment ago, the world had been exciting, thrilling even, and full of possibility.

They had almost kissed. She could still recall the heat of his body, the scent of it.

And now, with the absence of one person, life had lost that momentary luster.

"Are you all right?" Sarah asked.

Char did not know how to answer that question. Then again, she did.

She knew what was expected. She filled her lungs with the cold evening air and released it before taking a step inside and rejoining her aunt.

"I'm fine," she said, and she actually sounded that way. "If you will excuse me, I shall say good night. It has been a long day." She nodded to Lady Baldwin, who was gently snoring in a chair before the fire in the hearth, her feet propped on a footstool. "Do you need help seeing her to her bed?"

"I can manage." Sarah took a step close to her, concern in her eyes. "Is something wrong?"

"Why do you ask?"

"I know your moods, Char. You know you can confide in me."

"I know, Sarah. Nothing is wrong."

"What are you holding in your arms?"

Char held it out so that she could see the shape of the hat.

"What is it?" Sarah asked, confused.

"This is what a slain dragon looks like." Char turned. "I'm going upstairs now." She started up as fast as she could but Sarah stopped her.

"Wait. You'll want a candle."

Char did. She came down a few steps so she could take the wax stub Sarah picked up off the hall table where they kept the bits and pieces from around the house. Sarah lit it from a candle in the front room and carefully brought it back to Char. She offered it to her.

As Char accepted the candle, Sarah said, "The duke is a good man."

"I know."

Sarah waited a beat and added, "Choose the good man, Char, the one whose character is well known."

"I understand my responsibilities, Sarah," Char answered. "I know what is expected." With that, she turned and went upstairs.

Inside her room, she lit the lamp by her bed and blew out the candle.

"I know what is expected," she whispered to herself as she looked at Leo's hat that had been the pride of his wardrobe.

However, when she finally fell asleep that night, her dreams were not full of dukes . . . but of a man whom she had confided in. A man who had proved not only that he could be trusted, but that he would fight for her.

This had been what her father had meant.

Chapter Fifteen

*J*ack did not return directly to Menheim after leaving Charlene.

He walked and walked, hoping that in movement he would take ahold of himself. And failed. He realized the futility of what he was attempting to do close to midnight when he found himself in Hyde Park.

"I'm in love." He spoke to no one. There were few out and about at this hour on a Sunday night or, at least, no one who would give a care to a man speaking to himself, and he was tired of pretending. "It isn't just her looks that intrigue me. I love *her*."

Yes, her—Charlene Blanchard. His kindred spirit.

After Hope's death, he had believed he'd never love deeply again. Her loss had almost crushed him. What man would willingly suffer the possibility of such pain again?

This one.

Years ago, when he'd been Leo's age, he'd done what he must to direct his own life. He'd made a rash decision, and yet he had fearlessly carried on. He'd survived. Both good and bad had come out of his leaving, but he derived a great deal of satisfaction in knowing that the choices had all been his.

Charlene was a survivor as well. She was not afraid to break with tradition, to do what she must to live life on her terms.

With her spirit, she would take over Boston. The local society would not know what to do with her candor and they would adore her.

He would adore her.

In one fell swoop, Jack could imagine her as his wife. He allowed himself to think of children again. Their sons and daughters would be strong-willed and brave. They would also be imaginative and full of dreams. . . . just as their parents were.

Best, Jack's days would never be dull. Nor his nights.

The thought of having her in his arms, holding her, making love to her . . .

Jack gave himself a shake. Charlene had awakened a part of him that he'd thought he'd lost with Hope. It was more than desire or even lust. She had rekindled in him the sense that life in all its circumstances was worth living, and living fully.

But she was not his.

Gavin had staked his claim. Gavin wanted her.

And that was the crucial point of the matter.

He'd come to realize that the person who had been the most affected by his leaving years ago had been his twin. Jack could see now that, back in school, he had been a tether for Gavin. His leaving had left his brother feeling isolated with only their father for guidance.

Jack had no doubt that Charlene returned his feelings with an intensity that rivaled his own. He was also certain that those who loved her would discourage her from him.

In truth, even *he* would advise her to choose Gavin. Jack's law practice was growing but struggled. He had just hung his shingle when Strong had tapped him for this mission. For years, he'd been living modestly, and who knew if he could support a wife?

However, there was something about the way she'd looked at him tonight that had made him feel a hero. A warrior. She had held Leo's ratty hat as if it was a trophy. He had saved her from blackmail. For one unguarded moment, he'd seen mirrored in her eyes the same strong, vivid emotion that now ruled his own heart—*love*.

And did the sage not claim that love could conquer all?

"So what shall you do about it?" Jack asked himself.

The answer was silence.

On the morrow, he would take part in the most important meeting of his life. The stakes were high. Whether the British realized it or not, war hung in the balance.

This was no time for Jack to be moony-eyed. Or to place personal desire, even love, over what was right and just.

He stood in the dark of an empty park in the middle of a vast and powerful city and realized he must keep his distance from Charlene. It was the only honorable thing to do and, to Jack's surprise, he was honorable.

It had been bred into him.

The driving, restless need to move after seeing her vanished when met with brutal honesty. He could not, must not press his suit with Charlene.

It would irreparably damage his relationship with his twin. Gavin might have yielded to Elin falling in love with Ben, but Jack knew his twin's ego was every bit as strong as his own. Gavin would not take kindly to another betrayal, not from the black sheep of the family. Especially after all the Fashionable World knew his intentions.

Therefore, if Jack loved his twin—and, surprisingly, he did—*and* if he loved Charlene— passionately—then he must step back. He must accomplish what he'd set out to do and return to his life, leaving these two good people to their happiness.

Damn, being noble was a sword thrust to the heart. But Jack would recover. Hope had taught him that lesson.

And now that he'd reached his decision, now that he knew what he must do, Jack felt exhausted. Depleted.

If he was going to make sense on the morrow, he needed to find his bed.

Menheim was a short distance from the park.

Jack entered the front door shortly after midnight. He was tired but he wanted to review one more time the speech he'd written that he would be presenting at the meeting.

He opened the door, and found Gavin sitting on the stairs, waiting for him. The flickering light from the wall sconces reflected on an empty glass in his twin's hand. He appeared relaxed. He had abandoned his jacket and untied his neck cloth, but Jack could feel the tension around him.

"Hello," Jack said, giving his hat and coat to a nervous-looking footman. "Waiting up for me?"

Gavin looked down at the empty glass before saying, "I did wonder where you had gone off to."

He knew. In that uncanny way twins had of reading each other's minds, Jack knew that Gavin was aware of exactly where he'd been. And why.

"Do you still have Perkins following me?"

The footman had taken Jack's coat and hat to a closet. He had started back into the front hall but at Jack's question, the servant stopped mid-stride, and then quite wisely retreated away from the brothers.

"Do I need to do so?" Gavin countered.

Jack shrugged, having no problem meeting his brother's distrust with his own honesty. "I never felt the need to be followed in the first place."

"Tomorrow is an important day for you," Gavin said, changing the subject. "There will be men there who believe you could be a traitor."

Jack's first impression had been that Gavin has sensed his desire for Charlene. Now, he wasn't sure. Was Gavin having doubts about lending his support to the United States cause? "A traitor to what? Not to my values. Not to what I believe is important."

Gavin held up his empty glass as if it was a symbol. "They see you as an Englishman, Jack. They don't trust that you speak for another country. They question your *allegiance*."

The last word hung in the air between them. Jack spoke, "Especially since I once turned my back on my family?"

Gavin rose. "Or are you about to turn your back again?"

"What is it you are really asking, brother?" Jack tried to speak lightly. Gavin spoke in riddles. That he was angry was clear to see, but why?

"Whether or not I can trust you. Is that not clear?" Gavin came down the stairs but did not cross the floor to his twin. His jaw had hardened. "Because I am not certain, Jack. What do you want? Do you want what I have? *Is that all you have ever wanted?*"

"You can trust me as much I can trust you." Jack took a step toward him. "There was a time I was jealous of you, when I railed against the unfairness of it all. Two equal minds, two legitimate rights, and one came out of the womb before the other. You are duke because of a twist of fate. No more, no less. I have come to terms with the past."

"But is your allegiance with this family?"

"Why do I sense this has nothing to do with the family and everything about what is between you and me? I am the outsider, Gavin. I always have been, even when we were boys. Do I wish you harm? No. But I must live my life my own way. Are you wondering if I have love for you? I do. And none is more surprised than myself. When I was younger, I thought I had to rail against what I perceived as unfair to find the freedom I wanted. Now I understand that my leaving had nothing to do with you or Mother or Ben or even Father. I had a desire to wander and explore. It was born into me. I've always longed to know what was on the other side of a hill or where I would go if I followed a road.

"I sense your distrust, Gavin, and I can accept it. We do not know each other well. As twins and brothers, we have been at cross purposes more than we have agreed."

Taking another step toward Gavin, Jack added, "Yes, I have adopted another country and I understand that in some men's eyes that would make me a turncoat. But I'm not. I've simply chosen another way to live. By representing a country whose values I respect, freedoms that appeal to me—I'm not rejecting the land of my birth. I'm making a choice that pleases me. If I had no value for England, I would not be taking this time from my life to promote peace and understanding between us. Does that set your mind to rest?"

Gavin's answer was "Stay away from her."

So, this *was* about Charlene.

Having given his edict, Gavin turned and started up the stairs. As he climbed, he threw the glass he held in his hand against the far wall. The crystal shattered as if in warning and Jack's temper snapped.

The self-pitying bastard. Who did he believe he was to dismiss Jack after he'd spoken from his heart?

"So you *did* have Perkins follow me," Jack called up to him.

Gavin turned on the step. "No, it was your long-winded answer that gave it away." He went back to climbing.

Jack watched him a moment and then charged after him, taking the steps two at a time.

Gavin had already reached the hall. He walked toward his bedroom, a lumbering bear of a duke, the flickering wall sconces sending his shadow ahead of him.

With long strides, Jack passed him and blocked his path. "There is nothing between Charlene Blanchard and myself." He could say that with good conscience because he had made his decision.

Gavin's narrowed eyes informed Jack that he didn't believe him. He made as if to step around Jack.

Jack raised his arm to push against his twin's chest. "Did you not hear anything I said downstairs? Tomorrow is one of the most important days of my life. I have come to London to avoid a war, Gavin. Yes, I admire Lady Charlene. You are a damn lucky man. But I won't be the one who stands in your way for her."

"You won't?" Gavin's forearm slammed Jack's arm away. "Then what were you doing this evening?"

"I was seeing to a matter of some importance. Oh your behalf, I might say." That was true. That Charlene was being blackmailed might have evolved into a dangerous situation for Baynton.

Gavin's mouth flattened in disbelief. "Tell me. I am interested in what you have done for *me*."

Jack could not answer, not without betraying Charlene, and he would not do that. "It is no longer a concern. The threat is passed."

"Ah, 'the threat is passed.' How good of you, brother. I shall go to my bed and sleep well." He started toward his room but swung back around. With the repressed rage of a mongrel dog, he pointed his finger at Jack's chest and said, "Stay the bloody hell away from me and from her."

"Wait." Jack grabbed his arm as Gavin started to leave.

Of course, no one laid hands on a duke without

permission. The look Gavin gave him would have withered lesser men, or anyone English—but Jack was past that. There was not a man walking the face of this earth who could cow him.

"I need you on the morrow," Jack said. "You promised you would be there. This meeting is bigger than your jealousy."

"There will be no 'meeting' on the morrow. You should have understood that downstairs. I've called it off. And I want you gone, Jack. I want you and your delegation out of *my* country. We are done."

"You can't do that. Gavin, this is larger than any argument between us—"

Gavin punched him hard in the mouth. Caught unaware, Jack lost his footing. He stepped back, his own fist clenching, but Gavin had reached his room. He slammed the door.

Jack tasted blood. His whole jaw would be bruised in the morning.

Henry the butler materialized out of the shadows. "Lord Jack?"

Stunned by what had transpired and how quickly, Jack rubbed his jaw. "Yes?"

"I had orders to remove your belongings to the lodging of your fellow Americans. I am also to see you there as well."

Raising the back of his sleeve to his cut lip, Jack

knew the meeting was done. Everything he had hoped to do was in shambles.

A door quietly closed down the hall. The door to his mother's room. She had heard all.

"Of course," Jack said to Henry. "There is nothing left for me here."

Chapter Sixteen

Today was the day of Whitridge's meeting.

That was Char's first thought upon rising. Her hand touched Leo's hat folded under her pillow. The moment she felt the worn leather, she had an ominous feeling.

Discomforted, she sat up. She pushed her braid back over her shoulder. Something was wrong. Perhaps it had nothing to do with Whitridge.

She expected to see him that evening at Menheim. The dowager had planned a dinner party for the Americans. The duke would be sending his coach for Char and Lady Baldwin.

Pulling the hat from beneath her pillow where she'd kept it all night, she held it for a long moment . . . and thought of the duke.

She would never feel for him the rush of excitement she had for Whitridge. She heard Sarah's cautions. Her aunt wanted what was best for Char, and yet Sarah did not know Whitridge. *Jack*. His name was Jack.

For a moment, Char tried to conjure the memory of her mother's face. She could not remember her smiling. For years before and after her husband's death, Julie Blanchard's expression had been one of disappointment, fear, resentment.

But Jack Whitridge was not her father. Her father had terrible weaknesses. Her mother had suffered because of them.

There was *nothing* weak about Jack. And nothing staid and predictable about the life he led.

What she did know was that she could trust him. There was a connection between them, the very beginnings of a bond that, she believed, would grow over time.

And then there was the duke.

Char began unbraiding her hair, her thoughts troubled. She caught a glimpse of herself in the mirror on the wall over her washstand.

Her breath stopped, and she knew. She would never feel for the duke what she felt for his brother. Nor could she allow herself to accept the unacceptable the way her mother had.

And now that she had an inkling of what love

could be, she knew she must be honest and tell Baynton that her affections lay elsewhere. The sooner she told him, the better.

She also needed to tell Sarah.

Char dressed quickly, taking a moment to carefully place Leo's hat in her wardrobe. She went downstairs. She found her aunt in the kitchen breaking her fast while reading a book. Char stopped in the doorway and studied Sarah a moment. She owed her so much.

"That book must not be interesting," Char said. "You haven't turned a page."

Sarah startled and looked up. Her eyes were heavy-lidded, tired. "How long have you been standing there?"

"Long enough to tell you aren't really reading. Dull book?" Char walked into the kitchen.

"Um, yes, it is. Tea?"

"I would like a cup if the pot is still hot. I am going to toast bread. Would you care for some?"

"That would be lovely. Thank you."

"Is Lady Baldwin still abed?" Char placed a griddle on the grate over the fire to heat while she sliced the loaf of stale bread.

Pouring tea in a cup for her, Sarah said, "No, she left very early. She is excited about this evening and wanted to prepare. Are you ready for an important evening? Someone told me that Baynton's chef is French. Take special note of the dishes he prepares. See what he does differently than we British. I might try to copy one of them."

Slicing into the loaf, Char carefully said, "I wish you would go with me this evening. The duke keeps asking about you."

Sarah smiled as if pleased and then shook her head. "You don't ask the woman he believes is your maid or one who is in truth an actress to a dinner party of the top peers in the country. Not to say I wouldn't be able to hold my own." She leaned over and placed a loving hand against Char's cheek. "I'm pleased you would want me there, but let us wait until he is so hopelessly in love with you, he'll forgive a bit of subterfuge."

"I always want your presence, Sarah. You saved me. Who knows what my uncle Davies would have done if you hadn't intervened?" She placed the bread slices on the hot griddle.

Sarah did not argue. "You have been a blessing in my life as well."

"I don't know if that is true. You could be with a troupe and perhaps have your plays staged out in the countryside. London is too rigid. It doesn't seem right that they label you an understudy or a costume mistress while they use your talent. You have been fearless, Sarah."

Sarah laughed. "That is true. It took great courage to settle you down and teach you to read."

"I was shockingly uneducated."

"But you are wise in what is important," Sarah assured her, reaching up and smoothing back Char's hair.

"I wish I never had to disappoint you," Char said. There, she'd started but was suddenly unable to meet her aunt's eye. A knot had grown in her throat.

"You won't," Sarah answered confidently.

Char said, "I can't marry Baynton."

There, she'd done it.

Silence fell over the kitchen.

Char forced herself to breathe.

Sarah sat, her hands on the table, a line of worry between her eyes.

"I shall tell him this evening," Char said. "I know that your life would be immeasurably easier if I was a duchess—"

"This isn't about me, Char—"

"Then know that *I* can't marry the duke when I love another."

"The man last night? Who is he?"

"The duke's brother. His *twin* brother."

Sarah's jaw dropped. She closed the book, pushed it aside, turning away herself.

The smell of burned toast started to fill the air. With a cry, Char turned back to the griddle and, using her fingers, gingerly plucked the bread off the hot metal and tossed it onto a plate on the kitchen table.

Sarah was very quiet.

Char busied herself buttering toast. "It is a bit black but not too terrible." She offered the plate to her aunt, who did not move. "You are unhappy."

"Concerned is a better word."

"There is something else you should know." Char was ready to confess all.

Sarah swung in her chair. "It can't be worse than what you've just said. You are in love with the duke's brother? This is messy, Char. The sort of stuff that hounds people's reputations forever."

Char nodded. "Would you prefer I be dishonest with Baynton? That I pretend?"

"It would be safer."

"But at what cost? Could you have pretended with your husband?"

Sarah rose abruptly. "Let us leave Roland out of this. He's dead. Gone. While your gentlemen are very much alive and *related* to each other. Why could you not have found a different man to choose over the duke?"

"It was not my intention to fall in love with Jack. It just happened—"

"Wait, is this the American? The one who has everyone in uproar because he had once disappeared and then just turned up."

"It is."

"Oh, Char, he's using you. Can you not see that? I've heard the gossip. They say he and his twin never really rubbed well."

"That is not true," Char answered. "I have seen them together. They are as all brothers."

"And you know this because you have sisters? And so much experience with siblings?" Sarah queried. Her tone said she wanted Char to think.

"I know because I love Jack. He is honorable, Sarah. He is good. We tried to avoid this."

Her aunt threw her hands up in the air.

"There is more," Char continued.

"I don't believe I can take more," Sarah snapped.

"Uncle Davies has not been paying the money for my support."

"What?" Now she had Sarah's attention. "Are you telling me he is going to stop?" She moved so that the table was between them.

"He hadn't started since he quit sending funds months ago."

"But he sent money. There was that purse—"

Char shook her head.

"You told me it was from him," Sarah pointed out.

With a deep breath, Char admitted, "I lied."

"Then where did the money come from?"

This was not going to be easy. "I picked a few pockets."

"What?" Sarah almost knocked the table over in her shock. The teapot, cups, and saucers wobbled on the table before she settled it with a hand. Coming back around, Sarah sank into her chair. "Charlene Blanchard, you must tell everything."

Char did. She started by explaining about being afraid they would be tossed out by the landlord.

"A real fear," Sarah conceded. "Of course, now he is waiting for you to marry the duke so that he can collect favors."

"Which is despicable of him," Char announced. "Be that as it may, I saw this lad in the market pick the pocket of a wealthy man. I mentioned it to Lady Baldwin and she said she knew how to do it. She has had a rather colorful past."

Sarah groaned aloud and buried her head in her arms on the table.

"It really isn't Lady Baldwin's fault. I begged her. I was rather good—"

Her aunt groaned again.

"I tried to be careful in choosing my marks. I gave you the money and told you it was from Uncle Davies."

Raising her head slightly, Sarah said, "So that heavy purse was stolen—?"

"From a friend of Mr. Whitridge's and now you know how I met him. He caught me, but I escaped him and, well, the important part of the story is that some of what was in that heavy purse should have gone to Leo—"

"Who is Leo?"

"He oversees the criminal territory of this area. He leads a group called the Seven because there are seven of them. They are all quite close. They are boys actually but they can be very menacing, especially when they are together in a pack. They do most of the pickpocketing and some general thievery in our section of town."

"Interesting."

Char knew Sarah didn't mean that. She could tell her aunt was overwhelmed, and yet she needed to know all. "They were a bit of a problem for me. They were trying to blackmail me, and then they would have eventually blackmailed the duke, but Mr. Whitridge talked to Leo and now all is fine."

Sarah sat in stunned disbelief. Char placed a comforting hand on her arm. "I am sorry for all that I've done. I was trying to help us stay in this house. Before Lady Baldwin managed an invitation to Baynton's ball, everything had seemed so bleak and you were working very hard just to feed us—" She took a deep breath and released it. "Oh my, I am so happy to have that off my conscience."

"And on to mine."

Char shook her head. "Why? You have done nothing wrong."

Sarah didn't act as if she agreed. She lightly danced her fingers on the table as if thinking.

Char watched her carefully. "I'm sorry, Sarah."

Her aunt reached for her hand. "I wish you had confided in me sooner. Or hadn't been so worried over the rent. It will all work out, Char."

"I know it will. Mr. Whitridge will see to it."

At the mention of Jack's name, her aunt gave a thin smile, but she didn't comment.

"I plan on telling Baynton of my feelings this evening," Char said. "However, I believe I should talk to Mr. Whitridge first."

"That is a good plan," Sarah agreed, but she was not happy. Actually, she acted distracted. However, before Char could question her, she picked up her book. "I need to go to the theater." She walked to the door, and then stopped. "Char, I feel I've failed you. Your parents would never have wanted you to rob people."

"I didn't consider it robbing, Sarah," she confessed.

"How did you think of it?"

"I considered it a retribution of sorts. There are

those who stole all my father owned, including his dignity, and called it gambling. And here we were, going into debt and in danger of being tossed into the street. I was not right to do what I did. I lost my way. But, I must confess, it was a brilliant adventure—"

"*Charlene.*"

Char shrugged. "It was. For a span of time, I felt as if I had some power in this world. You talk about how it is hard for women to manage alone. However, when I was out on the street, moving along, I felt strong, alive. That being said, I've promised Mr. Whitridge I have set aside my breeches and I shall be all that is feminine from this day forward."

"*Your breeches? You have been parading around town dressed in breeches?*"

"Of course," Char said. "You didn't believe I would go pickpocketing looking like this. I'd not be able to close in on a mark without being recognized. I needed a disguise."

"Close in on a *mark*?" Sarah shook her head in outrage. "Oh, Lady Baldwin has much to answer for—and you will not do anything illegal again. Do you hear me?"

"Yes, ma'am."

"I mean it, Char. I don't know what I will do if I catch you in that sort of behavior, but I will do something."

Char tried to look contrite. "I promise I will behave."

Sarah appeared doubtful. She took a step and then rounded back on Char again. "And don't be too hasty in rejecting the duke. See what Mr. Whitridge does. Time helps us discern the true character of a person. Will you promise me that you will not do anything rash or foolish until you talk to Mr. Whitridge?"

Since that was Char's intention, she nodded, and yet her aunt did not seem mollified. "Is something the matter? I meant what I said about never doing something like picking pockets again."

Sarah shook her head, a small, tight movement. "I love you, Char, as if you were my own. Let me tell you something I have never spoken of to anyone else—I can never have children."

"How do you know this?"

"First, at four-and-thirty, I am too old."

There was that.

"But Roland was not a kind man. I do not like speaking of this. He could become violent. He threw me down the stairs once. I was at the beginning of a pregnancy. I was young. No older than you."

"You lost the baby?"

"Unfortunately. The midwife said that I would never have children after that. I'd lost too much blood. It took quite some time for me to heal. It was a very lonely time for me." She looked to Char. "Roland put me in an asylum."

"Why?"

"I was suicidal, but I grew better. When I was released, Roland was gone and then later I heard he came to a bad end, which seems justice."

"But you've always told me you married him for love."

"And now you know how poor a judge of character love is, at least when it comes to men. But not when it comes to nieces. I have no regrets in taking you on. I love you as if you were my own child, the one I will never have. Remember that."

Char nodded. "I love you as well, Sarah," she said. "I hated lying to you."

"You should. However, now you know more of my story, you can understand why I want you to marry a good man. And why I wouldn't want you to be so far away from me like in America where I couldn't help you if I was needed."

"Jack Whitridge is a good man," Char promised.

"I pray for your sake that is true." Sarah left.

The remainder of the day passed slowly for Char. Her mind was never far from Jack's meeting. She did her tasks around the house and prayed it was going well, that his hopes would be met.

Finally, the hour arrived that she could prepare

for the dinner party. She took extra care with her dressing because she wanted to look her best when she saw Jack.

Lady Baldwin arrived. "Don't you look lovely," she said with approval.

"Thank you. I have something to tell you." She drew her friend into the front room. "I told Sarah about the pickpocketing."

"Oh dear."

"No, you needn't be distressed. I took full responsibility. She is upset but at me. Not you."

"That is what you believe. I will reserve judgment for when I see her."

A knock on the door told them the duke had arrived. Char opened it. Baynton filled the doorway. He was remarkably handsome this evening, and yet her heart belonged to his twin. Jack could never match his brother in looks, but he made up for it in character.

"You are lovely," the duke said. He seemed quiet, subdued.

She curtsied. "Thank you, Your Grace. You are very handsome as well. It is kind of you to come fetch us."

He smiled a response to her pretty compliment but the expression was weak. He seemed preoccupied.

"Well, shall we be on with it?" the duke said,

and they went outside. "When is your aunt returning?" he asked, once they were settled in the coach.

"Soon," Char answered.

Lady Baldwin just smiled.

"I am anxious to meet her," the duke said. "I am certain you know that I am anxious to speak to a family member that you trust about a matter of some importance."

He was obviously referring to a marriage offer.

"She cannot return fast enough for me," he admitted, "as I believe you know."

Char smiled her answer. She couldn't speak. The duke was a fine man. He would not be happy with her confession. She was anxious for the evening to be done. However, first, she must speak to Jack.

"How did the meeting go today?" she asked the duke.

His gaze slid away from her. "Not as any of us planned."

Now she understood why he was so subdued. Char was even more anxious to see Jack.

The dowager received Char and Lady Baldwin in the family quarters. She was there with her great friend Fyclan Morris, who also acted quiet.

"You are looking well this evening, Your Grace," Char said in greeting. The duchess appeared regal, poised, and a bit distant. Her smile did not reach her eyes . . . or Char could have been mistaking the matter.

"As are you," she answered, nodding to Lady Baldwin, who had gone into a deep curtsy and always had difficulty rising when she did. Baynton held out a hand for her.

"Let me tell Henry we are all here," the duke said and left the room.

"We are small party tonight," the dowager said. "Elin is not feeling well so she and Ben have sent their apologies."

"Where is Lord Jack?" Char asked. "I am anxious to hear the results of his meeting."

For a second, the duchess's careful composure seemed in danger of cracking. Her mouth tried to smile and yet failed.

Alarmed, Char said, "I am sorry, Your Grace. Did I say something to upset you?"

"It is not you. I'm just weepy this evening. Jack is leaving for the United States on the morrow and I have no idea when I shall see him again. In fact, he has already left Menheim. He is staying at the Horse and Horn with his American friends. Here, don't let Baynton see me upset. It would make him angry."

Char's mind reeled at the information. "Did he tell you he was leaving?"

"Yes." The dowager smiled bravely. "I can't believe he would run off again but that is the way he is. We did have good conversations. I had thought there was an understanding between us, a forgiveness . . ." Her voice trailed off.

Stunned, Char murmured, "I am surprised as well. He spoke of enjoying the time he spent with you."

"So the duke said. We are both rattled by the matter and yet, Jack has made up his mind."

Dinner was announced then. Char was seated next to the duke. He was as attentive as he could be. Lady Baldwin carried most of the conversation at the table.

Char struggled to eat the carefully prepared dishes. Her appetite had deserted her. Jack had left. He'd abandoned without a farewell.

Or had that almost kiss on her step last night been his way of saying good-bye? It would have been her first kiss. He had been the one to pull away. She had been eager and ready.

Perhaps she had misread everything. Perhaps he had not returned her regard? She tried her best to be present at the dinner table but she found it difficult to smile, to be polite . . . and to breathe.

This was what poets meant when they spoke of a heart breaking . . . she'd always thought it a figure of speech. Now she knew it was real.

And she was not the only one distraught. The dowager was very reserved. No one at the table appeared to notice, not even Mr. Morris. He and Baynton became quite involved in a conversation of differing political opinions.

This news also explained the air of distance around the duke. He was probably as sad as his mother was and Char couldn't help but feel some empathy for him. How tragic it must be to have a brother, a twin no less, reject the family twice.

In fact, the more she thought upon Jack's desertion, his selfishness in leaving—her heartbreak evolved into anger.

She had not imagined there had been a connection between two such strong emotions. Between the soup course and the cheese, she found herself boiling with anger. She coped by being as attentive as she could be to the duke.

And he was pleased. He even, at one point, took her hand. It was an unusual gesture for him. He was always right and proper, but then, they were around family. Why should he not take her hand?

She just wished Jack were here to see it.

The evening came to an end at eleven.

The duke helped Char into her cloak. "Thank you, Gavin," she said.

He squeezed her shoulders. "You finally said it." His voice was close to her ear. "It was not that difficult, was it?"

She tilted her head to him. Their lips were inches apart. "No, it was not."

"Good. I may not be able to wait for your aunt to return."

It was on the tip of her tongue to tell him that he needn't wait. She could answer for herself, but she held back. She had done too many impulsive things over the past weeks. The time had come to be wise.

The ride back to Mulberry Street happened quickly enough. Lady Baldwin thanked His Grace for his hospitality. To Char, she said, "I'll step in and give the two of you a moment to say good night."

So, here she was, once again on the step with a gentleman.

"That was kind of her," Gavin said.

"She can be thoughtful," Char agreed teasingly.

"It gives me a moment to do this."

He was going to kiss her. She knew the thought had been on his mind ever since that moment with her cloak. He leaned toward her—and Char found it took all her will to let him come closer and not turn away. It was the strangest emotion. He was handsome and honest and everything Jack wasn't.

His lips pressed against hers.

Her first kiss.

Her back tightened. She held her breath, and fought the urge to jerk back. She wasn't repulsed. She had no feeling at all. It was as if she was kissing her aunt's cheek. She felt affection but didn't experience the overwhelming feelings lauded by poets.

What a disappointment.

Apparently, he'd liked it.

He took his time breaking the kiss. "Thank you for that."

Char nodded. She opened the door. "Good night."

She didn't want to give him the impression she was running but she did need to escape.

"Wait," he said. "May I see you on the morrow?"

"Yes," she answered, because she didn't know what else to say. She gave him a wave of her fingers and shut the door.

Lady Baldwin smiled sleepily at her. "Nice evening. I think you have him."

"Possibly. I'm tired. Do you need anything? I'm ready for my bed."

"I am as well. Sarah will be home late?"

"There was a rehearsal tonight. I don't know when she planned to return. She may already be in bed."

"Then I shall be quiet upstairs."

Char locked the door and lit candles for herself and Lady Baldwin.

Upstairs, in the sanctuary of her room, she threw off her cloak, tossing it on the edge of her bed. She then sank down on top of it, burying her face in her hands, and the anger she'd felt earlier returned full force.

Damn Jack Whitridge.

How dare he leave without saying a word to her? Or did he think those words they had shared the night before over Leo's hat constituted meaningful conversation? And what had gone wrong?

Here were questions she would never have an answer for because Jack was not here. Oh, what she would give to have him in front of her.

Or to be able to give him a shake and tell him how rotten she thought his treatment was of everyone who cared for him, most of all her.

Or did he think she preferred the duke? There was a thought she had not considered.

Char rose to her feet and paced the length of her room, practically distraught over the idea that perhaps Jack hadn't realized the depth of her affections for him. By the time she had reached the other side of the room, she'd discarded that worry.

Jack had known she cared. He. Knew. And there was no excuse to leave the country without telling her.

Her eye went to her open wardrobe door. The wardrobe where her breeches and boy's disguise were still hidden.

The house was quiet.

A daring plan took form in her mind. Jack owed her an explanation and there was only one way she could receive it. Furthermore, she owed him a good setdown.

Before she could question the wisdom of her actions, Char pulled her breeches from the wardrobe and began changing.

The Horse and Horn was not that far from Mulberry Street. She would say what she had to say and be back in an hour.

However, to give herself time in case Sarah decided to check on her, Char used her cloak to create the impression that there was a body in her bed under the sheets. She quickly braided her hair, wrapped the braid around her head, pinning it carefully in place, and pulled her wide-brimmed felt hat low over her eyes.

She blew out the candle and tiptoed down the stairs. Cold air rushed through the house when she opened the door, but it did not deter her. She took off into the night with one thought in mind—to find Jack Whitridge and let him know one didn't trifle with Charlene Blanchard and walk away.

Chapter Seventeen

*J*ack could say that he had given Gavin's men a good fight. In the wee hours of Monday morning, when Henry and the footmen had escorted him to the inn, Jack had been compliant. Why should he not be?

However, when he saw Perkins and realized the intent was on keeping him prisoner in a locked storeroom in the basement, Jack's good humor ended. Then they had a fight on their hands, right there in the public room of the Horse and Horn.

Jack was proud that his first blow broke Perkins's nose. He might have broken a few more in the melee. In the end, they had overpowered him. It had taken six grown, strong men. They had accomplished what the Seven had been unable to do.

Of course, no one witnessing the fight offered

to help Jack. Certainly not Silas or Matthew. Silas had actually watched the furor as if pleased. Jack didn't know where Matthew was. Probably playing with his knobby. That took up most of his brainpower as it was.

The footmen had bodily carried him down a set of stairs and had thrown him into a storage room full of odds and ends like brooms and buckets. There was a window, but it was close to the ceiling and too small for a grown man to climb out of. They hadn't been too nice about tossing him in, either.

Jack had landed heavily on his shoulder. He'd stayed where he was, bruised and humiliated.

Perkins had knelt over him, a kerchief held up to his bloody nose. "Rest easy. We'll come for you before your ship leaves Tuesday evening on the tide."

"My meeting," Jack had ground out.

"There is no meeting. His Grace canceled it."

Perkins left the room. A key turned in the lock and Jack lost consciousness. When he came to his senses, the light from the window let him know that Monday was well advanced.

He had tried to escape but there was no way out that he could find. He'd banged on the door to make a disturbance that could have caused attention to his plight but no one came. He had tried to barge through it. He had then threatened and cajoled and prayed . . . and still he'd been trapped.

That Gavin had done this out of jealousy gnawed at Jack. His mother had been aware of the argument. Did she know about this as well?

Damn his family. Damn all of them.

Evening fell. Daylight through the window was replaced by pale winter moonlight.

Gavin would be dining with Charlene. He was probably telling her that Jack had left London without so much as a farewell. She would not understand. She believed the very best of Jack, but this could break the bond between them.

It was one thing to ruin his reputation with the powerbrokers of London, but destroying Charlene's opinion of him was a different thing. She'd trusted Jack. He knew without being told that trust was not something she bestowed on many, and he had no idea how to reach her before it was too late and the damage was done.

He cursed repeatedly for not having told her Sunday night that he loved her. He should never have returned to Menheim without saying those words to her. He should have gone to Mulberry Street and roused her out of her bed.

And then she would say she loved him, too, and Gavin would never be able to part them.

He had no doubt that Perkins and Baynton's footmen would physically carry him to the ship. He'd probably be placed in the brig for most of the journey.

Nor did he want to think of facing Governor Strong when he returned to Boston. They'd both had high expectations for this trip.

Now any talk of negotiations was doomed. Jack had no doubt that Lawrence would happily take this tale to Congress. Jack's treatment would be considered an affront to the United States. The war hawks would be stamping their feet for Madison to declare war—and all because of Gavin's jealousy.

His twin's many machinations would have made their father proud.

Jack tried to keep his focus. He was hungry and thirsty. That worked against him, but this was not the first time he'd been a captive and he'd managed his way out of that one.

Sooner or later, they would come for him and when they did, Jack would have an opportunity to break free.

And then what? Would anyone in London care that the duke had locked up his turncoat brother? Most would cheer him on.

Jack sat on the floor, legs bent, his head resting on his knees. He kept his sanity by thinking of ways he could pay back his brother. The hour grew late. Past midnight by his calculations.

He might have dozed, but woke at a sound coming from the door. It wasn't that of a key turning in the lock but then he heard a click.

In the darkness, the door quietly swung open.

A shadow appeared in the door and a soft voice said, "Whitridge?" She stepped into the moonlight, a slender youth in breeches, shoes without their buckles, and an oversized hat that hid a wealth of glorious hair.

"God help me," he said under his breath, uncertain if he could believe it was she, and then going into a panic, because it *was* she. Where were the guards? What if they discovered her?

He jumped to his feet, put his hand out in the dark, and felt her. He pulled her into the room, soundlessly shutting the door. He almost choked on his joy. She smelled of the fresh night air and her own sweetness.

"What are you doing here?" he asked.

"I was wondering the same about you," she whispered. "There are men sleeping in the hall wearing your brother's livery."

"That is right. My brother put me here."

"No," she shot back. "He told me you left. What is this about? What of your meeting?"

"It is done, my lady. There will be no meeting.

Gavin will have me taken to the ship in a few hours and see me gone to Boston. How did you come here?"

"I was angry," she said. "I came to give you a very angry talking-to."

"Because?" he prompted.

"You were going to leave. You were going to leave *me*—"

He broke off her words with a kiss. He must. Dear merciful Lord, he must.

And she kissed back. Her lips had been together, but at his insistence, they parted ever so slightly, just enough for the kiss to deepen.

Jack had kissed more than his share of the fairer sex but nothing was as pleasing as kissing Charlene Blanchard.

She must have liked it, too. Her body leaned against him. Her breasts flattened against his chest. His hand drifted to her waist and then lower. It couldn't help itself. From the moment he'd first seen her in breeches, he'd longed to caress the curve of her buttocks . . .

But, infuriatingly, there was something more important he needed to think about and that was escaping. He brought the kiss to a close. She tried to follow his lips, her body pliant.

He leaned back. "We must be out of here, my lady."

"Oh. We must," she agreed, sounding very much like someone returning to awareness. She stepped back. "You kiss much better than the duke."

"He kissed you? No, wait, don't answer that. I'll be forced to tear the lips off of his face, and right now, we need to leave here." He walked over to the door. "You said the guards were asleep?"

"Yes, I walked right by them."

"How did you know I was here?"

"I overheard some men talk in the taproom. There are some broken tables. One man asked why and another said there was a huge fight early that morning. He said they had the man who had started it locked up in the storage room. Once I saw the duke's servants at the foot of the staircase, I guessed where you were."

"Did you steal the key from them?"

She held up her hand and he saw the hairpin in the moonlight. "Another trick Lady Baldwin showed me."

"Bless Lady Baldwin."

He kissed her again, a hard, grateful buss on the mouth. She deserved it. "I have something to say to you, but let's leave first." He would have opened the door but she pulled him back.

"No, wait, say it now."

"Let us escape first."

"What if we don't? I'll be returned to my aunt but who knows what will happen with you? I'll never hear what you have to say. I almost lost the chance to kiss you and I would never have wanted to miss that."

Both touched and gladdened by her candor, he cupped her face with his hands, marveling at the smoothness of her skin. How could anyone have imagined her a boy?

"Very well. Here is what I have to tell you. I love you, Charlene. You are simply incredible. You're bold and brave and I can't imagine giving my heart to any other."

"I am thankful that you said that," she answered, leaning into him. "I would never have wanted to live another second without hearing those words."

"If we make it out of here, I plan on telling you that every day."

"I pray you do. Whatever happens, Whitridge, you are taking me with you. If you go to Boston, I go to Boston. If you go to the moon, I go to the moon." And then she threw her arms around his neck and kissed him with all the passion in her being.

Had he thought the earlier kiss special? He'd been wrong.

What her kiss lacked in experience, it made up for in enthusiasm. She kissed him long and hard and he was powerless to pull away. Gavin could have led a host of guards into the room, and Jack would not have moved.

Charlene finished this kiss. Her eyes had been closed, her lashes dark against her cheeks. She now opened them. Sounding as content as a cat, she said, "I love you, too. I came here to tell you how rotten you were. I'm glad I was wrong."

"We shall finish this," he said, more of a promise to himself than to her.

She nodded. He took her hand and slowly opened the door. There was one window at the end of the hall that led to a staircase. The light from the window rested on the sleeping figures of two Baynton footmen. Jack recognized them as lads who served in the dining room. They were really not meant to perform this sort of work.

He moved Charlene up in front of him. Leaning close to her ear, he said, "I want you to walk right by them. You go first. Leave the building and I will come second. If they wake, don't stop. Run."

"What will happen to you?"

"Nothing as long as I know you are safe."

"I want *you* safe," she shot back.

"Then move." He gave her a small shove. "I shall meet you on the street."

She slipped into the hall, her movements noiseless. One of the guards gave out an abrupt snore, but neither woke. Jack saw her shadow turn the corner for the stairs.

He did not leave immediately. He wanted her to have a good chance to flee in case he was not as successful. He forced himself to be patient and when he was certain she'd had enough time to be outside the inn, then he moved.

In truth, Baynton's servants were apparently not afraid of him escaping. Babies slept lighter.

However, Jack was not sure whom he would meet at the top of the stairs. Perkins might have set a guard there as well. Now he was doubly glad he'd broken the man's nose. That had been a good moment.

He reached the stairs and climbed them two at a time.

All was quiet in the main part of the inn. Travelers who could not afford a room slept on benches in the taproom. No one was at the desk and there was certainly no sign of Baynton livery or the sort of man Perkins employed. Apparently, they thought they had Jack corralled.

Jack shoved his hair back from his face. He wondered where his hat had gone. He walked out of the inn as cool as he pleased. Moving out of the shadows, Charlene fell into step beside him. They did not speak for several minutes. Out on the streets, parties of men made their way about their business and Jack realized exactly what Charlene had risked coming for him.

She broke the silence first. "So, what do we do now? Are you going to confront your brother? Tell him how wrong he was for preventing your meeting?"

"No," Jack answered. He paused on a corner. "The Coachman's Inn is down this way." The Coachman's Inn was another posting inn.

"Why do you want to go there?"

"We need horses. How is your riding?"

Charlene hesitated. "I'm fair in the saddle."

"No worry. I'm a ripping good rider. I'll see you through." He started walking in the direction of the Coachman's.

She skipped to catch up. "The wharves are in the opposite direction."

"We aren't going to the wharves. That is what they will expect and I'm not ready to leave Britain yet." Jack stopped so quickly, she almost ran into him. He took her in his arms. "Were you truthful when you said you wanted to leave with me?"

"Were you truthful when you said you loved me?" she countered.

He laughed. "My Charlene, always hedging your wagers. Yes, I was honest. I love you, brat. I can't imagine not having you in my life. Although I prefer you in dresses."

She laughed, the sound very feminine, and Jack had to glance up and down the street to ensure they were alone. He turned serious.

"My lady, will you marry me—"

"*Yes*." The word was out of her before he could finish his sentence. She would have leaped into his arms but Jack held her off.

"Careful," he warned. They did not need to draw attention to themselves. Suitably chastised, she stayed where she was.

"My aunt will not be pleased. Sarah was trying to discourage me this morning. However, I like to think that once she realizes how happy you make me, then she will come round."

"My family will probably never come around. When we marry, Charlene, it will be without their blessing. There will be those who will tell you that I married you out of spite, but that isn't true. I'm marrying you because you have made me believe in love again." For a second, gratitude humbled him. "After Hope died, I vowed never to risk my heart on another. The pain of loss was too great. But, right now, I can't imagine my life without you."

He reached for her hand and laced his fingers with hers. "We are going to Scotland, love. I want us married on British soil so that no one can ever claim that I kidnapped you or forced you against your will or that our marriage is not valid. Do you understand?"

"I do. Isn't Gretna Green a long ways from here?"

"Not that far on horseback. Fortunately no one took anything off my person. I have the money to hire two horses. We can reach Gretna within the week, maybe less."

"Then let us be gone." She spoke without hesitation.

"You shall make an excellent American wife."

Her answer was a lovely grin. "I can't wait for the adventure."

"Follow me then." He stepped back onto the street. "We have to keep up the ruse a bit longer. We are two mates out on the town. Of course, this helps us. When Gavin starts looking for us, and he will, he will be looking for a man and woman."

Within the hour, they had hired two horses, and as the sun rose, they were well on their way out of London.

Chapter Eighteen

Gavin did not have a good night's sleep.

His conscience bothered him, as it had the night before. He had only to look at his mother to feel the pangs. She had not taken Jack's leaving well.

Worse, Gavin had lied to her. He was not a liar by nature and the sin did not rest well on him. It was compounded by his suspicion that she had heard their argument. She knew.

Last night, he had never wanted anything as much as he'd wanted Lady Charlene. Sitting across the table from her, he'd pictured her as the mother of his children and the partner in his bed. His body had ached for her.

Of course, Sunday night, the knowledge that she favored Jack and they were meeting behind Gavin's back had stirred an emotion in him that he'd never experienced before—jealousy. Festering, evil jealousy.

Because of it, Gavin had dashed his twin's chances to accomplish his reason for being in London—although, in truth, or to assuage his conscience, Gavin believed the grievances Jack had planned to present would have been met with stony gazes and cold shoulders. Gavin could build a case that he'd actually saved Jack from making a fool of himself. No one wanted to hear the American complaints, or feared going to war with them. Some, especially in the Admiralty, were even anxious for a chance to reclaim those lost colonies.

Gavin rose from his bed. He walked over to the window overlooking the garden. The sun had just risen. If he was of a mind to, he could go to the Horse and Horn and talk to his brother.

They might have a reasonable conversation and then Jack would board the ship on which Gavin had booked passage for him and leave . . . and then Gavin recalled the kiss he'd given Lady Charlene.

That kiss had kept him awake most of the night. He'd brooded over it. He'd liked kissing her but he was aware that she had not been, well, what was correct word? Impressed? Thrilled? Comfortable?

Charlene Blanchard was a well-mannered lass. She had pretended, except he'd known she was pretending.

And now his conscience returned to his miserable treatment of his twin.

He could even hear his father chastising him for having a care. There were traits Gavin had admired about his father, but he distrusted his sire's selfishness. A selfishness that apparently lurked inside Gavin as well.

Without ringing for his valet, Gavin dressed for riding. Exercise was what he needed. He'd been cooped up in London too long. He couldn't remember when last he had visited Trenton, his family's country estate. Certainly the world could do without him for a few weeks?

He could invite Lady Charlene and Lady Baldwin for a sojourn in the country. Lady Charlene would be impressed with his estate, and because things were always less formal in the country, they could have a chance to know each other better.

Lady Charlene's traveling aunt could join them as well. Trenton was far closer to Manchester than London was.

He liked his plan. He jotted a note to Talbert to prepare the invitation. He would personally deliver it later today.

Outside, the air was cold and brisk. His horse Falcon was fresh and ready for an adventure. For a good two hours, the horse kept Gavin's troubled conscience at bay and it felt good.

By the time he returned home, he'd convinced himself once again that he was completely justified in his actions toward Jack. After all, his twin had rejected his family once. Why could they not reject him?

After an hour with his valet, Gavin was ready to face the world. He broke his fast on beefsteak and coffee. Talbert sat with him, outlining his schedule for the day. But Gavin wasn't listening. Instead his mind was on his brother. The *Lucky Lucy*, a merchant frigate, was due to sail on the high tide that evening. Jack and his compatriots would be on board.

There had been no complaint from the two other members of Jack's delegation in accepting his offer to purchase their passage home. Like all governments, the United States didn't pay in a timely fashion, and those in its service rarely knew when to expect money. They would probably turn in the expense of their tickets anyway. Few were as moral as Gavin—

His conscience cut off the thought. That could no longer be said, could it?

Gavin lost his appetite.

"I did include the opportunity for you to pay a call on Lady Charlene between three and half past the hour," Talbert finished.

"Good. Have flowers sent."

"Yes, Your Grace."

A knock on the door to the breakfast room interrupted them. Perkins stood there and he did not look good. Gavin had not seen him since early Sunday evening. His nose was swollen and his right eye was a deep, unhealthy color of purple.

"Talbert, leave us," Gavin ordered.

He waited until the secretary had left the room and closed the door before he said, "What the deuce happened to you?"

"Your brother has a good right," Perkins answered. He stood at the end of the table, his hat under his arm, his coat still on his shoulders.

"When did he do that?"

"Monday in the wee hours. When we took him to the inn. He saw what we were about and fought hard."

"What you were about?" Gavin repeated.

Perkins had the grace to look uncomfortable. "You did not expect him to willingly follow your orders and docilely leave the country, did you, Your Grace?"

"I anticipated that he might be unhappy, but if

he was confined to his quarters, there would be little he could do."

"And how did you expect us to confine him? I warned you this would be messy. We couldn't put him in his room. He would have climbed out of a window. He is a resourceful man."

"What did you do?"

"We locked him in a storeroom in the inn's cellar. There was no way he could escape from that room."

"You expected him to stay there for two days?" Gavin would have gone half mad being shut in for even a day.

"We had no choice. I said he was difficult."

Gavin nodded. He knew. He also discovered that knowing his twin was confined in such a brutal manner did not set well with him. His already roiling conscience became even more restless.

"However, what we did does not matter, Your Grace," Perkins said. "He has escaped."

"*What?*"

Perkins nodded, his expression bleak. "He left sometime in the night. I came here because I feared he would come for you."

"He hasn't."

"Thank God." Perkins meant the words. "He is a fighter and he is very angry with you, Your Grace."

"Understood. If the door was locked, how did he leave? Did you not post guards?"

Perkins looked even more beleaguered. "I used two of the footmen, reasoning they would keep each other alert. They won't admit it but I believe they fell asleep. They saw nothing, which if one's eyes were closed would stand to reason. I then rousted the two other Americans from their beds. One had a local tart with him and I don't imagine he left her to save Lord Jack. The other, the older gentleman, has no love for your brother, Your Grace. He was well pleased that the meeting has been canceled and the delegation remanded, especially since Your Grace is paying their expenses and passage home."

"Where the devil could Jack be?"

"I have men checking the wharves."

"He wouldn't go there." Gavin pushed away from the table and stood. He found himself imagining he was Jack. What would he do?

Lady Charlene. If he were Jack, he would go to the true center of their conflict—to the woman they both wanted.

He strode to the breakfast room door and threw it open. *"Henry,"* he called.

The butler hurried from the front hall. "Yes, Your Grace."

"Have a horse saddled for me immediately and fetch my hat and coat."

"Yes, Your Grace."

Shutting the door, Gavin faced Perkins. "Keep searching for my brother. Try Whitehall. He may go there to salvage the meeting I canceled."

"Do you have any other idea where he is?" Perkins asked carefully, obviously suspecting by his actions that Gavin did.

However, Gavin had no desire to drag Lady Charlene's name into this. He could smell scandal. It was important to him to keep her reputation safe, and having his men surround her home would only raise interest from his enemies and the gossips. He needed to go alone, especially since, considering how perceptive she was, he knew she would ask uncomfortable questions.

So Gavin now added to his list of sins lying to one of his most trusted confidants. "No, I don't. However, I must see to another matter."

Perkins did not believe him. However, he did not argue. After all, Gavin paid his wages. He bowed. "If I may leave, Your Grace?"

"Yes, go. Take whatever men you need from the servants."

"I may need all."

"Fine."

Alone again, Gavin sat in the nearest chair, his mind busy. A footstep at the door caught his attention. Ben stood there. He frowned.

"I just saw Perkins. He does not look well."

Gavin shrugged.

"And I've had a conversation with Mother." Ben entered the room. "She told me you have ordered Jack to leave. What I gathered from what she is *not* saying, you used a manner similar to how Father sent me away years ago."

Uneasy, Gavin rose.

"What the devil at you doing, brother?" Ben asked. "You even canceled the meeting we've spent weeks setting up for Jack. Why?"

Gavin's first instinct was to shut Ben down. No one had ever dared to question their father. He stood still, struggling within himself.

"You are a better man than this," Ben said, his voice losing its censorial tone. "Do you not recognize what losing Jack again means to our mother? I mean, I had no problem with shutting down the meeting. No one was interested in hearing the Americans carry on. Without your support, most of them consider Jack one step away from being a traitor. But I was led to understand this was Jack's decision."

"It wasn't. I decided."

"And you have decided the time has come for him to leave as well?"

"I didn't know you were so damn close to him," Gavin shot back.

"I thought *you* were." Ben took a step back. "You have been behaving funny lately, Your Grace. One moment you are a true leader and in the next, a petty despot. There is an air in this house today, even amongst the servants. Something has happened and they are not proud of it."

"Are you done?" Gavin kept his voice neutral. Ben's words were sharp darts.

"Apparently. Let me know if you need me, Your Grace. My wife is indisposed and I need to take Mother to her." Ben bowed and left just as Henry came to the door holding Gavin's hat and coat.

"Your horse is waiting outside, Your Grace."

"Thank you," Gavin said.

He prayed he did not find Jack with Lady Charlene. He did not know what he would do if that were true.

Less than a quarter of an hour later, he knocked on the door of the house on Mulberry Street.

The maid answered. He recognized her by her green eyes. Witch's eyes, he thought. They were hard to forget.

She was wearing a blue day dress that appeared nothing like the costume for a maid she had been wearing. She had also not donned her mobcap. She was a redhead. That surprised him. Her hair color was unique, rich, warm.

At the sight of Gavin, she started and then made a graceful curtsy. "Yes, Your Grace?"

"I am here to see Lady Charlene and Lady Baldwin. It is a matter of some urgency." He took off his hat and started to enter the house but she didn't move.

"Lady Baldwin is not here," she said. "And Lady Charlene is still abed."

"Please wake her. I will wait for her in the sitting room."

Still the maid did not move and so he stepped forward and she had no choice but to step aside. "I will be in here," he said, pointing to the sitting room.

"I don't believe this is correct, Your Grace," the maid said anxiously.

"I'm not worried about correctness right now. There is a situation afoot and I must see Lady Charlene immediately. Will you fetch her, or must I?"

Those words coupled with the right tone had the maid closing the door. "One moment, Your Grace," she said. She hurried up the stairs.

Gavin paced the length of the sitting room, his hat in his hands. He had not yet decided how much he should or should not say to Lady Charlene. Obviously, thankfully, Jack was not here.

However, at some point, he realized if he was ever to have peace again, he would have to tell Lady Charlene that he had asked Jack to leave. Yes, that was the term he would use. He'd *asked* Jack to leave and Jack had agreed—

The maid practically tumbled down the stairs. She leaned against the sitting room door and confronted Gavin. "Why was it urgent for you to see Charlene?"

Her subservient manner had disappeared.

"I beg your pardon?"

True concern furrowed her brow. "Your reason for this unannounced visit, Your Grace? What is it?"

"I believe that information is for Lady Charlene or her guardian." He referred to Lady Baldwin and so was caught off guard by the maid's next declaration.

"I *am* her guardian. I am her aunt. Mrs. Sarah Pettijohn. Now why did you seek my niece at this hour of the morning and with urgency? Tell me, Your Grace, *please*."

Her aunt had always been here? Pretending to be a maid?

"Your Grace, does your visit involve *your brother*?"

Now she had his attention. "I have some concerns about him," he admitted, confused by both her conjecture and her manner.

"Do you know where he is?"

Alarmed, he answered truthfully, "I thought he might possibly be here."

"He is not, Your Grace, but neither is my niece. Instead of being in her bed, she has shaped her cloak into the form of a body and covered it with blankets. I know of no other way to say this except honestly—there is a possibility that your brother and my Char are together."

She whirled around, going to hooks by the door where a red cloak and shawls were hanging. She chose the cloak. "I pray they are still in the city."

"Do you mean they could have eloped?" This possibility had never crossed Gavin's mind.

"Exactly that." She threw the cloak around her shoulders. "We must go to the wharves and search the ships. I can't believe she would do this. Charlene is not a flighty child. She knows that eloping would upset me, and yet she can be willful. Wait, I must send word to the theater that I will not be in today." She had been speaking to herself and came back into the sitting room, going for the desk by the window where several of his arrangements of flowers sat. She started pulling out paper.

"The theater?" Gavin said, trying to make sense of what was happening.

"Yes, I'm an actress."

"And not a maid?" he repeated dumbly, attempting to wrap his mind around her change of status.

She pinned him with a sharp green gaze. "I do answer the door and clean the house." She put her attention back to the note before blowing on the ink to dry it.

"Who exactly is Lady Baldwin?" Gavin asked. In truth, he'd always thought Lady Baldwin a bit odd.

"A family friend. Well, more than that," she clarified as she folded the note and addressed the back of it to someone. "Lady Baldwin is Charlene's mother's godmother. She is very dear to us."

"But she is not what I was led to believe?"

Mrs. Pettijohn straightened. "She *did* chaperone Char to routs and parties and as her great-godmother, so to speak, I believe her actions are completely proper. It would have not been out of place." She started for the front door, her note in her hand—

"*Stop,*" he ordered.

She did. He walked over and took the note from her. He looked at the address on the outside, recognizing the handwriting. "You were the one who sent the note to me Sunday evening about your concern that Lady Charlene was forming an attachment for my twin. Not Lady Baldwin."

Mrs. Pettijohn swallowed. "I did." Her shoulders slumped. She raised a hand to her forehead. "Dear Lord, I did. What did you do with that information?"

"I confronted my brother."

"Did you tell him the note was from this house?"

"He believes I had him followed by a man I use for such purposes."

"And he said?"

"He did not deny he was here." Gavin took another step away.

"Then what happened?"

"I had him removed from my house. My men took him back to the inn where he had been staying. When did you last see your niece?"

"Yesterday. I was at the theater very late last night. It was quiet there and I had some writing to do. As you see, my desk is useless here." She nodded to the piece of furniture displaying the flowers that Gavin had been sending. "I know she and Lady Baldwin had returned before I arrived home. I could hear Lady Baldwin snoring. I thought Charlene was in bed. Her door was closed but I did not check. You do not know where your brother has gone?"

"No, but if he and Lady Charlene are at the wharves, then my men will see them. They are searching ships even as we speak."

"Wait a moment," Mrs. Pettijohn said. She ran back upstairs. After several minutes, she returned. "Char did not take anything with her. Her toiletries are right as they always are. The wardrobe was open but full of her clothing. Oh no, oh no, oh no."

"What is it?"

"This is terrible," she muttered to herself.

"*What* is terrible?" Gavin demanded.

Mrs. Pettijohn sank into a chair as if her legs could not support her. "Yesterday, Char told me she had been picking pockets and this gang called the Seven had threatened her. But then your brother talked to them and they were going to leave her alone. What if she is *not* with Lord Jack? She would have taken her personal items if she was going to run away. What if she has been *kidnapped*?"

"Pickpocketing?" Gavin repeated. "Lady Charlene is a thief?"

She waved her hand as if his question was of no consequence. "It is a long story. However, she became involved with a criminal element."

"Lady Charlene? The woman I have been escorting on my arm?" The young woman that was the very picture of propriety? That his aunt Imogen had approved? *That everyone expected him to marry?* "You allowed her to pick pockets?"

Mrs. Pettijohn looked up at him and frowned at the suggestion. "No, she completely deceived me. She told me the money was from Davies Blanchard, the current Lord Dearne. But yesterday morning she told me the truth. I'm sorry, Your Grace. I know this all sounds preposterous. It was not our intent to involve you in all of this."

"No, your intent was to trap me in marriage to a woman who lies and participates in reckless, criminal behavior."

Mrs. Pettijohn rose. "She is not a thief by nature."

"It looks very much that way to me, Mrs. Pettijohn."

"Charlene may have made some bad decisions but her heart was in the right place. We were just trying to survive."

"And make a fool of me at the same time."

"You were the man looking for a wife. You choose Charlene. Do you not remember?"

"I thought she was a proper young woman."

"She is. In fact, she is more than just proper. She was trying to help me. She went about it the wrong way."

"Then perhaps you are not the best chaperone for her."

Fire shot from Mrs. Pettijohn's green eyes. Gavin braced himself, ready for a fight. Right now he was angry at the whole world. He had done it again—fallen in love with the wrong woman.

A knock sounded on the still open door. "Your Grace?" Perkins said from the doorway.

"In here," Gavin barked. "At last, someone sensible to talk to," he muttered. As his man entered the house, Gavin said, "Have you ever heard of a gang of criminals called the Seven?"

"I have not, Your Grace. However, there are gangs all over London and every one of them has a name."

"Mrs. Pettijohn fears that Lady Charlene may have been kidnapped by them."

"Why, that is not good to hear," Perkins answered. "Although I don't believe they will hurt her. If anything, they might hold her for ransom."

"I don't have any money to pay a ransom," Mrs. Pettijohn protested.

"I do," Gavin answered, bitter and disgusted. *Gawd*, he was a fool.

"My poor Charlene." Tears came to her eyes. She blinked them back, thankfully. Gavin didn't believe he could handle tears in the middle of this tempest.

Perkins didn't appear comfortable with a weeping woman, either. "I do have news of your brother, Your Grace."

"Did you find him at the wharves?"

"I had another idea and while your men were searching the docks, I started at the Horse and Horn asking questions. Someone saw a man answering Lord Jack's description leave. However, he did not go to the wharves but in the opposite direction. I started making inquiries and at another posting inn, learned that Lord Jack hired two horses."

"Two horses?" Mrs. Pettijohn said, taking heart. "Why would he need two horses?"

"Apparently, there was a young lad with him."

"That's her. That is Charlene," Mrs. Pettijohn cried.

"She is a man?" Gavin asked, incredulous. "Are you saying now that the woman I have been escorting is a pickpocketing man?"

"She is a woman," Mrs. Pettijohn responded tartly. "However, she is disguised as a boy. Your Grace, I now understand what is happening. They are eloping."

"Which means Scotland." He looked to Perkins. "What time did they hire the horses?"

"Very early this morning. Say three o'clock."

"So they haven't been gone long. I can catch up with them. Good work, Perkins. You can tell them to stop searching the waterfront. I'll take care of the rest of this myself. I'm sure you understand the importance of discretion. See that the servants helping us are justly compensated."

Perkins nodded and went out the door. Gavin started to follow.

Mrs. Pettijohn had the audacity to reach out and grab his coat. "Where are you going?"

"To stop an elopement. My family does not deal in scandal."

"And what about my niece?"

Gavin did not want to think about Lady Charlene. She'd deceived him. She'd let him believe his feelings were reciprocated. She'd allowed him to make a fool of himself in front of the *ton* and then she'd run off with his brother. The betrayal from both of them cut deep, deeper than he wanted to admit.

He had loved her.

"She's brazen enough to fend for herself," he answered.

"I will not let that happen. I'm going with you, Your Grace."

"No, you are not. I'll be driving my phaeton. It is not a comfortable ride."

"But it is a fast one and time is of the essence."

"Agreed, however, you are staying here. I've had enough of our acquaintance."

Her grip tightened on his coat. "If it is scandal you wish to avoid, then you had best take me with you. That is the price of my silence. I must protect my niece. Otherwise, I will stand on the highest roofs and tell everyone what I know of this story."

"You would be destroying your niece as well."

"Those of us who have little are not afraid of what others say."

"Amazing. Blackmail, pickpocketing, thievery, and deception. Is there no end to the talent in your family, Mrs. Pettijohn?"

Her manner equally cool, she answered, "I take your question to mean that I am going with you." She let go of his coat. "Let us not delay."

Chapter Nineteen

Jack wasn't certain where Gretna Green was but he knew to ride north and trusted he would find his way as they came closer to Scotland. His main concern was to throw anyone who possibly followed their trail off the scent.

Charlene was game for whatever he suggested. Her concern was mastering sitting astride a horse. The animal chosen for her was docile enough but her lack of riding experience began to show. They did not make the progress traveling Jack would have liked.

After following the Post Road for several hours, Jack began taking country lanes and riding across fallow fields. It would take longer to reach their destination but he felt they were safer. He had the uncanny feeling that Gavin knew what they were about.

There was little conversation between them. In the beginning the road had been busy and it had been wise for Charlene to be silent lest someone detect the lad riding with him was a lass. Now that the path they took was free of traffic, she was tired and, in truth, so was he. Soon, they must either change horses or find a place to rest. They also needed food. He'd purchased some cheese and two mugs of ale mid-morning but that had only sharpened his appetite. Gavin's men had not been concerned about feeding him during his stay in the storeroom.

He'd also purchased a lap rug for Charlene to wear around her shoulders. A blanket would have been better but beggars on the road could not be choosers. The cold didn't affect him that much but she felt the chill. However, after hours of riding, she tried to fold the rug and place it between her seat and the hard saddle. It was not an effective solution. Only rest would help both of them.

When they reached a good-sized village, Jack inquired if there was someone about who let rooms to travelers for the night. He was directed to the tidy cottage of the Widow Fitzwilliam.

Dismounting and handing his reins to Charlene, he knocked on the widow's door.

"Who is there?" a pert voice said from the side of the house. A rotund, energetic woman with smoky brown hair under her hooded cloak came around the corner to see who stood at her front door. She held a basket of feed, and was followed by a clucking peep of brown chickens anxious for her to finish her task.

Jack removed his hat. "I'm told you have a room you can give us for the night."

"I might. Who are you?"

"I'm Jack Whitridge and this is my"—he had to think fast—"nephew, Charles Blanchard."

Charlene did not remove her hat but kept her distance by the horses and bowed subserviently to the widow.

"I see." The widow looked Jack up and down. She was a shrewd one. He doubted much escaped her. He was glad his boots weren't run down at the heels.

Apparently she was satisfied with what she saw. "Twenty shillings a night and that includes a meal and something to break your fast—"

"That would be excellent," Jack said, scarcely believing his luck, but she held up her free hand to let him know there was more.

"For that price, I will be expecting a favor of you, Mr. Whitridge. A tree fell in my garden. I need the wood chopped and stacked."

"I am happy to do whatever you wish," he said. "The boy is tired—"

"No, I'm not," Charlene called. "I can help."

She'd gruffed up her voice a bit and for that Jack was thankful—still, he was not pleased to be countermanded, especially when he was trying to protect her.

Then again, Charlene was not a hothouse flower who let others do her bidding. She would make a great success of it in Boston.

So he didn't argue but respected her enough to believe she knew her own mind.

"There you have it, we both work," he said. "Let us settle our horses and we will see to your tree."

"I own a shelter in the back next to my hen-house that will house your horses if you wish to put them up."

"May I hobble them to graze?"

"Whatever you like if you take care of the tree for me. Are you partial to chicken for your supper?"

The way his stomach rumbled just at the suggestion answered her question. She laughed. "Let me show you the tree."

The tree wasn't actually that difficult a project. It was only fifteen feet tall and a little less than two foot in diameter, but it had landed across her garden and she couldn't have cut it alone.

"The roots were rotted," she explained. "Fell last night and, while my neighbors are always happy to help, this will be one less problem for all of us, thanks to you."

Jack truly didn't need Charlene's help but she picked up the wood he cut and split, stacking it where the widow indicated. The chickens clucked around their feet and offered suggestions. The widow came to her back door from time to time to check their progress. The smell of a good stew kept Jack working.

Within an hour, it was almost dark and he was done. If he and Charlene had not been tired before, they were now.

He moved the horses to the shelter, closing them in for the night. The widow nodded after surveying his work. "I have food on the table."

"We'll eat it out here," Jack said. If they went inside to eat, the widow would expect Charlene to take off her hat and that would be a mistake.

"After all the work you did for me? You will eat in here. If you are thinking that your 'nephew' will need to remove his hat, you are right. However, I already know he is a female. Now come eat."

"How did you know?"

"I've eyes, don't I? Are you telling me you *didn't* know?" She didn't wait for an answer but said, "Come along now."

Charlene looked at Jack as if she half expected

them to continue running. He offered his hand. "Let's trust her."

"I'm so grateful you said that," Charlene confided. "I didn't want to leave, not without having something to eat. Hot water also sounds good right now."

"Aye, and I'm a bit ripe."

She laughed. "Your stay in that storage room did you no favors."

"Thank you, nevvy." He held the door open for her and Charlene rewarded him by removing her hat. Her braid fell down her back.

"You are a pretty one," the widow observed in that frank way women had for one another. "There is hot water in that bowl and a good soap for you to wash. She began ladling a thick chicken stew into the three bowls she had set on the table. There was a loaf of bread and a bit of cheese as well. "Here, help yourself."

Both Jack and Charlene were happy to sit down and do so.

"I used to be as lovely as you," the widow continued as she poured out mugs of apple cider. "You can't tell it now though. I'm an old woman. But when my husband was alive, he looked at me the way your gentleman looks at you, as if he'd do anything to keep you safe. So, are you two eloping?"

Charlene glanced at Jack and he decided to be honest. The woman had treated them well. "We are on our way."

"You are a lovely couple. Your secret is safe with me as long as you promise to call the first baby Elizabeth, Libby for short, after me."

"If it is a girl, that would be a lovely name," Charlene said, and Jack was so grateful for the woman's good humor, he could honor the request.

They ate their fill and then, at Jack's request, the widow let him heat more water for them to use to bathe. He wondered if she was going to insist they sleep separately. He wanted Charlene close to him.

As if reading his mind about her sensibilities, Libby said, "Oh, go on now. You are a lovely couple. I've a good feeling about you. I've been a widow for two years now and I miss my husband every night. Widowhood has taught me we must all make the most of every moment. You can say the words to each other or you say them before the anvil priest in Scotland." She referred to the blacksmith priests who were reputed to make a fine living witnessing the marriages of English couples. "What matters is, do you care for one another? Will you be kind? Generous? I watched you work on that tree together. The two of you will do fine in this life. Trust me."

Beneath the table, Charlene reached for Jack's hand and gave it a squeeze.

"Be good to each other," the widow offered as a last piece of wisdom before rising from her seat and picking up their empty bowls.

The water over the fire was starting to boil. As Jack moved it from the fire, the widow said, "Let me show you the room."

It was neat enough with a bed big enough for two, a wood floor, and a side table and a chair. Perfectly serviceable with a washbowl on the table. There was plenty of room for him to sleep on the floor, if need be. He didn't know what Charlene was thinking and he loved her enough to be patient.

After the widow said her good night, Jack offered to pour hot water in the bowl for Charlene to use in the bedroom. "I'll wash in the kitchen." He set about doing exactly that.

Rubbing his jaw, he realized what he needed was to shave. He thought he'd have to wait until they reached Scotland and married to do something about it, but Mrs. Fitzwilliam had laid out a razor, a strop, and some soap that had probably belonged to her husband.

Jack took advantage of her generosity. He shaved and scrubbed off as much of the travel dust as he could. Tomorrow would be another day of hard travel but at least they wouldn't look like ruffians.

He returned to the room and tapped lightly on the door. "Are you ready for me to come in?"

There was the sound of light footsteps, the rustle of sheets. He imagined Charlene climbing into bed.

"Yes," her soft voice said.

He opened the door and refused to look at the bed. He was having trouble enough keeping his randy side contained. Soon, she would be his. Very soon.

It didn't help to see her shoes, stockings, jacket, and breeches neatly folded over the chair.

He had removed his jacket in the other room. His shirt was damp from where he'd used it to dry himself but he put it back on for Charlene's sake. He sat on the chair and pulled off his boots.

Jack blew out the candle. The room was saved from blackness by the soft moonlight flowing in from the window. He stretched and then reclined on the hard wood. He should have asked the widow for an extra blanket. He'd not take one from Charlene. He did not want her to feel a chill. At least this floor was cleaner than the one in the storeroom. His muscles protested. They knew the bed was right there.

The bed ropes rubbed together as she moved.

He could feel her close. "Why are you on the floor?"

"We need our sleep," he lied, turning on his side away from her. Sleep was the last thing on his mind. His eyes were gritty with exhaustion but the sound of her movements on the bed stirred the other parts of him that were never too tired.

"We could both sleep in this bed. There is room."

"It would not be wise, Charlene."

There was another rustle of movement . . . coming closer to him. When she spoke, he knew she was right at the edge of the bed. "I was thinking the widow was right. We could speak our own words. It may not bind us legally, but what are legalities in the sight of God, and it seems somewhat silly to pretend."

"Pretend what?"

"That I don't want you here beside me. I'm not certain, Jack, how one goes about it, but I want you as close to me as possible. I want to know you in all ways. I'm tired of waiting for my life to begin."

Her hand lightly touched his shoulder. "Come to bed, Jack. Come to my bed. Then no one will ever be able to take you away from me. Even if your brother catches us, I will already belong to you."

Jack rolled onto his back. It was as he suspected,

she was right at the edge of the bed, the moonlight catching on her glorious hair and turning it to silver. "I'd not let anyone take you away from me either way," he vowed.

"Yes, but should we not be comfortable?" She lifted herself as if to move to create room for him beside her. The covers fell down from her shoulders and he discovered it was as he suspected, she was naked under those sheets.

All noble thoughts fled his brain.

Jack came to his feet. He unbuttoned his breeches because he needed the space there first, but he didn't remove them. Being noble was a damn trial, especially when Charlene threw back the covers and there she was in all her glory.

"Char, you are killing me," he whispered. Her skin glowed. Her breasts were firm and perfectly made. The line of her waist flaring to her hip was smooth and feminine in its curve.

He could see her blush even in the moonlight. "Really? You want me to cover up? It seems silly but Lady Baldwin said that on my wedding night I need never worry. If I was naked, my groom would know what to do."

"For once in her life, Lady Baldwin is right."

And he could no longer hold back the lust inside him.

Jack pulled his shirt over his head and tossed it

aside. He didn't know what his young bride would think about his very obvious desire for her, but he was about to find out. He slid off his breeches and tossed them in the direction of his shirt.

He knew Charlene had never seen a naked male by the way her eyes widened at the sight of his full arousal, and then she came to her knees. He half expected her to ward him off.

Instead, she whispered, "May I touch?"

That request almost brought him to *his* knees. "I pray you do."

She placed her hand upon him and, God help him, he was almost unmanned. "Gentle now," he warned, covering her hand with his. "When we first met, you almost gelded me. I wouldn't advise you to try it again." He showed her what he did like.

Charlene was an inquisitive student. She curled her fingers around him, ran the pad of her thumb over his tip—

Jack grabbed her hand, bodily lifted her up, and kissed her.

And it was every bit as sweet as he'd dreamed. He liked the taste of her and the way she trusted him. She was eager and open to his lead. He pressed his body to hers, letting her feel him as he explored her mouth—and yet, this seemed wrong.

Jack broke the kiss.

"What is the matter?" she asked. He could feel her heart's wild beating. It matched his own. His blood sang for her.

"The words," he ground out. "This isn't just a coupling. The Widow Fitzwilliam is right. Words count." He held her from him. Lord, she was so finely made, so delicate and yet strong and resilient. She might even be stronger in spirit than he.

Hope had been. His late wife had taught him much of love . . . and through Charlene, he'd found the will to love again. Was any man more blessed?

Jack struggled to keep his masculine impulses in check, to clear his lust-driven brain. *The words, the words, the words . . .*

"Charlene Blanchard, I take you for my wife. I want you by my side, always. I wish to hear your voice every day, to see your face light up in the morning and your head on my shoulder at night. I ask you to bear my children and know that my affection for you will only grow as the years pass. This I promise you."

Her eyes had grown serious as he'd made his declaration. Did she realize how seductive she was? Or how he valued the gift of her trust?

Their hands were still joined. She now placed his palm against her left breast. "My heart is yours, Jack Whitridge. You are the only one who knows me and has not tried to change me."

"I would not have you picking pockets," he had to admit.

She laughed, the sound the music of angels. "I promise I will never stoop to crime again."

"Thank you. It would not do for a lawyer's wife to be a petty thief."

Charlene's eyes softened. "A lawyer's wife. There is no finer title that I want. I am yours, Jack. I love you all the way to my soul."

Ah, yes, blessed.

Jack kissed her. He must. The kiss between them grew heated. Her tongue now tasted him.

His hand covered and stroked her breast as he introduced her to the other places that should be kissed. The bed became their school. Charlene let him push her down into the covers, his leg resting on her thigh.

He kissed her cheeks, her nose, her eyes, but when he nibbled his way to the sensitive skin below her ear, she practically cried out her astonishment.

Jack smiled against her skin. "You like that," he whispered. "What of this?" He kissed her breasts. She gasped, then sighed her pleasure.

Her voice became a purr. "I like that very much."

Jack took his time. Reveling in the taste and feel of her skin. The warmth of her body was his haven.

He ran his hand over her hips and down along her thigh. She immediately opened to him. She was that honest and willing . . . and so he slid his hand up intimately.

Charlene did not flinch but arched herself for him. Her hand returned to his hardness. He stroked and she mimicked the same movement against him and he was the one almost undone.

Jack could delay the moment no longer. He needed to be in her, to feel himself surrounded by her. He rose over her and pressed her back into the mattress.

"If the hurts, even the slightest bit, tell me and I shall withdraw," he said.

"It won't," she answered. "You would never hurt me."

He was not so certain. Her trust humbled him.

Slowly, he entered her. Her body warmed to his. She reached up for him, placing her hand around his neck and drawing his weight down to him. Their lips met and melded. Jack pulled back and thrust deeper.

He felt her tightness, the breaking. She shifted, a sign she'd experienced something, but she would not let him leave. "Please, love, stay," she whispered.

Jack began moving, his every sense attuned to her. This was the way it was meant to be between two people who loved each other. This was no fleshy act but a sacred moment between a man and his love.

He sensed her quickening; his own desire picked up heat. Together they moved, striving for that moment, that little death where all cares are erased—

Her hold on him tightened. She said his name, repeating it. Her body arched. Her words became inarticulate. He kept driving, knowing what she needed, letting her ride to that one point, that pinnacle, that glorious completion.

Only then did he allow his own release and it was magnificent. For a span of time, he was lost in her.

And then slowly, he regained his focus. He felt the sheets around them, the softness of the mattress, the curves and secret places of the woman he loved. Jack rolled onto the bed, gathering her up into his arms. She snuggled right into him, holding him tight.

"We did it," she whispered. "We are no longer alone."

Her last word caught him by surprise. Since

Hope's death he *had* been alone. Love's grace had once again rescued him. "You are my life. *My* life."

She burrowed even closer. "Yes," she agreed, "because we are now one."

In that manner they fell into sleep.

It was close to midnight somewhere in the Midlands on the road to Scotland when the duke almost ran his phaeton into a ditch.

Sarah had been trying to sleep as best as one could on the rickety seat of a sporting phaeton. Why men wished to drive these uncomfortable contraptions was beyond her.

She had suggested while there was still daylight that they find a place to stop for the night. The duke had instead purchased a lamp that he hung from his vehicle as if that would light the horses' way.

The journey was exhausting, especially with His Grace, Duke of Sour Words, for company.

They'd rarely spoken to each other and she liked it that way—although, in truth, she had been praying for just such an incident as the ditch. Then she would be right about the need to stop and he would be wrong, and *that* would give her great pleasure.

The man was arrogant and far too focused of purpose for her comfort. That he thought the worst of Char upset her, even if what he might be thinking could be the truth.

Charlene had certainly surprised Sarah with her questionable choices. Then again, while riding beside the Bitter Duke, Sarah had started to reflect on what role she might have played in Char's decisions. Her conclusions were not comfortable.

The vehicle swayed as the wheel rolled along the top of the ditch. The tired horses faltered at the sudden imbalance.

Sarah would have been flung off her seat if not for Baynton's quick hand grabbing her cloak. He threw both of their weights in the notoriously unstable vehicle to his side. The wheel beneath her found the road and the horses regained their footing.

The duke brought the horses to a halt and released his hold on her garment.

"We almost toppled," Sarah said, breathless as she realized the extent of the disaster that could have overcome them.

"But we didn't," he snapped.

"But we could have."

"We're *fine*."

"Yes, so fine that you'll kill both of us by weaving back and forth across the road."

The moment she spoke the words, she wished she could call them back. Baiting the Beast was not in her best interests.

He proved her concern by flicking the reins to urge the horses forward, and then just as abruptly halting them so suddenly, they pranced and she almost fell off the seat that way. "*What* would you have me do?" he ground out. "You sit there completely critical, judging my every endeavor and find it lacking—very well, what do *you* think we should do?"

Sarah struggled not to answer in kind. She could point out that she hadn't spoken at all for the last two hours. Instead, she said calmly, "Sleep. We both need sleep."

"As you can see, we are in middle of nowhere."

Because of your obstinacy. She forced a smile. "Then let us drive on a bit sensibly and, hopefully, we shall find shelter."

By the hard set of his jaw, she could tell he'd heard what she'd not said, proof that he could be perceptive if he had a mind to it.

And, as if wishing a tacit truce, the duke stoically moved the horses forward. A half hour later they came upon a yeoman's cottage. He set the brake and jumped down to knock on the door.

No one answered as one wouldn't to a knock in the dead of the night in London, but this was the country and along a busy road.

Sarah picked up the lamp to give him some light. "The cottage appears deserted," she said.

He pounded again on the door and then tried the handle. A moment's inspection led him to say, "It is nailed shut."

In the deep night, the ring of light extended far around them. She noticed dark shapes. "There is a barn. Perhaps it is open. I'm certain they won't mind our sleeping there and caring for our horses for the night. This close to the road, they are probably accustomed to travelers."

He didn't respond but went off into the darkness to investigate. A few minutes later, he returned. "The building is open and there is hay. I don't know where we will sleep." His words had come out on puffs of chilled air. He had the decency to take the lamp from her and offered his hand to help her alight from the vehicle.

She pulled her cloak around her. "Do you need help bringing the horses?"

"Hold the lamp," he ordered, which she did. She was so tired, she had to stamp her feet to stay awake while he pulled the horses and vehicle to the side of the cottage and then quickly unharnessed the team.

The horses were spent. She knew Baynton had

planned on changing them along the way but when the time had come, he had not been pleased with the quality of the stables they had passed. His grays were prime stock and he was wise to be cautious with them.

The barn was more than suitable for their needs. There was a good stock of hay in a hayrick that took up half the barn. It wasn't musty smelling, which was a relief. The horses needed something.

The other half of the barn had stalls with dirt floors. There had not been an animal in them for some time which led to Sarah to wonder if the cottage was abandoned and the barn was being used by the neighbors to store fodder.

They spread some of the hay in the stalls and turned the horses into them. During this time, she and the duke did not speak. They both understood what needed to be done.

Sarah then saw to her own needs. Returning to the barn, she found the duke had already climbed onto the hayrick and had made a nest for himself, using his coat as a blanket, which was exactly what she'd been intending to do. He'd even hung his hat and the lamp on the poles of the hayrick.

"Do you need help up?" he asked her.

"I believe I can manage," she answered, but when he offered his hand, she didn't refuse it. "Thank you."

He nodded.

Squirming around, she found her own soft space in the hay. It was not uncomfortable. She nestled into her cloak.

He blew out the lamp, plunging them into the darkness one can only experience in the country. She let herself relax.

"I'd forgotten how comfortable this is," she murmured, not realizing she'd spoken aloud until he answered.

"You have done this often?"

"When I was younger I traveled with an acting troupe. I've done this many times in fact. I would place a wager you haven't."

Her comment met with a moment of tense silence, and then he said, "I am not as pampered as you may think."

Of course, he took it as an insult. He was that touchy. "Oh, I'm certain you are," she answered. "But I have become that way as well. It takes having nothing to finally realize how much one truly has."

"Is that another veiled insult or are you philosophizing?"

"Philosophizing."

"What set you into that mood?"

"This trip. I'm starting to realize how my ambitions for Char might have encouraged her decisions." The comment had flowed out of her. The darkness invited confidences she would never have thought of sharing with him an hour ago.

And why not be open? What did she have left to hide?

"Such as?" He had a good voice, a deep, masculine one with the right touch of culture to it.

"My worry over money. The house on Mulberry Street was a bit too dear for my income, which is always precarious at best."

He didn't answer immediately and she began to believe he'd fallen asleep until he said, "Didn't Dearne have a brother who took the title? And the responsibilities?"

"An angry brother with an empty title, Your Grace. He had agreed to pay a portion of Charlene's expenses but he has conveniently forgotten his obligation over the past six months or so."

"What of the courts?"

"Courts cost money for representation. Besides, I didn't want the world to think her penniless. I wanted her to have the life that was rightfully hers."

"Is that what she wants?"

"There is the question. Obviously not. I wanted her to be safe and secure, and money is power. A woman is mere chattel without it."

"The law sees them as chattel to protect them, Mrs. Pettijohn."

"Or is it to keep us in our place, Your Grace? Isn't that the reason men like you want virginal wives with little experience of the world?"

"No, we don't 'want' such a thing," he replied, his voice tight. "However, there are standards."

He was probably whipping himself into a lather of offense again. Sarah didn't care. She was too tired. "Yes, yes, the rules—the ones everyone of power flouts. My Char may be ruined when all is said and done, but let us not forget your brother is playing a role."

"My *twin*." A wealth of anger colored that word.

She looked toward him in the dark. He radiated tension. She didn't answer but waited.

He did not disappoint. "This is a second betrayal," he said as if unable to stop himself. "The first was over a decade ago when he left. He never said a word to me that he was planning to leave. There wasn't even a sign. He just went off and all of the responsibilities fell on my shoulders. Sometimes, I hate it. I feel trapped in my own damn life. There are those with expectations all around me and the one person I should be able to trust rips my faith in him open to the core."

He would never have spoken these words without the darkness, and now she understood: This journey was not so much about stopping an elopement as it was about confronting a traitor.

"And when you see him?" she asked. "What do you intend to do?"

There was a long period of silence and then he said so quietly she could have imagined the words, "I don't know."

Chapter Twenty

Char did not want to leave the haven of the Widow Fitzwilliam's house, especially to ride horses. Between her riding the day before and the lovemaking that she and Jack had reveled in, she was discovering muscles she didn't have before.

Mrs. Fitzwilliam surprised her with a dress. It was deep loden green and far from fashionable, the sort of thing a maid would wear, but as the widow said, "I thought when it came time to stand before the minister, you'd like something a bit more fitting to your sex."

Char thanked her profusely and wore the dress at the end of each day as they walked around the villages they came upon looking for places to stay for the night. As far as she was concerned, Jack was her husband. They even signed themselves into the registries at two inns as "Mr. and Mrs. Whitridge."

Jack would ask if anyone fitting the duke's description had been this way. The answer was always no and they began to relax. Still, they did not dally.

The sores she had earned in the saddle subsided and her body happily adjusted to lovemaking. They had little in the way of money. Jack's funds were growing limited and he still needed to pay their ship fares to Boston, but she couldn't remember ever being so content. The old sense of desperation that had led her to pickpocketing had left her. One way or the other, she and Jack would manage. She trusted him.

She also enjoyed listening to his stories of his past adventures. Or hearing him describe Boston. She made him create word pictures of the street where he lived. She quizzed him on how he lived. He talked about his friends including Governor Strong, who had asked him to petition on behalf of peace.

"I dislike disappointing him," Jack said.

"*You* didn't. Your brother did. He was the dishonorable one."

"War will come, Char. There are too many hotheads in Congress. You understand we will be on the opposite side? You are all right with that?"

Char reached for his hand. "I've made my

choice. And, who knows? Perhaps cooler heads will prevail."

"Perhaps." He did not sound optimistic.

At last, they reached the Scottish border.

Char once more changed into her dress, Jack standing guard of the thicket where she'd gone for privacy. She didn't rebraid her hair but twisted it into a chignon much like Sarah wore. She placed her hat on her head, tilting the wide brim to a jaunty angle.

"I'm becoming quite good at making this dress stylish," she bragged.

"You could make a sack stylish, my lady," he answered, and she laughed.

"Are you ready to marry?" he asked. "We are almost there."

"I've been ready," she informed him wearily, and held out her arms for him to help lift her up into the saddle. She would ride sidesaddle into Gretna, a proper lady.

"Then let us do this," he said, and started down the road.

Gretna Green was a lovely village of white-washed cottages and a good-sized smithy. There was also an inn. Jack observed that the smith probably didn't make as much money from his forge as he did from marrying couples in front of the anvil.

People nodded at them as they rode into the village. There seemed to be no question that Jack and Char were a couple ready to marry and the locals were welcoming.

The day was a bit overcast but a good one. The weather was the least of Char's worries. She wanted the marriage done.

The smithy itself was a number of buildings connected by walkways. They were greeted at the door by a jovial lady who introduced herself as Mrs. Lang.

"We are here to marry," Jack said. "The sooner the better."

"A long trip you've had of it, eh?" Mrs. Lang said. "Let me fetch my husband. He went home for a wee nap."

"Please do," Jack answered. "Also, how much is the fee?"

"It will be fifteen guineas, kind sir. I will return in a moment."

"Fifteen?" Jack drew a breath and released it.

Char knew he was thinking of the ship fare. "We shall manage," she assured him.

He nodded. "Wives are expensive." There was no heat in his voice.

"And I only have one dress. I pray thee wait, I may become more expensive."

He laughed and kissed her hand. "There are

always breeches. We shall be fine once we return to Boston."

Mr. Lang, "Bishop Lang," was a handsome, officious man with a lighthearted attitude. "I married a couple this morning and thought I was done for the day. All right, shall we be on with it? We'll have you stand right over here in front this anvil."

Jack took Char's hand, but before they could move there was a commotion of horses outside. A glimpse out the window showed the team.

Matched grays.

Char gave a start. She might have run if not for Jack's steadying presence. He squeezed her hand. *Courage.*

"Let's be on with it," Jack ordered Mr. Lang.

Mr. Lang accommodated him. "Please tell me whence have you come?"

"London," Char said.

"Boston," Jack answered.

"This is a long way, sir," Mr. Lang replied.

"And I'm in a hurry to return," Jack assured him.

"Yes, well, then, let us begin." Mr. Lang looked at Char. "Will you state your full name—?"

The smithy's door flew open. The Duke of Baynton in greatcoat and boots ducked under the door and came striding in followed by a very worried Sarah. "Stop any ceremony," he commanded. "This young woman is under age and I have her guardian with me."

Sarah was heartily tired of traveling and overjoyed to see Char. She would have hurried to her, except Lord Jack had stepped forward, placing her niece protectively behind him. More telling, Char accepted him as her protector, even moving closer to the shelter of his body.

The gentleman who had appeared ready to perform the marriage ceremony closed his book and calmly informed the duke, "Sir, I need tell you, this young lady is legal under the laws of Scotland. Her guardian has no say." He had obviously given this little speech before.

"Where are you in the vows, sir?" Sarah demanded.

"We haven't started," he answered.

"Yes, we have," Char countered.

Lord Jack's attention was on his brother. They glowered at each other like angry tigers. "*You* are not welcome here."

"I didn't expect to be," Baynton answered. "What the devil are you doing? Is this how you have plotted to strike back at me, Jack? By humiliating me through marriage to Lady Charlene?"

"This has nothing to do with you," Lord Jack

answered. "I met her long before you did, brother. More important, she's *mine* now."

Baynton reared back as if his twin had physically struck him.

Sarah, too, was stunned.

Mine now. She understood exactly what Lord Jack was saying. There would be no turning back for Charlene. She'd given him her virtue and Sarah could have wept. His claim echoed words Roland Pettijohn had said to Sarah the first time she'd tried to leave him—*mine*. Then again, Roland had been a liar and a fraud. If the duke had been confronting him, Roland would have pushed Sarah in front of him, expecting her to save him.

Lord Jack gave every sign that he would shield Char with his life.

However, what truly jarred Sarah was Baynton's astounding response.

"Yours? Like chattel?"

When they had come within sight of Gretna, Sarah has promised herself she would keep calm. She could see the duke was growing more aggressive as he neared his quarry. They were both tired, exhausted, actually, and she knew one of them needed to be the cooler head. Her purpose was to be there for Charlene.

However, the duke taking her ideals, ideals that he had repudiated repeatedly on their journey, and twisting them to use to his own advantage destroyed all good intent. They also gave her a convenient target since contemplating the irrevocable choices Char had made with her life was far too distressing. "That was uncalled for," she informed the duke.

Without bothering to look at her, since his glare was saved for his brother, Baynton said, "What was?" He spoke as an aside.

"Mocking my principles."

"They are mockable," he responded, annoyed enough at her interruption to give her a stern frown and an unvarnished opinion. "I did not appreciate them being foisted on me."

"And yet you just used them on your brother."

Now she received the duke's full attention. "Are we here for the same purpose? Do we not want the same result?"

"Not at the cost of my principles."

He looked at her as if she had stepped on his last ounce of patience. "I'm merely making use of all the nonsense you have been foisting upon me."

"We have been together for days. We had to talk about something."

Baynton lifted a brow. "Aye, we did. And may I remind you that you don't like my politics, my views on religion or the role and place of women—"

"What intelligent woman would admire the

opinions you hold, Your Grace?" Sarah answered with false sweetness.

"Many women do," he answered. "Hosts of women."

"So you keep telling me." She looked to the minister. "This is Scotland. I could use of dram of whisky or maybe three after traveling with him for days on end."

"Thank you, Mrs. Pettijohn," the duke said, speaking to the room at large and making his exasperation clear. "Advocate of Mary Wollstonecraft and bluestockings everywhere."

"You are *so* annoying," she replied. "However, I must credit you with knowing who Mary Wollstonecraft is. I am amazed. Simply amazed."

Baynton growled his response. "Thank you again, Mrs. Pettijohn. May I say, I preferred you as a maid? You weren't so opinionated."

Char had come out from behind Lord Jack. She stood beside him, her gaze turning worried as she followed the argument from the duke to Sarah and back again. The expression on her face brought Sarah to her senses.

In truth, her niece did not look the worse for wear. Her hand had found Lord Jack's and their fingers were laced together. Something about seeing them this way eased the knots of fear and doubt Sarah had been harboring.

"His Grace is being sarcastic," Sarah assured Char.

"I wasn't being sarcastic," Baynton shot back.

Sarah harrumphed her answer. After all, a good harrumph was unanswerable. It said so much without saying anything.

And gave her the last word, something she knew the duke would not appreciate.

Lord Jack spoke up. "I'm actually starting to feel sorry for you, brother."

"I don't want your pity," Baynton answered.

"That *was* sarcasm," Lord Jack informed him, and his dry quip startled a laugh out of Sarah . . . and once she started, she couldn't stop, especially when the duke gave his brother one of his lowering looks he'd been directing at her whenever she'd dared to question his opinions.

And this whole trip had been for naught.

Yes, she was glad she was here to protect her niece. . . but she needn't protect her from Lord Jack. Even a blind woman could tell he loved Char. And Sarah, whose principles had included a belief that a woman should do exactly as she wished, had come to realize she had no right to stop Char. Not from this marriage or from going to Boston. Char had had more faith in herself than Sarah ever had.

Sarah just wished she'd realized all this before

having to spend days in Baynton's insufferable company. She had probably lost her position at the Haymarket by now because she had been gone so long—and faced with her own culpability Sarah could only laugh all the more. It was all so absurd. Who was *she* to tell Char whom to love?

"Are you all right?" Char asked.

Sarah tried to catch her breath, to bring herself under control, but then a burly blacksmith in his leather apron and big clopping boots walked through the room on his way to another, and she started laughing again. Only in Scotland could this happen.

Char noticed him as well and she began to chuckle. Laughter could be infectious. Then the minister and his wife started laughing and they all seemed to feed on each other.

The only ones not joining them were the brothers Whitridge.

Sarah tried to explain. "It is all so incredible," she said, gasping for breath. "We're in Scotland and it took days for us to arrive here and now we are here and why? *Why?*"

"She's daft," the duke said to Lord Jack. "That is what happens when women read too much, and she reads. She reads everything."

Yesterday when the duke had said that, Sarah had been so angry she'd threatened to walk back to

London. Today, right now, it struck her as hilariously funny.

And then the duke really sent her into laughter when he said to his brother, "Do you really want to marry into this madness?"

"I do," Lord Jack answered. He shrugged as if he could not help himself and he began to laugh as well—and the duke lost his temper.

"*Then the devil with all of you.*" He turned on his heel and went walking out the door.

That sobered Sarah.

"Wait—" she started, but he was gone. She wouldn't put it past him to drive away. She looked to Lord Jack. "Go talk to him. Now. *Go.*"

"I will not. He has ruined everything I've tried to build with his jealousy. He wants to claim the woman I love."

"Do you truly love her?" Sarah asked, watching him closely.

"With all my heart," he answered without hesitation.

"And you, Charlene. Have you thought this through? You do realize that if you marry him, we may never see each other again." A hardness formed in her chest. "He's been very clear to Baynton and everyone that he considers himself an American."

"I love you for what you've done for me,"

Charlene answered, and then added with a new maturity, "but this man has become my family. Sarah, I can't imagine living without him. My home is with him. I would have you come with us—"

"Oh, I won't do that. I can't. My plays . . . George promised Sunday that he is thinking of staging one this summer. This is my chance. I've worked hard."

"Our door will always be open to you, won't it, Jack?"

"Absolutely."

Sarah placed her hand on Char's shoulder. "It hurts to give you up. My life was empty until you came into it. And now, well . . ."

"I love you, Sarah. I can never repay you for what you've done."

"Yes, you can," Sarah answered, realizing a truth. "You can repay me by living your own life fully and completely. You have my blessing, Char. Be happy with your life."

Any response to her gracious words was cut off by the sound of shouting outside. It was the duke. The horses were apparently protesting being asked to move after finally reaching what they had hoped was their destination. They had been ready for a good rubdown and their dinner.

Sarah turned back to the couple. "Actually, there is one request I have, Char. Ask Lord Jack to make peace with his brother before it is too late."

"I did not invite him up here," Jack answered.

"He had Jack locked up in a storage room," Char agreed. "He kept him prisoner."

"And he is your *family*," Sarah said. "Your twin. I agree that he is infuriating. After the first day with him, I thought Char was wise to run. However, don't let matters end this way, my lord. Family is important. You and your brother both know it. You are just too stubborn to cry quarter first. However, once you've settled the matter, I'll serve as witness to your wedding."

One thing Jack had learned over the past days with Charlene was how much she admired and loved her aunt. When she spoke about Sarah Pettijohn's bravery in confronting the current Lord Dearne and how much she had taken on to protect her niece, his opinion of this woman had soared.

And now she was telling him he needed to make peace with his twin.

"He will not want it," Jack predicted. "His actions have been inexcusable and he knows it."

"Then all the more reason for you to be the larger man," Mrs. Pettijohn said. "Go."

Jack walked out of the smithy, not for Charlene but because Mrs. Pettijohn had let him see reason.

The day's light was waning. Only a fool would

set out on a trip at this hour, and Gavin definitely qualified for the description.

His team was balking. They were tired and didn't wish to work together. Consequently, Gavin had rolled over a small stacked stone wall and caught the back left wheel. Jack was well aware of what such a silly accident could mean to such a reputed whip.

The woman who owned the wall was not pleased, either. Gavin had climbed down from the vehicle and was trying to speak calmly to her. Jack went to the horses, who stamped nervously.

"I will pay to repair the fence," Gavin told the woman.

"I want it repaired right now," she demanded. "I don't need money. I need my fence mended."

"I will help you," Jack called out.

"I don't need *your* help" was the answer.

Jack took a deep breath and tamped down his temper.

Seeing his brother in this disarray made him realize that Mrs. Pettijohn was right. "Well, you have it anyway." He began unhitching the horses. "Seriously, Your Grace, you are a pain in the arse."

"It takes one to know one."

Jack stopped, his hand on a leather lead, at the childish rejoinder. "Did you really just say that?

Please, promise me you haven't said that since we were boys."

His twin ignored the barb. "Stop unhitching my team. I'm *not* staying here." He was reaching in his pocket for his money purse. "How much for the damage to the wall?" he asked the woman.

"I've never known you to not think of your horses," Jack continued. "You can leave, but you'll have to do it without this team. They are spent." He whistled over some lads who had gathered to see all the commotion. "Take these horses up to the inn's stables. That man will pay you handsomely," he said, pointing to Gavin.

Meanwhile, the woman said, "I don't want money. I want you to *repair* the damage."

What was there for Gavin to do?

He pulled out some coins and gave them to one of the boys waiting expectantly. The lads took the horses.

Jack walked over to inspect the injury to the wall and the wheel. "You are lucky. The wheel is fine. We just need to lift it up and over. The two of us can do that easy enough."

"And my wall," the woman said. "Repair my wall."

"We will," Gavin assured her.

He'd said "we." Jack took that as a good sign.

Gavin went to the other side of the vehicle. "Lift on the count of three."

Jack complied and they picked the phaeton up and over the low wall. For a few coins more, the boys pulled the lightweight vehicle to the inn as well.

About twenty stones had been knocked over. Jack started stacking them back into place. Gavin came over and helped.

On the tip of Jack's tongue was a comment about the duke dirtying his hands . . . and then he realized that wasn't what he wanted to say to his brother. Yes, he was angry at his twin. Furious, even.

But he was also tired of resentment between them. He would have been crazed with fury if Gavin had won Charlene. Loving her had filled an emptiness inside him, a longing he'd not been willing to recognize until she'd shaken him up.

Perhaps Gavin had hoped she would fill in the same way. Disappointment was always a bitter pill and, for Gavin, this one came with the humiliation of knowing all his contemporaries had watched his courtship and would know he'd been rejected.

Both he and Gavin reached for the last stone at

the same time. They found themselves practically eyeball to eyeball. Jack stood.

Gavin placed the stone. He looked to the disgruntled cottager. "Is this correct?"

She took her time reviewing their work and then said, "It will be good enough." On those words she marched back into her home and shut the door.

"Well," Gavin said, imitating her manner with a bit of humor. "We shall keep this incident between us."

Jack laughingly agreed.

The two of them faced each other. They did not move.

Gavin's gaze drifted back to the smithy. "Lady Charlene is a true pearl."

"Aye, she is, but she is also a willful lass. I don't doubt for a second that she will play me a merry tune and yet I love her. I'd do anything for her."

"Even lock up your own blood?" The humor had left Gavin's eyes. A tight muscle worked in his jaw.

Jack braced himself, not knowing what to expect.

"The trip up here has given me time to think," Gavin said. "I'm not proud of what I did."

"Why did you do it?"

"I felt betrayed. I wanted to hurt you the way

you wounded me. I wanted to break you. I'd opened myself to you, Jack. I shared what I would not tell anyone."

"Are you speaking about telling me you haven't slept with a woman—"

Gavin took a step back, tensing as if he didn't even want mention of the subject. "It is an odd place to be, my age and not having experienced what almost every other man from the rat catcher to the king has."

"It is nothing to be ashamed of and easily remedied."

Gavin ignored him. Instead, he continued. "When I found out she preferred you, it raised old emotions. And it was like when you left years ago. I was shocked then, Jack. I'd always thought you shared everything and then you just left. For a while I wanted to believe you were dead because then there was an explanation. However, I knew in that way we have that you were alive."

"Did you tell Father?"

Gavin shook his head. "No."

Now it was Jack's turn to feel uneasy. To explain. And how does one put into words rash behavior and make it sound palatable? Especially when he had no regrets.

"I have no explanation for why I left, Gavin, other than a belief I'd go mad if I had to spend more time with books and being under Father's thumb. I hated being the cupbearer. You are the one he valued. Ben and I were just spares in case something happened to you. And he was a hard taskmaster. I will say he was more demanding of you than he was with us."

"He had to be with me. His standards were high."

"Maybe, or maybe not. You don't want to be a paragon, Gavin. There is no breathing room there. You can't live your life meeting a dead man's expectations." He paused a moment and then added, "Any more than I discovered I could spend mine in your shadow. Our wills are too strong, brother."

"But to give up your country?"

"I've lived out of it longer than I've lived in it. However, the adventure of carving my own reputation suits me. And here is my advice to you, live the life you want."

"A duke cannot be that free—"

"That is nonsense. There are hosts of them who are rascals and rakes."

"I'm not cut of that cloth."

"I imagine you could be if you gave yourself half a chance. I was and I bet Ben has had his moments. Gavin, you deserve happiness. Even Mother has Fyclan Morris."

"Not actually. She was telling me before all of this nonsense started that they were having a parting of the ways. She told me that although they are friends, Fyclan may never recover from his wife's death. He loved her deeply and Mother doesn't wish to be Jenny's shadow."

"I can understand. Although he may change his mind with time. I never thought to love again after Hope. If anything happened to Charlene, I would go mad with grief. However, is Mother all right? She appeared to enjoy having an escort when she went out."

"She told me she wants to be free to find a man who will give her all of himself." He fell quiet a moment. "Do you remember telling me that I needed to be attentive to Lady Charlene?"

"You wanted me to entertain her whenever you were called away."

"Is that when I lost her?"

"No, Gavin. I would not be so dishonorable. However, what lies between Charlene and me started when we first met, which was weeks before your ball."

"Weeks?"

Jack nodded. "I caught her picking Matthew Rice's pocket."

"You knew she was a thief?"

"Did you?"

"Not until Mrs. Pettijohn informed me. I was shocked."

"I was shocked as well—first when I actually caught her and tried to shake Rice's purse out of her. *That* is when I discovered she was female."

"Did she give you back the purse?"

"No, she almost gelded me."

"Oh," his brother said as if this was new, and troubling, information.

"The second time I was shocked was when I recognized her on your arm," Jack confessed.

"You could have warned me," Gavin said.

"Would you have believed me?"

He didn't even have to consider the matter a second. "Probably not. I was bowled over by her. However, now, hearing what you have to say, I may be lucky she chose you."

Jack laughed his agreement.

Gavin took a step back. He looked tired, weary. He held out his hand. "Can you forgive my actions in London? I've cost you your opportunity to make your mark."

Jack pushed aside the hand and he gave his brother a hug. "My mission was a wild shot from the beginning. Lawrence and Rice had been forced upon me to undermine me."

"At least they sent you. That was good. You did try and your cause is noble. But in the end, Jack, I didn't have anything to do with your delegation. No one wanted to listen to even me speak about the grievances."

"Will they be surprised when my country declares war?"

"Sometimes I suspect it is the only way to get men to think."

"A pity."

"Yes and a waste." Gavin turned again to the smithy. "Well, shall I go witness your marriage?"

"I would be honored."

"Then let us do it."

Side by side, they walked toward the building. Jack felt compelled to say, "My actions have never been against you, Gavin. Ever. I was just trying to be my own man."

Gavin nodded. He might not have been convinced. Jack would have to give him time.

But a new thought struck him. "Mrs. Pettijohn is a widow. Do you not find her attractive?"

Gavin's answer was a sharp bark of laughter.

"Well?" Jack pressed.

"You would wish on me an old actress with the tongue of a harpy?"

"She's our age, brother."

"No, she is older than we are. I know because at one point I made her so angry she said that never in her four-and-thirty years had she met a man who made her want to bite through nails. I took it as a victory of sorts."

Jack shrugged. "She is a redhead. They are known for strong personalities."

"True, but I'm not going to marry one. A man needs peace at home."

And on that note, they entered the smithy together.

Charlene had been watching for them. She approached them and Gavin took her hand and apologized for all that he had done.

"If it wasn't for you, Your Grace, I would not be here marrying the man I love."

Gavin released her hand. "You are lucky, Jack."

Jack clapped a hand on his brother's shoulder and said quietly. "It will happen to you in good time. Have faith, brother."

Gavin's smile turned rueful. He looked to Mr. Lang, who sat on a stool waiting. "I'm ready to witness my brother's marriage."

The vows were said quickly. Sarah and the duke signed as the witnesses, and Jack and Charlene were legally married.

There was one awkward moment when Mr. Lang asked for the groom to place his ring on the bride's hand as a sign of his commitment. Jack didn't have a ring.

"You need a ring," Mr. Lang said, with Scottish bluntness. "It is part of my ceremony."

Of course, the Langs had rings he could buy. "We are always prepared," Mrs. Lang said cheerily.

The problem was, Jack was very low on funds, something he didn't want to admit in front of everyone, and still needed to pay for passages to Boston.

Gavin seemed to divine the situation. "Here, for the ceremony, you can use this." He removed his own signet ring. "The blessing is over the two of you, not the piece of jewelry."

Mrs. Lang appeared ready to argue but a shake of her husband's head reminded her that no one countered the Duke of Baynton.

The signet looked heavy and bulky on Charlene's hand, but it served the trick. After the ceremony, she happily handed it back.

Gavin then hosted a delightful meal at the inn in honor of his brother and his bride. Jack could find no rancor in him and was not only astonished but deeply grateful.

Later, Gavin stunned Jack and Charlene when he announced that his wedding present to them would be passage to Boston from Glasgow, a sure sign that his blessing had been given to their marriage. He even settled the accounts at the inn for their entire party and also generously paid for Mrs. Pettijohn's trip home by private coach.

That night, Jack opined to Charlene that Gavin might have done that for some peace for his own trip.

They were entwined in the middle of the four-poster bed in the inn's finest room when he made his statement. The extra night for their enjoyment before they started the long trip home had been another gift from his twin.

The mattress was by far the best they had tried and they had given it several good goes already. The Widow Fitzwilliam would be proud. They might have even created their little Libby.

"They are oil and water," Charlene said. "I've never seen anyone annoy Sarah so easily . . . although after the ceremony, I did overhear her tell him that his lending us his ring gave her hope for him."

"What was his answer?"

"I believe he growled at her."

Jack laughed. "It is of no matter. Their paths will never cross again. I can't imagine Gavin at the Haymarket. He rarely attends the theater other than to watch the occasional Shakespeare."

He yawned. "It is good that Gavin had some business in Edinburgh. His trip up here chasing us is not a waste. By the time he returns to London, everyone will have forgotten who we are."

"Does he ever take time for himself?" Charlene

asked. "He always seems to be busy, always working."

"My brother is not like most men. He keeps himself on a tight rein and that is unfortunate because no one can expect to be moral and capable all the time. Sooner or later, he will rebel. I did."

"Perhaps then he'll find a woman who will force him to see a different way to live. And then he will want to slay dragons for her . . . just as you did for me."

"And I always will," he promised. He gathered his wife closer, marveling at the warmth and the scent of her. Whatever the future held, all that was important to him, all that mattered was right here in his arms.

Life was indeed a blessing.

April 10, 1812

Dear Sarah and Lady Baldwin, since I know she will read this,

I hope this letter finds you well.

We arrived safe a week ago. I must say I did not enjoy ocean travel. Jack has his sea legs but I took to our cabin from the first day almost to the last. My stomach would not settle.

Boston surprised me. It is like London, a bit smaller, and just as exciting. There are squares and parks. Jack and I take a stroll every evening as do most Bostonians although I find the weather a bit too cold for my tastes. Our new friends assure me that this is spring, though they warn we could have snow even into May. Can you imagine? Snow when we should have strawberries blooming?

Jack has introduced me to many of his friends including the governor and his wife. Her name is Sarah as well. I am proud to say my husband is well respected. As you know,

Jack was disappointed that he could not set up a meeting with our two governments. Apparently, afterward, a Mr. Lawrence went to Washington and delivered a report that was not true. Jack will be leaving for Washington in two weeks to defend his record.

Our home is the size of the house on Mulberry Street. I have a small garden with which Jack says I may do whatever I wish. I take notes when I visit friends of what they have done to their houses. My husband has been a complete bachelor and there is much work to be done to the public rooms and our private spaces. I shall find myself very busy.

You would be very comfortable here, dear Sarah. There are many Independent Thinkers in Boston. Jack's friend, a Mr. John Park, has founded a school for the Education of Young Ladies. He joined us for dinner on Monday night and I was interested in all he had to say. He believes in the Intelligence of Women and insists that education is a necessity. I spoke to him about your plays and he said he would like very much to read one.

I need to close this letter. A friend of ours offered to carry it to London for me. His ship is sailing this evening and he is most anxious for me to seal it and hand it over to him.

I keep both of you in my thoughts and prayers.

Please know that I am happier than I could ever have imagined. Jack is the most perfect of husbands. Together, we will build a good life for our family.

With much love and affection, my dearest ones, Char

Author's Note

Dear Readers,

I must share a few notes over what happened after my story ended.

The War of 1812: It gave us the "Star Spangled Banner" and the term "war hawks"; saw the White House burned to the ground; and almost gave the British the chance to reclaim their former colonies.

The United States Congress declared war on Great Britain on June 18, 1812. A coalition of war hawks, mostly from the Democratic-Republican Party (yes, that makes me smile, too), pushed President James Madison toward war for causes that I lightly touched on in this book.

The war was unpopular. There were many

strong voices in the United States, including Massachusetts Governor Caleb Strong and Virginia Congressman John Randolph, who opposed it. However, the war became a test of our national character. We were either going to pull together or pull apart. It is good to remember how young the United States was. Our government wasn't even thirty years old.

For two and a half years, British troops were once again tramping over our countryside. Both sides won major victories; both lost some. It was a bit of a stalemate.

Finally, on December 23, 1814, the United States and Great Britain negotiated a treaty and the war was done . . . save for an important battle in New Orleans that became the making of a future president.

Happy reading, my friends,
Cathy Maxwell
September 30, 2015

The Duke of Baynton is still searching
for the perfect bride . . .
but will he ever make it to his date at the altar?

Don't miss the next
Marrying the Duke novel by
New York Times bestselling author
CATHY MAXWELL
A Date at the Altar

Read on for a sneak peek . . .

A Date at the Altar

Sarah Pettijohn could not believe who stood on her doorstep—her least favorite person in the world, the mighty Duke of Baynton.

And she was also certain he held little love for her as well. Therefore, the only reason he could be here is if he had bad news that could not be conveyed in any other way than in person. Fear for her niece in Boston gripped her. "Is all well with Charlene?"

"May I come in?

"Yes, of course." She opened the door wider.

He removed his hat as he stepped inside. His size and presence filled every nook of her small apartment. He looked too fine for the room and its mean furnishings. "This is different from your house on Mulberry Street. I'm surprised you moved."

"The landlord and I had a difference of opinion," Sarah said, crossing her arms against the uncomfortable feeling of having him this close and in such a confined space. "He wanted the rent and I couldn't pay him."

"Which is why you were in the Naughty Review last night?"

Heat warmed Sarah's cheeks. Baynton had recognized her through her disguise. She brazened it out. "I'm an actress, Your Grace. I perform on stage."

"Funny, I hadn't thought to see so *much* of you." He mimicked her clipped, unwelcoming tone. "Or your breasts."

"They were covered—"

"Barely."

"It was the costume the part called for."

"Ah, yes, the naked damesoielle role."

"*Half* naked," she corrected, turning from him. She'd hated the costume, hated that she'd had no choice but to wear it. "What is your purpose, Your Grace? If something has happened to my niece, tell me now."

He looked contrite. "I did not mean to alarm you. As far as I know, all is well with Charlene and Jack."

Her temper flared. "But you let me imagine there

might be a problem. You knew I would not let you in under my roof for any other reason, no?"

"Guilty. I did not want to discuss our business in the hall."

"*Our* business?"

"*I* have a business proposition for you."

"What sort of business proposition do you wish to make, Your Grace? It can't be the usual. Everyone knows the Duke of Baynton is no mere mortal man. He is above earthy matters."

"And everyone is aware that Mrs. Sarah Pettijohn is no mere actress. She has principles. She'd never stoop so low as to sing away while pumping her legs on a swing over the heads of a pack of hungry lords behaving like dogs."

For a bald second, Sarah was tempted to pick up the fireplace poker and skewer him with it. The thought of his blood running free on her floor gave her great pleasure. Nor would she defend herself. She had a good reason for participating in the Naughty Review and she refused to explain herself to His Haughtiness. A woman did what a woman must to survive. "A pack of dogs in which you were a member," she reminded him archly.

"I was there," he conceded. "Nice legs."

"Go to devil."

"I might."

She walked over to the door and opened it. "Thank you for your call, Your Grace. Now leave."

He didn't move. "Hear me out."

"I've heard enough."

"I wish to spend the night with you."

"*That* fact was established when you mentioned my breasts, Your Grace, not to mention complimenting my legs. You will not be surprised by the answer—no. Now good day to you." With a sweep of her hand, she urged him to go through the door.

He did not move. "Hear me out, *and*—" he continued as if knowing she would not be convinced, "if you still wish me to leave, then I will do so."

"*If?*" But in spite of her sarcasm, Sarah had a kernel of curiosity as well. Baynton had never taken a mistress. What did he have in mind? She closed the door. "Speak."

"You don't like me. I understand," he hurried to add. "But I am not set against you. I find you headstrong and wrong thinking, but I believe that is no crime."

"How generous of you, Your Grace."

He ignored her falsetto sweetness. Instead, he began pacing the small confines of her sitting room. "I have a problem. I must marry. I will. I have money, I'm a duke, some woman will want me."

"Two have already said no," she silkily reminded him.

He stopped. "Yes, they have and that is part of the difficulty. You and I know that I've done the honorable thing to let them marry the men of their choice. It was not because they faulted me. However, the rest of the world does not know the full story." He paused as if wrestling with himself and then admitted, "They see me as less of a man."

"That is nonsense," Sarah answered.

"And yet it is true."

She wanted to refute his claim . . . then again, she realized he was right. She'd heard whispers, knew they were unfair to Baynton, however, what could she say that would help? Who cared what an actress thought?

"And so you believe spending a night with me will—what? Improve your image? I doubt it. My advice is to ride out the gossip, Your Grace. You are strong enough to do so."

"There you are wrong, Mrs. Pettijohn. First, last night you created a vision every man in that theater wanted. They ran backstage for you."

That was true. She had been a sensation. "I did not encourage them."

"You needn't. Men are covetous. They see; they want. Having you on my arm will do much to restore my reputation."

"I am not a whore."

"This is a business proposition," he replied steadily.

"I. Am. Not. A whore," she reiterated.

"I would never call you that." He took a step toward her. "However, you have created an impression—a false one, perhaps—but people think what they will."

"And for that I'm to sell myself?"

"Or use this moment in time to your advantage. What do you want that you can't have, Mrs. Pettijohn? How about a lovely house to call your own? The security of knowing no one can ever toss you out of it."

Tempting. Still . . .

"There are a half a dozen birds around London men would be jealous to see you with, Your Grace. Why me?"

"I require someone who will not be foolish. I do not want bastards."

He was being smart. Baynton was wealthy. He

would be honor bound to support any child he bred. A mother could find herself set for life.

"I also need someone upon whose discretion I can trust."

"And you believe that is me?" Sarah asked, incredulous.

"As a matter of fact, I do. You actually *do* have principles, Mrs. Pettijohn."

"Thank you, I think."

"You think?"

"Yes, you have me confused. You wish discretion and yet you obviously plan on letting everyone in London know we have been lovers. What game are you playing?"

"No game, Mrs. Pettijohn. I need help and you are the only one I can trust."

"Because?" she prompted.

"Because I'm a virgin, Mrs. Pettijohn."

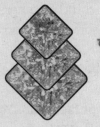

AVONBOOKS

*The Diamond Standard
of Romance*

Visit AVONROMANCE.COM

Come celebrate 75 years of Avon Books
as each month we look toward the future
and celebrate the past!

Join us online for more information about our
75th anniversary e-book promotions,
author events and reader activities.
A full year of new voices and classic stories.
All created by the very best writers of romantic fiction.

*Diamonds Always
Sparkle, Shimmer, and Shine!*